MOONLIGHT AT CUCKMERE HAVEN

The Wentworth Family Saga
Book Four

Graham Ley

SAPERE
BOOKS

MOONLIGHT AT CUCKMERE HAVEN

Published by Sapere Books.

24 Trafalgar Road, Ilkley, LS29 8HH

saperebooks.com

ISBN: 978-0-85495-617-3

CHAPTER I: LURED INTO A TRAP

London, Summer 1796

Loic sauntered past the house, pausing below the brightly lit window through which elegant figures could be glimpsed: some lively, others languid, glasses held up or dangling from fingers. The sound of laughter and raucous banter spilled out through the half-open casement and the gap between the imposing front door and its jamb. Loic set one leg at an angle, casually stretching his arm along the length of the iron railings. He allowed himself three minutes, counting the time off mechanically like some old school exercise. He had no timepiece; but Coline had made him and Françoise practise counting off together with her.

He knew that he was being looked at before he turned round. He let the feeling rest on the back of his neck for a while, before he swung his shoulders, pushed back his hair from the one side of his face, and stared fixedly along the top of the railings. He left his arm where it was, the blouse buttoned at the wrist, bagging out just above the waist, the earring with its ruby-red stone prominent below the curls in the new, shorter cut she had given him. He had a dark green satin neckerchief loose around his throat, and Coline had found him a silver ring for his finger. Oval buckles sat above the flat shoes below his silk stockings, but he had refused to wear white breeches, and so his were of a russet-brown worsted, clasped at the knees by smaller relatives of the buckles on his shoes.

But it was the face that fascinated, always the face above the body — and so he swung it abruptly upwards to gaze almost insolently in at the window, grasping the rail and challenging the viewer. The young man who was staring at him, one hand resting lightly on the window-pane, his nose almost touching the glass, jumped perceptibly, making as if to turn away but trailing his fingers across the condensation. For a moment their eyes met, and outside Loic deliberately pursed his lips, and opened them slightly. He then tossed his head, in a move he had been practising and felt he had now perfected, and languidly strolled off without a look behind him.

The young *émigré* inside at the window breathed shallowly, and beads of sweat trickled down around the angle of his chin. He drank his wine in one swallow, set down his glass and pushed past his joking companions into the hall, where a strong-scented woman in dark satin and heavy jewellery said something to him which he ignored, but at which her companion laughed. There was no one by the door at that moment; he pushed it open and ran lightly down the steps into the street.

The way was at first well-lit. In front, Loic did not slow his pace, which although it appeared languid was also lithe. He could hear the footsteps of his follower behind him in the relative silence of the narrow lanes, and what he wanted to do was to keep him at an alluring distance, rather than risk being accosted in the street. The heat of the night brought sweat freely to the pursuer's brow, and dampened the locks of hair that fell over it: he could feel it running under his shirt, which was silk, a nuisance now, as were the lace ruffles at his wrists. He was not gaining on the young man in front, but he felt sure his presence had been noticed, and the nervousness that the *gars* revealed by increasing his pace proved all the more enticing to his alerted senses.

The alley bent round to the right, and the overhangs of an older building made the moonless night for an instant even more impenetrable. The footsteps in front became muted, and then ceased altogether. The pursuer slipped around the corner, hugging the wall. The lane stretched on ahead, with no sign of his prey. He edged along it to the opening of a court on his left, and peered round the rough stonework of the entrance to it. A dim light at the far end of the court picked out the lace on his delicate hand as it gripped nervously on to the stone.

Loic had waited at the end of the court. This was the final gambit, but he was already sure of his man. The secret was not to look at him, to be desired intensely at this final, short distance, yet to be neither solicitous nor sweetly coy. The lighting was a brilliant touch. He allowed himself to fumble with the blunt piece of metal that passed for a key, clanked the latch loudly but unnecessarily, and eased the door back. He slipped out of sight through it, and closed it slowly behind him, almost tight but making sure it was just ajar.

The young *émigré* waited, and then ran across the smoothed cobbles of the court. His blue Morocco slippers, which like the silk shirt he had retained amidst all the other deprivations, made no sound on them. After looking around, he peered at the door, and his eyes reflected the uncertainty, at this last threshold of intractable impulse, whether he might dare to tap on it. He set his mouth firmly, and raised his knuckles, but his other hand rested lightly on the furrowed wood and he felt the draft from inside as it creaked slightly open. The stairwell was dark, the stairs creaky, and the heat felt oppressive. No sound of a door shutting, no tread on flights higher up. The *émigré* took out a handkerchief and wiped his forehead, his foot poised on the first step. He then edged up, with the stairs leading at first towards the back of the house, and then turning through a small landing back to the front. There was a window on this second landing, but the shutters were clamped down in place.

He trod on and upwards, listening all the time for a sound from a room, until he brushed up against another body, standing still against a door in the angle of a turn of the stairs. The body was warm and scented: but it was not that of a woman. It remained still. He ignored the beating of his heart and eased himself slowly round to press himself gradually more closely against it. He raised his hand slightly, his fingers searching out the other's hand for the ring that he had seen from the window, and he sensed rather than heard the breathing.

His arousal was now beginning to overpower his self-control, and the fear he felt was becoming a stimulus rather than a constraint. He remembered in a flash the dark, recessed wall-cupboard in the deserted seminary, on that stolen afternoon, and his naïve astonishment at the urgency of lust: his companion's laughter, his greater experience and sensual assurance. He now might be the more experienced companion to an *ingenu*, the leader in the dance, the initiate subtly summoning the confused senses of the novice. But what he heard was 'No, not here', spoken in a dull English, while a flattened hand pushed firmly against his chest. In his infatuation he grabbed hold of that hand by the wrist and tried to pull it lower down his body. But the *gars* had a very strong arm, and behind him the door opened into bright, almost dazzling light into which he slipped noiselessly away.

The young man followed him, scarcely acknowledging the candlelit interior, which was handsomely furnished with brocade and velvet. A sumptuous sofa was all he needed to see, and the *gars* did not resist as he took him by the shoulders, unbuttoned the blouse and pulled it out from the waistband of the breeches. He swung hurriedly out of his own coat and waistcoat, and pushed the voluptuous body of this lithe Adonis backwards on to the ample cushions without encountering any resistance. He laughed at the joy of it all, passed his hands through those enticing black curls, along the edge of that ivory chin, and then began to wrestle, urgently but incompetently, with the cursedly tight fastenings of his own sleek pantaloons.

He heard the door opening behind him, but he did not hear the key click in the lock. Coline did not always believe in doors that locked, but for this particular scheme it had been plain from the outset that a lockable door was essential. Their search had soon found a very suitable room, and Françoise had enjoyed herself in filling it with second-hand furniture and knick-knacks, covering old cushions with scraps of fabric she found in a market. Later, Loic emerged from a chandler with a wrap of wax candles stuffed under his coat while Françoise engaged the owner in a complicated conversation about tallow. They were all lit now, some in bent candelabra, others merely stuck in bottles, but the young *émigré* had no concern for that.

Coline's fingers closed around the key. She caught Loic's almost despairing eye, and simultaneously stamped her foot on the ground for the sake of the noise and shrieked '*Mon Dieu!*' At that signal, Loic threw the young man from him with alarming strength, and stepped past him and the sofa into a corner of the room, where he buttoned his blouse with urgency, casting reproachful glances back over his shoulder at the bewildered villain of the piece. Coline swirled herself round dramatically in a full gown of deepest purple, a hand raised in distress and horror to her face, hoping that the lavishly ostrich-feathered hat that she and Françoise had chosen would give her the dignity she now needed. Loic rushed across the small room to her, and buried his head in her shoulder.

'*Ma soeur*, my sister!'

'*Mon frère!*' So much to avoid any misunderstanding: he must accept unequivocally at this point that they were brother and sister, and that they were French. The young man had gathered himself together to a certain extent, and recalled those long, weary years of good breeding. He bowed slightly, and uttered '*Madame, monsieur...*' and made to walk past them resolutely to the door.

Coline raised her hand imperiously, while Loic cowered into her shoulder:

'Wait, scoundrel!' Loic lifted his head slightly: by Saint Corentin, she was good — or if not good exactly, then impressive.

The young *émigré*'s face went pale. He hesitated, and Loic went to the door, put his back against it and spread his arms across it in a display of a freshly discovered defiance mingled with a lingering show of fear. Coline almost spat at the pale young man:

'You have insulted the honour of my brother, and of our family. No doubt you have sensed our distress, our weakness and lack of protection here in this alien land, and believe that you can run riot like a stinking Jacobin over our paltry defences against abuse. But —' and here she hissed, leaning in towards him — 'I shall denounce you. It is our only recourse against such as you are.'

And the word she added to this, finally and almost in a whisper, drained what last vestiges of blood there had been in the young man's face. He resorted, rather hopelessly, to bluster.

'How dare you! I… I…' But words failed him. He knew how easy it would be to let a suggestion slip out here or there, to speak casually but purposefully to a gossip, to lay a festering sneer amongst servants or maids, or, more boldly, to slander him in loose company, knowing that word would happily spread.

'I… I might be of service to you, madam. It seems that there has been a mistake —' now this felt better — 'which we would do well…' But here again, he could not think of how to conclude this sentiment.

Coline relaxed her posture, and beckoned Loic forward from his place by the door. She motioned to the young man to sit on the sofa, which he did. She herself remained standing, while he stumbled to find some helpful words.

'That is, we would do well to keep such a misunderstanding within the realms of apology. Yet, no —' looking at her glowering face — 'I can see that no matter what the explanation of these strange circumstances in which we all find ourselves might be —' she was glaring straight at him — 'it will be a matter of honour to make amends to you. That is, to you and your brother, to both of you.'

She had turned away in grief, as it seemed, clutching a handkerchief to her eyes. Loic went to her side, and scowled at his assailant over his shoulder. The woman sobbed, almost inarticulately.

'We wish to leave this country. For good.'

There was silence. Then, when she faced the young man once again, with reddened eyes, she was angry, and embittered, and completely clear.

'I know your mother! I have left my card at her house. We were a respectable family, before the times changed. I am not afraid… I can speak to her confessor, to bring correction on you before it is too late.' She calmed a little. 'It will not be too late, for your eternal soul.'

He became resolute in the moment. 'You say you wish to leave this country.' He stood up. 'So be it. It must be my duty to help you. There are those who travel to Scotland…'

'America. We are to go to America.'

He swallowed. The thought of his mother was utterly unbearable. 'I would be indebted to you if you would do me the great honour of accepting ten guineas of English sterling.'

'Fifty guineas.' The elegant, dangerous brother spoke sharply, and for the first time since his seemingly seductive acquiescence in the corridor. 'My sister is a good friend of the Abbé Carron from Jersey, as is your mother. Ten of those guineas for the hospice he will be opening over in Somers Town. Anonymously.'

'Fifty guineas? But how…?'

'Gambling. You have English friends of dubious character. It is well known. Your mother will be aware of that. They gamble. You have lost. Your reputation is at stake: you must honour your debts.'

As he spoke, Loic took the key from Coline's unfolded hand, and placed it in the lock. The young man came up to him and looked at his deceptive beauty, closely, within breathing distance, for the last time.

'You have a week. My sister will be here, alone, and you must come alone. At six o'clock of the evening, shall we say. When all has been settled between you, I shall come up here and hand over to you a letter that is addressed to your mother. Should you not appear…'

They listened as his footsteps clattered down the stairs, and the door into the alley banged down below.

CHAPTER II: TIME TO LEAVE

Brittany, the Manor of Kergohan

Old Gwen rode in to the manor at Kergohan on the same donkey that had carried Babette's aunt to Kergohan for Babette's marriage to Daniel back in the late spring. Daniel Galouane had been brought from Saint-Domingue in the Caribbean to look after the manor, and had soon met Babette, who entranced him from the beginning. Daniel's niece Héloïse had followed him across to Brittany, and together with Gilles, who had been brought up by Babette since childhood, they had all worked hard to set the manor back on its feet again.

The *domaine* of Kergohan now belonged to Laurent Guèvremont, who had provided mortgages for the Galouane plantation in Saint-Domingue, and so become acquainted with the owner of the plantation, Octave Argoubet. It was Guèvremont who had brought Daniel across to Kergohan, not long before Argoubet was killed in the fighting in Saint-Domingue. Eighteen years ago, Octave Argoubet had freed both Daniel and his sister Saba, who had been slaves on the Galouane plantation along with their sister, and had kept Saba with him as his mistress until her death; Héloïse was the daughter of Saba and Argoubet, and was cared for by her uncle after her aunt had been crushed by a cart in an accident.

Gwen was chatting and gesticulating to the impassive old man who was leading the donkey, but ceased abruptly when she caught sight of Babette waiting for her by the well in the yard. She scrutinised her mercilessly, while remaining firmly wedged on the donkey's back between two panniers, which with a worn sheepskin formed enough of a seat. Babette pushed her hair back from her face, while Gwen slid down from the donkey's back and shuffled off purposefully towards the kitchen. She stopped to stare at the large bread oven standing outside, which had been repaired by Gilles before he left to live in Auray with Guèvremont as his ward. Gwen put her head inside the cavity, sniffed, and headed on into the dark doorway of the kitchen, moderately satisfied with what she found.

Babette and her husband Daniel bustled around thinking of refreshment, found some cider and put it in front of her. But Gwen pushed it away and asked for spirits, for *lambig*, and when they said it had all been taken from the manor she scoffed at them, and sat there mute, her eyes half-closed, for a good, long while. Then, quite distinctly, she said the one word: '*Glaou*-koad'.

Babette and Daniel looked at each other. Gwen opened her eyes.

'*Glaou-koad.*'

The old woman closed her eyes again. Daniel whispered to Babette: 'What is she saying?'

'*Charbon, charbon de bois.*' The old woman opened them again, spoke sharply to Babette and laughed, closed her eyes again, and rocked back and forth on her seat.

'What did she say?'

'She said... She said you should fetch the charcoal.'

Daniel was up and out of the door. 'I'll go, I know where to go,' he said over his shoulder. The old woman opened her eyes, and stopped rocking, and suddenly laid a folded piece of cloth on the table, which she opened: it was the leaven. They had brought her here for her leaven, to start them off in the new oven, and that had been the tradition in the villages around. It was said Gwen's mother before her had the blessed touch too: but for all that, it did not look much.

'Chop it up, warm water. Leave it. Strain it.'

As if at a signal, the man who had been leading the donkey appeared at the door with the panniers from its back. Old Gwen continued in Breton.

'We'll use my flour. We add it, and leave it. I want that charcoal in the oven and lit over the same time. It's not been used, and I want it bone dry. Then we'll rake it out and start the fire again, when the bread is kneaded.'

Babette nodded, and took the panniers from the old man at the door. There was a sound of footsteps along the corridor, and Héloïse, Daniel's niece, came into the kitchen. Old Gwen stared at her, and snorted, 'How many are there?' Then she laughed, looking her up and down unfavourably, and now spoke out quite plainly in French. 'Still, just as well. The bread won't rise without a virgin in the room. No, won't rise at all. Just like a man's pizzle, it is.'

Héloïse opened her eyes in astonishment, and Babette began to curse silently about asking this old crone into her house. To distract herself for the moment, she smoothed her apron across her stomach slowly with both hands. The old woman cackled again, mercilessly.

'There's nothing in there yet. No good stroking it.'

The leaven had risen for the first time, the salt flushed out of it, and they had waited two days. The women had to work round Gwen, while Daniel had the dubious privilege of firing up the charcoal he had brought back from the woods, the old woman's cantankerous directions interpreted for him by Babette. Babette had sent out word not just to the village but to others who lived on the land, and a good crowd gathered in the yard. Some were certain that a first baking would be poor, Gwen or no Gwen, shaking their heads at hopeful excitement, others were willing it on now that they could feel an appetite growing in their bellies. Babette had risked baking some buckwheat biscuits in the smaller kitchen oven the day before, and they were put out in the yard with the brought-in cider that was still sweet, one barrel having gone off to vinegar, which would find other uses.

The fire was lit, under supervision, before many people had arrived and it had taken well, rising to a great heat, the plug-door proving effective, copied as it had been from the remains of the old one that had been found cast aside in the stables. Old Gwen ordered it to be lifted out of the way, and she poked around inside making noises about smoke and ash and soot which few could follow. Once the embers had been raked out, the oven was left to cool just a little before the loaves were placed inside, and the plug wedged back in place. Babette made sure to turn the hourglass watchfully, but Gwen had nothing to do with such contraptions. In due time she seized the peel, and Daniel stood by holding a tray as the flat wooden shovel slipped the loaves out and on to it. Gwen then swept in some biscuits of her own devising, but all eyes were on the bread. She took it back into the kitchen to cool a little, while the biscuits cooked.

When the first loaf was broken, they were all entranced: many swore there had never been bread like it. Héloïse was ecstatic and cut the loaves into thick pieces which she took out to the eagerly waiting villagers in the courtyard along with the butter. A song soon arose from one small group, under the influence of the cider on empty stomachs; one or two of the older men and women crossed themselves. Daniel wiped his forehead as he smiled at Babette, who kept repeating to herself the number of turns of her five-minute hourglass so as not to forget. Then suddenly Héloïse spotted Babette's friend Yaelle in the crowd, and her husband Grosjean not far behind, a great slab of the bread in his hand, licking the butter from his fingers. Yaelle pushed through to embrace Babette; Grosjean whispered in Daniel's ear, and they laughed. Héloïse saw Babette's solemn face, and almost by instinct glanced down at Yaelle's pregnant belly. A sudden pang of compassion swept over her for Babette, who was kissing Yaelle again on her cheek and listening to her excited talk, with pain in her smiling eyes.

'We say that to the lasses, y' know, when we can.'

It was Gwen, right by Héloïse's side, a smudge of ash on her forehead, her grey hair tied back with an old, black ribbon.

'Oh, yes, I dare say you do.' So, now it was French again; she did that when it suited her. Gwen reached out impulsively for Héloïse's hand, and grasped it tightly in her own bony fingers.

'It's a joke we old'uns make, but not too often. It catches them out. They blush and don't know where to look. Not so you. You held your ground. Your father, is he?'

'No, my uncle. My mother … was his sister. She's dead now.'

'Well, she'll have been a beauty, just like you. You be careful, lass. Like moths to a candle, they are, but it's not them that get burned. I'll be off now. I must get my donkey. Your uncle got the firing just right. First time. Never show someone twice.'

The old man appeared from the kitchen, carrying the panniers for the donkey's back; he was as silent as ever.

His mother saw the toddler pointing. The child had wandered off from all the noise in the yard and was standing by the corner of the manor house. A chunk of bread had fallen from his hand on to the ground, and there was butter on his fingers and around his mouth, which had stood open in the act of chewing. Nothing that his mother had not seen before, but she had never seen a carriage and horses like that coming up between the avenue of trees, stirring up the dust. She bent down to pick up the piece of bread and swept her toddler up on to her waist. Almost immediately groups began to disperse, and within a minute or two the stable yard was empty.

The carriage trundled through the line of elms and swung round into the turning-circle in front of the house. Its progress had been closely observed by the household, and they were prepared for it. The coachman jumped down from the box and unfolded the step. The door of the carriage swung back, and Laurent Guèvremont emerged from it wielding his ebony cane, followed at a respectful distance by his clerk, Fourrier. The front door of the manor opened to reveal Daniel, who had quickly assumed a cravat and coat over presentable breeches, stockings and good shoes. The coachman drove his carriage smartly round to the stables, where Babette was waiting with water for the horses. Daniel stepped forward to greet his guests, leaving the *patron* to have the first word.

'Ah, Daniel, I trust you are in good health? You must take Fourrier with you on a tour of the house later on, and let him make notes on what is to be done.' Guèvremont pointed vaguely with his cane, over to the stable-block. 'Was that your new wife I saw just now? She must learn to be an effective housekeeper. But let's not stand here discussing matters in the open air. I shall take a little refreshment, perhaps from a glass of the wine which I left for you. Fourrier here can go to the kitchen, where your wife might provide him with a piece of the farm cheese, of which I hear good things. And do I smell bread? I dare say he will like that. Come, lead me in, and to one of the cleaner rooms, if you please. Fourrier, you will find the kitchen round to the side. Daniel will come for you later.'

Daniel led Guèvremont through the central hall and past the staircase, which was in good condition, and then into what had been the former baron's modest cabinet. Here there was a small, rather worn oak bookcase with a number of volumes of various sizes rather plainly bound. But the major feature was an old deal desk, which now had one leg mended and a new front for one of its drawers. On it lay account books and two large ledgers, inkwells, pens, and a knife for them. Some correspondence under a glass millefiori paperweight completed the assemblage. Laurent was puzzled by the paperweight, since he recognised the type. He already had two of them at home which he had removed from the manor: he wondered where this third of the set had been hiding.

Daniel offered him a chair and left the room. Laurent gazed at the painting on the wall, a rare decoration in this house now stripped of all its character. It was a small portrait of a gentleman, in the older style, no doubt of someone from the de Guérinec family that had owned the manor, a predecessor of his cousin Sempronie and so of her son, Justin Wentworth. If that were so, then he could see no obvious family resemblance. Daniel reappeared, and noticed that he was looking at it.

'We found it in the attic, under dust and cloths. May I join you?'

'By all means, be seated. The refreshment?'

'Coming. I am afraid that we live rather hand to mouth here.'

'So I see. But Fourrier tells me that there are some good entries for his accounts, and that you yourself keep a ledger as you should. The grain appears to be firm and full, and the cattle are progressing. I know little of these things, but Fourrier seems content, and he can be a hard man to please.'

'Yes, I can show you. We had no notice of your visit, so…'

'Yes, yes, I quite understand, and that is not why I came. Let us just say that I am satisfied for the present, and that you may continue as you have been. I believe your wife is from the locality, and that will surely help with finding the labourers that you need. Fourrier will instruct you how to recompense labour, which will have to be more formal once the autumn is over, and another winter faces us. I should just inform you that my man, Le Guinec, who was steward of this property when you arrived, has been moved to other duties for the time being. So you will deal directly with Fourrier, who will have to be conveyed here from time to time. But enough of that. Ah…'

This mild exclamation was for the appearance of Héloïse at the door, who had knocked and shown her face above a small, neat tray just large enough for a bottle and two glasses. Daniel smoothed away a space on the desk, and Héloïse placed the tray down.

'Shall I pour the wine?'

'No, that will be fine. Please tell Babette that I shall be here for some time.' Daniel started to pour wine into the glasses carefully.

'I would rather your niece did not leave. Would you mind joining us?'

Héloïse glanced quickly and inquiringly at her uncle, who did no more than blink at her, and smile a little. Daniel plainly did not know why this Guèvremont man wished her to be there; but she did know that Guèvremont was the owner of the manor. Daniel handed a glass to him. There was a small, wooden chair tucked back at the side of the desk. She pulled it forwards, sat on it, and folded her hands.

'You are Daniel's niece, I believe? And your name is Héloïse? A fine choice of name. From Rousseau, I am sure. A prominent thinker, from whom we all have much to learn. Do you read, Héloïse?'

'A little. No, perhaps more than a little.'

'And what do you like to read?'

'I have liked the lives of the saints. And the bible. I have also seen some poetry. I did not like it much. I did not understand it. Oh, and some of the essays of the *seigneur* de Montaigne.'

'We do not have many books here. Not as yet.' Daniel could not know for sure that it was Guèvremont who had removed the collection from the manor, leaving many empty shelves, but he had wondered.

'I shall send some on from my library. You see, I have a daughter who is much the same age as you. Well, a little older.'

Héloïse said nothing. She knew of Joséphine Guèvremont from Gilles, but did not want to admit that.

'Now, Héloïse, you must listen carefully to me. Some of what I have to say may pain you a little, but it is necessary. We have left things a little too long. May I have your attention, and your indulgence for the moment?'

He was not a man who asked a question of that kind in order to be told 'No'. So she remained silent.

'Your father, *Monsieur* Argoubet on the Galouane plantation in Saint-Domingue and I here in Brittany were what we might call associates in business, or affairs. Do you understand what I mean by that? Such things are complicated, but they involve trust and obligation. For example, your uncle Daniel is here by an arrangement that I made some time ago with your father, and then you came over to join him. Subsequently, there was what we might call an unfortunate confusion, in which you were briefly caught up, but that has all been resolved and is firmly in the past.'

Uncle and niece both breathed quietly and deeply, and said nothing. From Rousseau and trust and obligation to shackles and an abduction, and a slave-driver's ruffian shot dead on a country road only an hour's walk away. Confusion? Terror and outrage, more like, but all now 'firmly in the past'.

'You see, Héloïse —' and here Laurent Guèvremont drank from his glass, and then held it in an unaccustomed posture for him, between the fingers of both hands — 'I have an unbreakable obligation to your father Octave, whom undoubtedly you loved and who was my friend. At least, that was what he became. Or something very like that.'

Loved? She had not hated him. He had been kind to her, in his way. She had loved her mother, and her aunt. And then Daniel. He was her father now. And what was this obligation? Would this prove to be a shackle of a different kind?

'I know your uncle will agree with me that we must make provision for you. You must recognise that you cannot stay here. We need to complete your education as a woman of France. Nor can you conceivably return to Saint-Domingue, which is a country now in turmoil. We must find a place for you to learn what you will need to know to be the wife of a man of standing. It is the least that you deserve. You cannot learn that here at the manor.'

Héloïse found that she was trembling. Daniel clasped his hands together and gripped them tightly. In the instant, neither of them could think of anything to say.

For the first time, Laurent Guèvremont smiled across at her.

'My dear young woman, this education will involve dancing, fine clothes, the society of handsome young men and attractive young women, even perhaps learning some harmless card-games. My own daughter might not expect much more. What do you say to that?'

Héloïse looked at Daniel, who spread his hands, encouraging her to speak. She knew there was at least one thing that she wanted to say, that nothing could prevent her from saying.

'I do not want to be married.'

The strange and unfamiliar man opposite with the obligation put his head back and laughed at her.

'My dear, I do not say that you will be married, to this or to that man, now or tomorrow, or even in the next year. No. But at some point you yourself, like my own daughter, will *wish* to be married, and that will not be possible if you are not prepared for that responsibility, as the other young women of France are now being prepared. That is all I am offering you. At present.'

Héloïse knew that she wanted to talk to Daniel, but she was also deeply afraid that he might in some way be persuaded to agree with this man, and that would upset her. It might be better if she made the decision for herself. Daniel would be so utterly miserable if he felt he had to persuade her of something against her will, and this man Guèvremont was after all the owner of the manor, which was Daniel's sole livelihood here in France. She took a deep breath.

'How long would I be gone?'

Laurent was a negotiator rather than a diplomat, and he preferred concession to extended discussion, which rarely produced a good result. Concessions might be adjusted later: in that respect, they were rather less of a liability than promises, which tended to have a disturbingly long life.

'Good heavens, in absolutely no time at all. Just long enough to enjoy the pleasures and excitement of a lively town. For a month. Let us say that.'

He began to sense success. The query that was on the young woman's lips, that might have hardened into an objection, faded as she looked across at her uncle, who opened his eyes wide and raised his eyebrows.

'I am so delighted to have your agreement. Your uncle and I must make a toast to your future. Daniel, stand with me and raise your glass, please. To Héloïse!'

Héloïse stared ahead of her, at the portrait on the wall. The old gentleman in it appeared to be looking straight back at her, but she had no idea what he might have been thinking.

CHAPTER III: FOR OLD TIMES' SAKE

Eugène Picaud detested and feared meetings with his father. And so the fewer there were of them, the worse they became in consequence of that, with his father suspicious that Eugène had something to hide, and Eugène certain that he would encounter that inevitable suspicion and the air of contemptuous indifference, punctuated by incendiary hostility, that went with it.

Eugène was of moderate stature, by no means tall, but his father was short, strong at the wrists and slightly bow-legged from his ancestry, as the family portraits could not always conceal, or boldly chose not to do. The vicomte's nose, too, stared out in many versions from all those revered and varnished paintings: some he had succeeded in bringing with him as an *émigré* from the crisis in France a few years back, others his judicious interests in London had seen re-located to the small townhouse the family had owned for decades in a fashionable street in Marylebone. Perhaps all this forethought was sufficient evidence that it was a nose that smelt trouble coming, and that it did not serve the unique purpose of allowing him to stare down it forbiddingly at his younger son. Still, Eugène reflected, at least the old devil had to tilt back his head to be able to do this, which is why he had declined his father's offer of a seat: no normal mortal could keep up that posture for long.

The Vicomte de Biel-Santonge fixed Eugène with his customary stare, and made up his mind as he always did to be kind to his boy. That was as the boy's mother would have wished, but it irritated the Vicomte to see his son wearing that loose cravat. The refusal to powder his hair was also an annoyance, but at least he tied it behind rather than cut it preposterously short like the appalling revolutionaries in Paris.

'Your brother is well.'

Eugène twiddled his thumbs behind his back. 'I am most grateful to hear it, sir.'

'He is living in Richmond, which is not to my taste, but his mother's income allows him an independence that many must envy in these straightened times.'

'Indeed, sir. Enviable.'

'Enviable? What is enviable?' His father's temper was rarely suppressed for long.

'Why, sir, his independence, as you just remarked.'

'Yes, yes, so I did, but is there any need for you to repeat my words? Are you looking to flatter me, sir? Or are you cajoling me? Is that it?'

'The saints preserve me from such insolence, Vicomte.' Eugène now wrapped his thumbs tightly around each other behind his back. His father liked the old-fashioned formality of his title, which Eugène's older brother made a point of using, as he did remarkably of bowing to him. Eugène recalled that the English had a word for this kind of thing, which was something to do with amphibians. It would not come to him: he would have to ask his friend Justin Wentworth.

His father snorted, picked up from the table a round, lacquered snuffbox which he had had from his grandfather, and rapped it down again angrily.

'And which saints would these be? Am I aware of them? Are they in the canon?'

Eugène flushed in anger, took his hands from behind his back and raised them in a despairing gesture before swinging on his heels and marching in fury and frustration to the door. His father took a step after him.

'Eugène! My son! Stop, stop! Come, my son, you must forgive your old father, he has missed you, feared for you.' The Vicomte walked quietly up to him, and placed his hand on his son's arm. He turned him and led him, still with his hand on his arm, to a chair, inclined his head and gestured to him to be seated. Eugène did so. His father swung himself on to a facing armchair.

'So, you must tell me. Have you been successful? You have been away, over *la Manche*, no doubt, Jersey — no, no, well then, *Bretagne*, no, you cannot say... Well, what have you been doing? Does it help our cause? Have you been to the *Prince de Condé*'s army ... no, you have not. So, you cannot say — so, what should I ask you, then?' The Vicomte had stood up by now, and was gesticulating, largely to avoid facing his son in the full flight of anger again.

'Father, what I do, and have done, is of no significance. I have come to see you because I believe — I am not as yet completely sure — but... I do believe that I wish to get married.'

His father's face froze. Being struck dumb was the last thing that his son had expected of him, and Eugène found himself completely disconcerted. The Vicomte reached out for the snuffbox on the table, fumbled it open, brought it over to his nose with trembling fingers, and took a pinch of snuff. The result was instantaneous: he immediately sneezed, coughed once and then began to look as if he had been seized by an apoplexy. Eugène rose to his feet in alarm, but the old man raised his hand to prevent him from intervening and took a deep breath. His voice when it came was small, like a door creaking on old, rusty hinges.

'And who, may I ask, is the fortunate young woman?'

'I believe, father, that it will be the sister of my close friend Wentworth. You recall Wentworth, no doubt. You thought well of him.'

'I am not at this instant concerned to think well or otherwise of *him*. The name of the lady, if you please.'

'Miss Amelia Wentworth, known to her mother as Amélie.'

'I see.' The Vicomte was silent for what seemed a long time. 'And tell me, what do you expect to live on, Eugène?'

Eugène coughed, and felt the blood rising to his face. He took a breath. 'Well, there I was hoping that you might be able to assist... I mean advise me, father. I have given some thought...'

'And does this young lady know of your tastes, Eugène? Of your proclivities, shall we say? Of the company you have chosen to keep, despite all warnings — no, despite all *prohibitions*, despite the danger of damage to your family's name...'

Eugène stood up. His face was red, and as the anger pinched his nose it was apparent that he shared at least one physical characteristic more than he would have wished with his father.

'I am in love with Miss Wentworth. I have foresworn all... I have pledged myself to her, and to none other. All I require is some assistance...'

His father's tone was cool. Had the heat of the day not ruled out such an easy assumption, it might even have been regarded as icy.

'Are you accepted? By her?' No reply was given. The Vicomte pressed on. 'Have your advances to her been welcomed? Is Wentworth apprised of the situation, of the great honour done to his family?'

Eugène looked around for his hat. He had brought none. He bowed.

'I shall bid you good day, Vicomte. Father.' The Vicomte lifted himself out of his chair.

'You may wait, my son. Yes, wait! Eugène, now come, my boy…'

But Eugène had gone.

After his father's savage treatment, Eugène felt in need of companionship, someone to whom he could bare his soul. That would restore him. After these quarrels, he could never get his father out of his head, the bandy legs, the beaky nose, the ridiculously outdated hair-powder, but above all the disdain that oozed off words and stuck to sentences. He thought inevitably of Dick; his good friend Major Francis Houghton was too far away in Chatham. If he told Dick all about it, Dick would listen patiently, understand what he had been going through. He had been walking heedlessly for some time, in a daze, but he noticed now that he was right next to Dick's house. Yet he was still undecided. He paused, and put his back against a row of railings. A young woman passing with her maid blushed under her bonnet and looked down, while the maid glanced back over her shoulder at him.

Impulsively, he swung off back down the street, pausing again at the foot of the steps to gather his thoughts, and trod slowly and deliberately up to the imposing door with its familiar brass lion and bell-pull and the arched fanlight above. He banged his fist on its panelling, and heard the footsteps approaching inside. The door opened, and the space was filled by Samuel, immaculately uniformed but without his wig, and with a broad grin on his face. He stood back, but as Eugène made to go past him put a massive hand on his chest, and looked down at him severely.

'And where do you think you are going, sir?'

Eugène stared at his face in shock, but Samuel withdrew the hand and stepped right back, restoring the grin.

'Mr Eugène, it is a long time since we saw you, far too long, sir. The company has been missing you, all the ladies as well as the gentlemen.'

Samuel closed the door, and Eugène waited for him. They walked together along the hallway, as far as that was possible with Samuel's bulk, and stopped at the foot of the staircase, which — unusually — ran up from the back of the house.

'Mr Courtenay is upstairs, sir, in his dressing room. We are still quiet at this hour. Tonight is one of our evenings for play. No dice, sir, just the cards. We have only two a week. Invited guests, of course. And then there is what we call our "salon". But you will remember that, Mr Eugène, I am sure? Shall I take word to Mr Courtenay that you are here?'

'No, thank you, Samuel. I am pleased to see you in good health. I shall run up myself and surprise him.'

Dick Courtenay's rooms were on the upper floor. He liked the air, the sky, and looking down on people and trees. The door from the landing opened into what he called his parlour, which led off through one door to his bedroom, and through the other to his dressing-room, which was also connected to the bedroom. All the rooms were wallpapered, oak leaves in the parlour as Eugène recalled, with a preponderance of mirrors with frames of different designs and eras hung arbitrarily — some gilded, some fretwork, some walnut, some mahogany. Eugène slipped through to the far side of the room, and decided it was better to tap on the door of the dressing-room rather than indulge himself and surprise Aunt Harriet.

Dick was sitting in front of the mirror on his dressing table, which was beautifully oval and hung from slender and graceful arms, all of which came back to Eugène in an instant, reminding him of how Dick held himself when at any of the *soirées*. He pivoted on the quaint, revolving stool which allowed him to achieve perfection in his *toilette*, and somehow spread both eyes and lips in a consuming smile in that astonishing way as he saw Eugène. But composure remained everything, and he pointed imperiously to his cheek.

'Come now, you naughty fellow, where have you been? You should abase yourself in front of your Aunt Harriet, but a peck will do.'

Eugène grinned across at him, but merely pulled up a chair and sat looking at him over its back.

'Since when would a peck do for you, Dicky? I see I catch you in a rare moment of peace and quiet.'

Dick, or Aunt Harriet as he liked to be called, had his hair tied back from his face, and his cheeks were both whitened and touched with the rouge brush. He favoured a style that was now *passé*, but he would not hear of criticism, and his rule was steely in his own house.

'Oh, my boy, we shall be heaving tonight. Georgiana may come to us. But did you hear the news of Albinia wherever you have been? No, I thought as much. Gillray has her in his sights with his cartoon, and that may be the death of us all.'

Eugène did not respond, and he had drifted off, his face blank. Dick took pity.

'Lady Buckinghamshire? Sarah Archer? The "Faro Ladies"? Gillray has them sketched in a pillory? No, nothing? Where have you been, poppet?'

'Don't call me that.' And then, more mildly: 'I can't tell you, Dicky, you know how it is. Mum's the word … yes, even to Auntie. Come now, tell me, how you have been?'

Dick had turned back to face the mirror, and was content to cast glances at him from the reflection.

'Oh, life goes on, much as before. But we keep our good humour here, through it all.' He looked more searchingly at Eugène. 'Been to see dear papa, have we? Had a go, did he?'

'That sort of thing. He does not change. I had something to tell him, but I might as well have pissed in my own ale. Not sure where to go and what to do, frankly, Dick.'

'So come to see Aunt Harriet.' Dick stood up, went over to a small cabinet, and took out a bottle of port and two small glasses. Eugène waved his hand in dismissal of the idea. Dick brought the bottle and the glasses over, notwithstanding, and poured himself a glass.

'A little early in the day, but I shall take some for you.' He sat down again. 'Now tell me.'

Eugène swung the chair round the right way, and sat down leadenly on it.

'You must not scoff, or I'll be off, d'y'hear? I know it sounds strange, but I've had enough scorn from my father, and a man has to make up his mind… I am thinking of getting married, Dick. To be more precise, I am in love.'

The other knew better than to make a joke of this revelation at this point. He paused for a while, and spoke mildly.

'And the object of your affections is…?'

'A gentlewoman. But I'm damned if she shows any interest in me. I don't know what I'm doing. My father ridicules the idea, dammit, and is what I'm feeling enough? God knows, Dicky, you know enough about me to…' He looked across despairingly at his companion, and spread his arms hopelessly.

'Is this wrong? I am all over the place. A woman, a woman, a woman! What shall I do?'

'You shall have that drink with me, Eugène, and we will talk about it.'

Eugène stood up, resolutely.

'No, I can't do that. I can't stay, I must go. It's just — where, I don't know.'

Dick got to his feet again, took the one or two short paces to come to his side, and placed his arm round Eugène's shoulders.

'Come, stay with me, my dear boy. We'll work it out. I have missed you. Just stay for a while. For old time's sake.' He removed his arm, but did not touch him further. Eugène heaved a sigh, almost like a sob, and sat down.

'Pour me that one glass, then. Just for old time's sake.'

CHAPTER IV: LAURENT'S TEA-PARTY

Madame Louise du Plessis, who now owned her late husband's bank in the bustling town of Auray in central Brittany, graciously accepted Laurent Guèvremont's invitation to act as a host for a tea-party he was to hold in his own house. Laurent had been a client of her husband, and since her bereavement he had always shown her the respect that she felt was her due. Guèvremont had come quite properly to call for her on the morning in question, and they had proceeded elegantly from her house to his, occasioning just the kind of notice that she would expect from other well-dressed citizens in the streets of Auray as they passed, both of them occasionally acknowledging a particularly significant acquaintance. Her hand rested quite appropriately on his levelled forearm, while he told her about the potential there was in a fashion for tea, and how Jean-François Mariage had taken the initiative in Lille, as he himself might now do here. She admired his sense of enterprise, while privately resolving not to invest a sou in it herself.

Laurent Guèvremont's butler, Bernard Sarzou had the door open before they had crossed the court, and *Madame* du Plessis had removed her arm discreetly as they came into the view of the house. Laurent handed her with due formality up the steps, Bernard bowing appropriately as they entered. Louise du Plessis glanced around her with satisfaction, noting the sheen of wax on the wooden stands in the hall and the slim vases of flowers, displaying carefully selected rose blooms of delicate shades. She looked towards the butler, tilting her head almost imperceptibly in appreciation, and then spoke to Laurent.

'Guèvremont, your man here has that rare ability to understand the taste of refined society. I have no doubt,' she added, 'that he is indebted to your own excellent judgment for that.'

Laurent took the compliment well, although he had entrusted the practicalities of decoration totally to Bernard. He had not become successful in business affairs without acquiring the confidence to delegate decisively.

'I trust that we may now visit the salon?'

The butler had already begun to move past them discreetly, and he was there again at the salon door to open it and reveal the improvements, to which Laurent had in truth not yet adjusted his own conservative expectations. He did not like domestic change, but he did want to create a good impression, and not just with this thoroughly respectable woman he had adopted as his hostess for this occasion. Bernard, because he felt it was his duty to do so, stood at the door and watched as *Madame* du Plessis conducted her inspection of the fabrics on which she had scrupulously advised.

'I do so like these drapes, Guèvremont, and I hope you are by now reconciled to them. Vimoutiers *cretonne* is all the rage, I am reliably informed, and I think it will soon be a talking point even here in our lamentably small Breton town. There is such a lightness to them.'

'Most certainly.'

'Oh, I do so approve of the side-tables in here! Walnut is such an attractive wood, and your man here has given them new lustre. They were lost and merely gathering dust in my old *petit salon*. And there can surely be no doubt at all that the *guéridon* is a wonderful centrepiece: I do like a round table of good proportions, and this is a Jacob, you know, with scarcely a mark on it. I see that your man has brought the sideboard in from the dining room, and that will do very nicely for serving the tea, while the *guéridon* will display our *pâtisserie* quite delightfully. The *pâtisserie* may be placed here now, do you not think?'

Bernard left the door slightly ajar as he went out. They were more than ready in the kitchen, and there had been no raised voices or tempers despite the nerves. *Madame* du Plessis might convey orders to the butler through comments made to her admirer, but she had the good sense not to presume in any way yet with the cook and the sacred enclave of her kitchen.

The door creaked from the hall, and Gilles entered the room. He had, in fact, already been in the kitchen, despite being dressed to kill or be killed, as the latest jokes had it, and although he had been forbidden to touch the small cakes and biscuits, he had been reassured by Bernard that they were about to be carried up to the salon. In typical fashion, and for no reason at all, Gilles had not anticipated that there would be anyone else in the room. So he came to an abrupt halt when he saw this elaborately dressed woman whose name he had already forgotten. Guèvremont came forward.

'Ah, Gilles. *Madame* du Plessis, may I introduce my ward to you, *Monsieur* Gilles of Kergohan?'

'At your service, *Madame*.' He hoped that would do; the bow was not too deep, he felt. *Madame* du Plessis let her hand drop; the bow would have to do for now.

Gaëlle came in with an immense tray, and placed the faience plates without further prompting on the round table. There were the macaroons and madeleines, Gilles could see, but also some *sablés* he had not expected. Glorious. Laurent unexpectedly put his arm around Gilles' shoulders and squeezed hard.

'Well, my boy, will you be excited to see your guests? How do you feel about my English tea party? Do you think it will catch on? *Madame* du Plessis has generously agreed to be our hostess this morning, and to chaperone the young people. We must acknowledge that we are in her debt, do you not agree?'

Which question was he supposed to answer? 'Yes' seemed the only thing to say.

The doorbell rang in the hall, and a loud, young male voice was heard. Théodore Bérard's pomade advanced into the room ahead of him, mingling in confusion with the perfume that rose from the handkerchief dangling from his ringed hand; there were yet more rings on the other. As Bérard stepped forward, Gilles stared open-mouthed at the extraordinary lapels on his coat, and the grotesque size of his cravat. Théodore was, indeed, everything *à la mode* that Gilles had failed to be, and his appeal to *Madame* du Plessis showed clearly in her eyes as he took her hand, brushed his lips deftly over it while accomplishing an elegant bow, and uttered the simple greeting — albeit with some suitably delicate, muted feeling — of 'Madame'.

A discreetly rung bell had Bernard looking in at the salon door and catching the eye of the *bourgeoise*, who broke off her *tête-à-tête* with Bernard and went through into the hall. She swept back into the room with her fingers lightly touching the dainty elbow of Clémence de Moire. Clémence was an acquaintance of Laurent's daughter, Joséphine Guèvremont, and this morning she was wearing one of those thin dresses which were all the latest fashion with the younger women. Hardly a surprise, then, that the *bourgeois* himself came right over to speak to Clémence, whose hair had been trimmed neatly, and who had those pink cheeks that some of them favoured.

When she finally made her appearance, Joséphine Guèvremont was sporting the same sullen look she had worn for weeks, ever since Captain Leroux had left his garrison duties in Auray to serve in the fighting, away and over the Rhine. Her yellow dress might seem old-fashioned, in contrast to the others, but she could carry off anything, and her hair was dressed in trailing ribbons, her shoes a matching yellow, and she carried a fan, one of those Chinese painted items which she liked a great deal. She and the *bourgeoise* curtsied to each other in due order, and her face relaxed no further when her father came up and kissed her affectionately on the cheek. She just went to sit down in one of the armchairs, placed her fan on her lap and folded her hands slowly on top of it, staring miserably straight out in front of her, limply, for all the world like a shot partridge.

Gaëlle came in again with the tea, which she placed on the sideboard. She was dressed nicely too, over and above the usual, but the only perfume surrounding her was that of sweet macaroons. The *bourgeois* spoke up.

'*Mesdames, messieurs*, tea is served. If you will be seated, your cup will be brought to you by the serving maid. The English take their tea sitting, I am told, and in this little entertainment of ours we shall imitate them in that, if not in any other particulars. *Madame* du Plessis, if you would supervise the distribution of this refreshment as our hostess, you would indeed do us a great honour.'

Théodore Bérard sat down on a chair between Gilles and Joséphine, and after glancing briefly at Joséphine's face spoke firstly to Gilles, complimenting him on his new breeches. Gilles looked surprised.

'I'm pleased that you think well of them. That damn fellow who measured me for them gave me some nonsense about whether I dressed to the right or the left, and before I knew what was what he was sliding his hand up my leg towards my best friends. I'd have had him by the throat, but apparently it's what they all do.'

Bérard laughed loudly, without replying, and jumped up to bring a plate of madeleines over to Joséphine, who declined them with the slightest motion of her head. Undeterred, he risked speaking to her.

'Tell me, *Mademoiselle* Guèvremont, do you walk out much in this delightful summer weather?'

'With my maid, but as little as possible. It is too hot.'

'It is true we have few parks, but our promenades, especially those by the river, are justly admired. Do you go to the river?'

'Not unless I cannot avoid it. The insects are troublesome.'

'Ah. I see. But do you ride, *mademoiselle*?'

'I detest the smell of horses.'

'But surely…'

'There is no *surely* for me, Théodore. Not any more. None at all.' A tear welled up in the corner of her eye. Bérard looked round for help, but none came. Gilles was intently studying an obscure portrait on the far wall, so Bérard blundered on.

'Have we heard anything more, *mademoiselle*, of our accomplished dancing partner, Captain Leroux? Of Nicolas? A little stiff in manner, perhaps, but…'

Joséphine stood up suddenly, spilling her tea on her lap, and gasped at the scald of the hot water. Clémence came quickly over to her, but Joséphine pushed past her in tears and rushed out of the salon, followed closely by Gaëlle. Bérard was deeply embarrassed; Gilles continued his close study of the portrait, even more intently than before. Clémence de Moire made an admirable effort to start a conversation, but Gilles completely failed to notice her and instead stood up and advanced intently to the *guéridon* to resume his sampling of the macaroons. The *sablés* were also quite magnificent: buttery, and crisp, and tasting of almonds.

He picked up the plate of *sablés* and went over to Clémence, who was standing quite still: offended, elegant, and slightly flushed. He noticed nothing of any of that, but gave her his best boyish smile and thrust the plate towards her enthusiastically.

'Here you are, *Mademoiselle* de Moire. Just try one of these. You will not be disappointed.'

CHAPTER V: THE DARK OF THE STREETS

Loic eased his way past the bustle just outside Brooks's club in St James's Street, crossed the street and walked on in the direction he was now sure his latest quarry would take. This was his third successful watch after two last week, and he was now completely sure of the route. What mattered was that the man would indeed pass close enough to the new room they had taken for the trick to be made, although in this case it was hard to see what the trick would be. Seemingly quiet and restrained, this fellow went during the day to various addresses, merchants, private houses, and at least one bank, and that was a fruitless and tedious trail for Loic. But in the evening, like many men of his class, he settled down to a routine, and he would go to this grand building which the link boys hanging around outside called a club: Brooks's, apparently. It looked like a hive for the rich and respectable, going in and out, escorted or taking carriages; his man always walked, and walked alone.

At the end of last week, Coline had decided to take a tiny room above a tavern, right on the fellow's line of progress from St James's, one with a side staircase up to it and just a small landing. They gave their usual story about a brother and a sister, and there was enough word around about Frenchmen down on their luck that it was easy to get it without more questions asked. Once Loic had returned, they sat on the two chairs they had brought with them, and Coline asked him again what time the man left the club, and where he walked, and how long he took, until Loic became annoyed.

'What are we doing with him? If you ask me, he's all wrong for the trade, and here we are setting up a new rendezvous just for him. I haven't seen a flicker of interest in him to help us. Head down, lost in thought, hands in coat pockets, hat crammed on head, doesn't look to left or to right. You should have left me to sniff a good one out, as I have before.'

Coline paid him little attention, and said: 'Here's the plan. This time, I want you to squeal out loud that you have been robbed.'

Loic looked in disbelief at her.

'What in the name of Saint Brioc is the good of that? You think he will start to fondle me just because I am squealing on a street corner?'

'Listen to me. It will be at night, on his way back, quiet, poorly lit, and I shall rob you. In a man's clothing. Don't protest, you know I can do it. I shall have a small knife, I think, to hold at your throat. Rings and a purse. You will be dressed up, as usual, but with a coat. You will squeal, I shall curse you, he will dash up and I shall run away.'

Loic recognised the tone of voice. It would be no good arguing with her. She already knew precisely what she wanted.

'I can do that. But what then?'

'He will ask you if you have been harmed, and you will tell him what has been stolen.'

Loic took a breath, before taking the risk of another question. 'How do I manage that?'

'Why, as volubly as you wish, in good, plain French. He speaks French.'

'How do you know that?'

Coline gave him one of her looks. He clamped his teeth together, partly in anger, partly to stop himself saying any more.

'Trust me.' The room fell silent, apart from the cry of a fruit-seller outside that drifted up the stairs. It was hot in the room.

She smiled at him. 'Well, you can speak, you know. You can ask "What then?"'.

He did not smile back at her.

'What then?'

'You will say, utterly distraught, that the thief has snatched your mother's ring, as well as all the money you have. You have just arrived from Jersey. He will understand.'

'And?'

'And you will run after me. No, the first thing is that he will say "Quick", or "Quick, then!"'

His puzzlement and incredulity got the better of him. 'How can you be so sure of that?'

The look that crossed her face was both wistful and frightening at the same time, and her voice was hard.

'Just take it that I am.'

He risked one more question. After all, method was everything, and she knew that.

'What about the knife? Won't he be scared of the knife? Why should he run into danger?'

'Just take it from me: he won't be scared of a knife. But more to the point, I must allow you time to get all that done, the conversation with him, the story. So, I shall stop not too far away, in a shadow or a doorway, and be counting the money. We shall pick it out when we choose the spot, so you know where I will be.'

Loic stood up, and stretched. 'I'm hungry. Let's map this out tonight, before he changes his habits.' He was still puzzled, but he hoped he could slip in one more question, casually.

'And what do we do with him once we've got him?'

She refused to look at him. 'Leave that to me.'

Eugène took a long walk, finding his way in the warm evening air and the half-light down towards the river. His mind was wrestling with his future, veering madly between Australia and the banality of the *imprimerie* Mame in Tours, where his father had acquired a significant interest, and a brand-new building was being constructed. His father always managed to think ahead, and had sold property and invested money before anyone of the *noblesse* near Tours had thought of doing so. And yet — as Eugène sardonically reflected — if sending his son to be educated in England was part of that *mentalité* of investment, it had not brought the advantages that his father might have anticipated. The net profit had been that, at times, Eugène could still not be sure if he thought better in English or in French, although the speech of his childhood with those familiar, local inflexions would always be comforting.

He avoided the south side of St James's Park, with its notoriety that he could not face, and cut into the broader thoroughfares of Whitehall and Parliament Street, the Abbey standing heavily in monumental obscurity in the distance. The inns off to the right could still be heard, but the approach to Westminster Bridge itself was relatively quiet, just one carriage trundling past and raising dust. The smooth, low arc of the bridge was remarkable, stretching out to an extraordinary extent, although who would truly want to cross over it to the timber yards and the fields beyond? It was surely a way *in* rather than a way *out*. Yet there was a mystery in the gloom, and he found at that moment that he craved the open space that the views up and downstream revealed. The lamps had been lit, and signalled across to other lights now glinting like stars behind fleeting clouds.

For the first time in some days he chuckled, at the sense of being a poet in his head at least, and as he turned back from a couple walking slowly ahead of him, arm in arm, he spied a lonely figure resting in one of the alcoves. Perhaps this was the poet, musing at the sight of London, wrapping his dreamy imaginings around the stark towers of Westminster Abbey? The figure stepped out into the light of one of the lamps, and Eugène found himself alarmed by his features and his dress. He was young, refined in manner, and muttering in a mad, aimless way; but, as the light caught them, both the cut of his coat and the style of his cravat sent a sharp and unnerving signal to Eugène about life back in France.

Yet enough of thinking. The boy — he was not much more than that — lurched forward and stumbled towards the balustrade on the far side. Eugène ran: he was nimble and quick, and in seconds he had grabbed hold of the lad and got between him and the edge of the bridge. The boy wriggled, crying, 'No. no, no!' at him, and trying to push Eugène away. But Eugène put his arm like a clamp around his shoulders, and bent his face to the other's.

'No, no, no — you have got that just right, young man. No, no, no, it is, and it will stay that way. Do you understand me?'

The young man looked at him, and then lowered his head.

Eugène released his grip, but tucked his arm tightly into the young man's and started to walk them both back off the bridge to the west. But on instinct he stopped, and took him over to the balustrade. The young man shrank back from it, but Eugène forced him forwards, now resisting, into looking over the edge.

'Have a good look. Do you see that? It's low tide. That's what the stink is. You would have ended face-down in the filthy mud: inglorious, smelly, and *ignoble*. Now come along with me.'

The young man became meek but as they stepped forwards in silence, leaving the carriageway of the bridge behind, he sneaked a look at Eugène's face. Eugène steered him to the back of the Admiralty, which he knew well, and they sat down on a ledge of stone, facing the now dim outlines of St James's Park. The young man took a deep breath, stood up, and extended his hand to Eugène, trying for his best English.

'I thank you, sir, with all my full heart.'

Eugène took his hand, without rising, and spoke to him in French:

'You're welcome, *mon brave*. I am at your service. Come, sit down.'

The young man sat down, a little stunned. He had felt extremely alone in an alien city, but here in this still, dusky setting it now felt as if he was partly back at home. Eugène decided that the conversation should continue in their shared native language.

'Well, here we are now, and for the moment the world is not so bad. We shall leave aside who I am for the time being, but I will surprise you more by saying that I believe I know your name. What do you say to that?'

'I think I will believe anything now. I do not know yours.'

'Ah, there you might just be wrong. But not to create more suspense — I believe you to be Alphonse. Am I right?'

'I think you must be my guardian angel.'

'Now, Alphonse, we shall sit here a little longer while I tell you that I think I also know that you are miserable, and that you have been quite recently in the house of a Mr Richard Courtenay. What I do not know is *why* you are miserable, and perhaps I can ask you to inform me of that.'

'I cannot.'

'I have to say I doubt that, Alphonse, and also that perhaps you owe me a little debt of gratitude, and that sharing your current, overwhelming affliction with me is what I duly request. You see, I too am acquainted with Dick Courtenay, and it is he who suggested to me, merely in passing in a conversation, that you might have run into trouble. How strange that is.'

'Exceedingly strange.'

'Yes —' and here Eugène stretched out his legs, and brought them back up close again — 'but some people learn to be very observant, watchful even, and they look out for others, and Dick is very much one of those. That is why he spoke to me, incidentally, of you. He had begun to be concerned for you.'

'But I hardly know him. I have been to his house…'

'…and gazed out of the window, I gather. Perhaps rather too often. Now that kind of thing can be dangerous, young Alphonse.'

'I am not particularly young. It is just my curse that I happen to look young, no matter what I do.'

'Well, I shouldn't worry about that.' Eugène stood up. 'We shall walk, and perhaps the closer we get to your home the more willing you will be to talk to me. Would I be right about that?'

'Let's walk, then. But not too quickly. Where is *your* home?'

'Not very far from yours. You see, I know your mother.'

CHAPTER VI: A FACE FROM THE PAST

Justin Wentworth let his eyes drift across the drawing-room at Brooks's as Charles Fox left a lively debate and headed, no doubt, for the cards, followed by a small entourage. Justin's companion, the dissenter Richard Sharp, picked up the slight sign of inattention, and followed his eyes briefly, but returned to their conversation on the sadly languishing cause of abolition.

'Stanhope, yes, I cannot think when we last saw him. Rather like you, Wentworth, out of sight of the rest of us. Head buried in his scientific projects, I shouldn't wonder. Do you see him down in Devon? No, of course not, or you would not be asking after him here.'

''Tis no matter. But I always found him a sympathetic man. Being married to Pitt's sister must have been difficult for one of his opinions in recent years.'

'They have been difficult for many, and for many of the just causes. Even Wilberforce is quieter. I do not know whether it is the excesses or the successes of France that have had the worst effect, certainly for abolition. Shall I see you for a breakfast with Samuel Rogers tomorrow? Samuel informed me that he hopes to have Fuseli there, and your sister Miss Amelia draws, you tell me?'

'My mother, too. It is kind of you to remember, Richard. I have little to keep me here longer, but a breakfast in such company would be a good parting.'

'Well, we may get Fox too, if he plays on into the night. It is only round the corner, which was a clever choice for bringing company together. I'll look to see you then.'

Justin was left alone, which suited him. The conversation at Brooks's was often enlivening, exercising at times, rarely difficult. But his general sense was of paralysis in reform, and of parliament's failure to learn anything at all from America or France, despite the lively and outspoken minds to be found on these premises. Still, he had a wife with child to consider, and he must be getting home to Chittesleigh. Another day of calls in London in the cause of abolition would have to satisfy his conscience.

It was not especially late, but as he walked north from the club in St James's the streets gradually narrowed, and the spill of light from lamps or inns and houses became less evident. He was aware that he had been followed on these walks from the club to his lodgings in the evenings; but the inconsequential and repetitive nature of the stalking removed the threat of a footpad, let alone a cutpurse. He had tried one or two old tricks, more intrigued than concerned, and thought he might just have caught sight of a young lad, and once at least a slightly older, perhaps stockier figure. What they were doing was anyone's guess. But times being what they were, and Pitt so febrile about insurrection, he supposed the company he was frequenting here in London might have attracted agents to him. Good god, was it that bad? It scarcely seemed possible, but what had happened at home in Devon last year, with a spy in his own house, had been at first inconceivable.

The evening air was close in the alleys, but he felt at ease in them knowing his way around each now familiar corner with its landmarks, oddly similar to following a track in the forests of the New World, with which he had become familiar in his military days. He knew that the street that ran across the end of this stretch was wider, and that was just after a small court on the left. A figure moved suddenly into his line of sight, perhaps coming out of the court, some thirty paces away, and then another rushed in headlong from the street, and grappled with the first, tumbling out of sight. Justin stopped for an instant, weighing up what he had seen: he heard an oath, and muffled sounds of a threat and of protest. The figures came into view again, in a struggle, and by then Justin had started running. The assailant stooped with his hands holding the other's wrists, and stared back up at Justin from under a three-cornered hat and a greatcoat. He shoved the slighter man back out of sight and ran off into the street at the end.

Justin reached the small court in an instant, bent down, and picked up the young man.

'My purse, my rings! He has taken my mother's rings!'

'Are you hurt?' The young man shook his head. 'Quickly now, follow me.'

The young man held his arm briefly. 'Be careful — he has a knife.' He had slipped into French, but the accent had been plain from the beginning.

'Never mind that. Follow me, but stay back.'

They ran, together. Or, rather, they had just started when a dark figure hurtled across the end of the alley, so they sped after him. He was quick, and in twenty paces he ducked under an arch to the right, clattered through an inner courtyard, and banged the outer gate at the end of it. But the hunt was on, and an astonished boy on a late-night errand stood back against a wall in fright as first one and then another man rushed past, followed closely by a young lad.

Justin reached a corner, came to a halt, and peeped around it just below a projecting stone. The new street was quite narrow.

He saw the thief slow down ahead, stop, and look over his shoulder. Justin reached out an arm for the young man following him, and pulled him in just behind the corner. The thief had taken off his three-cornered hat to run, but now had the confidence to put it back on, and saunter up some further paces into a doorway. They could hear the hinges and the latch in the stillness of the warm night air. Justin leaned his head in to the other's ear, and spoke softly in French to him.

'Shall we go and get your rings back, then? And your purse, you say?'

'Yes, if you please, if you dare.'

'He will put the knife down. He will take off his hat and his coat, and he will empty the purse on to a table or a chair, and look at the rings and count the money. He will not hear us coming.'

Loic thought of the sparse furniture in the bare room, and said: 'Yes, maybe a chair. How can you be sure he will not hear us?'

'Trust me.'

Justin walked down the street. He was feeling confident, contented to have action after so much city business, a chance to help someone who must surely be a young and naïve *émigré*. The trick was to be silent, of course, bare stockings on the inevitable stairs, but then straight for the knife. The boy could wait at the bottom, by the street door, to trip up the thief if he made a run for it. There was just one small thought irritating him, which was why the young French lad showed no surprise in being answered in his own language. And there was something a little odd about the thief too; but it was too soon to put his finger on it. No one by the door: a dead silence, no trace of a movement, and as he suspected, a staircase. He took off his boots, handed them to the lad to keep with the hat, and motioned him to stand by the outside wall, sticking out a leg to show him what he had in mind. The young man nodded.

Coline was standing on the far side of the small room, but had not yet taken off her hat or her coat. She had put some rings and a purse on one of the chairs. Her back was to the door, but she heard him soft-foot up the treads because she was keeping completely still, despite her pounding heart. The small knife lay on the other chair. She stayed quite still, and heard him move the knife, but when he seized her arms from behind he was not holding it. Something in her manner, her absolute stillness, made him drop his hands and stand back, alert but puzzled. Coline turned round slowly, removed her hat, and took the pins out of her hair, which she shook out. She knew she was flushed, and anger and desire surged in her now they were face to face, after what seemed like so many years, although truly it was no more than a few.

'Justin Wentworth.'

There was a sound behind him, and the young lad stood in the doorway. He tossed Justin's boots to the floor.

Coline spoke past Justin to him. 'Out. Walk for an hour, and then come back.'

Loic shut the door quietly behind him, suppressing an oath, and all was quiet, as Justin stared in astonishment at the familiar face in front of him.

Coline's eyes narrowed as she looked at Justin. He recognised her immediately, an indelible mark in the account that he might someday take of his life. He was better acquainted with her than he wished to admit standing in this bare, meagre room that was good for nothing as far as he could see. What on earth was she doing here? That she was angry was obvious, but he had last seen Marie-Rose Heaume standing at the back door to her father's house in Quebec, just over four years ago, in the reluctantly warming springtime of those regions. He had to speak, even if he did not choose to sit, which would surely have been capitulation.

'Marie-Rose…'

'*Mademoiselle* Heaume, if you please.' She sat down, and motioned him to the other chair. He did not move. 'Captain Wentworth, you will sit down because I ask you to do so. We have both been at exercise.'

He held his ground, and remained standing. His tone was severe, for the simple reason that was how he felt. 'Why have you brought me here? What is this deception?'

She stared at him incredulously, and burst out laughing bitterly. 'Deception? You accuse me of deception?' She then reclaimed her habitual *sang-froid*. 'Oh, a little trick, that was all. I thought you might enjoy it. The Queen's Ranger, the backwoodsman, the man who boasted of tracking down human quarry. By Saint Anne, I made it easy enough for you.'

'Who is the boy? Is he with you?'

'The boy is Loic. He is a Breton.'

Justin reconciled himself to a short conversation. He pulled the chair towards him and sat on it, taking her knife from the waistband of his breeches and placing it on the floor.

'I see,' he said. A meaningless statement: he saw nothing, but he was becoming extremely apprehensive.

Coline got to her feet, and took off her greatcoat, revealing a man's shirt and breeches. She pulled the shirt loose, and he caught a glimpse of her belly. Her hips were broader, and there was more flesh on her cheeks, but she had not changed. She caught him looking at her, and just for a moment felt a tremor of hope before she sat down again; but his face showed no trace of any residual warmth, let alone desire. His tone was measured.

'The whole retinue parted along with Lieutenant-Governor Simcoe, upriver for Kingston. I could stay no longer. I was his adjutant. You had left for the woods by then. I could hardly leave a message for you, with Berthe or whatever her name was at your father's house, still less a letter. It was not my choice.'

'Yet your company's departure was bound to come. You will have known of the preparations.' Her voice was dull, as if she recognised defeat, felt its numbing blow once again.

'How could we predict accurately when it would be? The conditions … the reports from upstream on the River Lawrence were uncertain, as you yourself know, the conditions vary year on year, and, anyway, you were gone.'

'So I am to blame, am I? I went on the trail in the lakes with my father, as the season was breaking, and you gave me no warning that you would be leaving too. The first trapping trip of the year: just as we had always done, father and daughter.'

'Simcoe was Lieutenant-Governor of Upper Canada, for God's sake! I was in Quebec by chance. Stuck there over winter. We were always due to go to our post up-river, once the freeze was over.' He was indignant because he felt the full weight of the accusation, now she was in front of him. He had allowed himself to believe that she would have forgotten him. It dawned on him that he had misjudged her from the beginning, and it was now far too late.

'You could have written. From 'Upper Canada', in your English words, with your English boundaries, from Kingston: Frontenac, my father always used to call it. You could have sent something.' Her voice had sunk to a whisper.

'How could I write to you after … what had happened? A letter from a young officer to a young woman? What would your father have said to that?'

'Or come to see me. After what had happened. Or is it the truth that you had lost interest, that you "happened" on me in Quebec by chance?'

'How could I have come to see you? I was at my military postings, on duty; there was no occasion to be absent for a month, no, for more, for much more! By the time we passed by Quebec on our way back home nearly two years later you had gone. There was no word of where, just that your father had died, and that you had left. I leave you to imagine the state of my feelings at that report.' He realised his voice had become strained, almost strident, like that of an officer. He glanced at her face, and felt true guilt. 'I am sorry. So very sorry. But I still do not understand why you are here, in London. What can I do for you now?'

She put her hand in a pocket of the greatcoat and came the few steps over to him. Quickly, she reached down, deftly took the knife from the floor and brought it up to his face. He flinched instinctively. She grabbed some of his hair tightly between the fingers of her other hand and cut off a curl. Then she stood back and opened both of her palms: a lock of dark hair lay in each of them.

'You can come and meet your daughter.'

CHAPTER VII: EUGÈNE STEPS IN

In the end, they walked up to Dick Courtenay's. Alphonse had been adamant that he could not go home to his mother's lodgings and had become quite distraught about it. So Eugène wheeled him about a little away from Marylebone, and then decided that Alphonse might feel protected where so many others did, in the place where he had previously found company and sympathy. On their approach to Dick's house, it was evident from the noise and the lights that a large company had gathered. Once Samuel had ushered them in, Eugène waved Alphonse off to lose himself for a while in the rout, while he wandered over himself to the window which had been the source of so much distress.

Something about Dick's flamboyance dictated that on rather too many evenings the curtains were not drawn across, shutting out the street, and Eugène reckoned that this above all had been the undoing of Alphonse. He had mentioned it before to Dick, who could be endlessly diplomatic when dealing in person with *le beau monde*, but all too readily rash and careless when confronted by those outside it. Eugène pinched his lower lip in thought. It was obvious that what seemed like Alphonse to be a disaster had been set up as a trap from the beginning, and the handsome young *gars* had been the bait or the lure. Someone standing by the railings below was easily visible from the window, since the front steps raised the floor of the house from ground level, and someone standing by the window was plainly conspicuous. After what may have been a long preparation, the lure had worked, and the young *émigré* had walked blindly into the trap.

All that was tawdry enough, but the young woman — for so Alphonse had described her, not that in his panic he had taken much more in — was something of an enigma. Even more so, the fact that this crooked pair had been French, and preyed on a French boy. It was not just that this was of *mauvais esprit*, in the circumstances now affecting all *émigrés* in this city of strangers: it seemed an unusual partnership in an unusual crime, daring as well as unscrupulous.

Madeleine came up to Eugène. She was particularly bewitching tonight, with curls freshly turned and extravagant earrings, a perfume that Eugène would have sworn came from Paris were that possible, and ridiculous quantities of lace to set off the powdered face in her antique style. She pouted her lips together to form a kiss, but had no intention of delivering it. She merely wanted to be admired, and Eugène provoked her because he was standing on his own, lost in thought, which was inadmissible. She tapped him with her fan.

'You naughty boy,' she said.

'I protest! No, I am not! No time to be naughty tonight, Madeleine. You will have to look elsewhere.'

'I have been looking and finding elsewhere for rather too long, as you well know. You have been absent from us, Eugène. And that —' another tap of the fan — 'is why you are a naughty boy, as you well know.'

'You are ravishing,' he said, in an attempt to placate her.

'Then ravish me, you fool!'

Eugène held up his hand, and smiled self-deprecatingly, at which she truly pouted, adding a frown to indicate her full displeasure, and with a dismissive wave of her hand swept demonstratively away from him in rejection, so that an elegant couple close by turned and laughed.

Alphonse appeared at his elbow, holding two glasses of wine. His eyes were brighter.

'So you know Madeleine, do you? Isn't she charming, and a little crazy? I am too shy, you should introduce me.'

Eugène took the wine, sniffed at it — for all his insistence on quality, Dick could dip from time to time with his white — and then tossed it back, leaving Alphonse to marvel at him.

'My father said that you should never do that...'

'Well, that,' said Eugène, 'is fathers for you. Drink up. We must go for a stroll.'

Alphonse's face fell. 'Why must we?'

'Because I say so, that's why.'

An older man put out a restraining arm as the young Frenchman passed him, but Eugène deftly came in between them without giving offence and moved out of the hubbub of the room. Madeleine studiously ignored them as they passed. On the steps, Eugène bent down and loosened the blade in his boot.

'Where are we going?'

'That, my boy, is what you are going to tell me.'

'What do you mean?'

Eugène threaded his arm through that of Alphonse, and walked in a relaxed way by the railings and along the street.

'I cannot help you, and you cannot truly help yourself, if we do not retrace your footsteps on that fateful night.' He tightened his grip as Alphonse instinctively tugged to free his arm. 'No, less of this impulsive behaviour and more self-compassion, my friend. Think. One way or another, we must be able to find that lodging again. And you, I suspect, were too agitated to record it precisely — either beforehand, from what you say, or afterwards, at the mercy as you were at those times of two very different emotions.'

The formality of the little speech had, as Eugène had hoped, its effect. Alphonse's face remained for a while expressionless; but then he nodded.

At the start, Alphonse showed a great deal of confidence in direction. The thoroughfares were relatively open and lit, recalling the time of night well and the shadows and shapes of houses and corners. At one crossing he hesitated, retracing his steps, and then regaining certainty chose the moment to leave the well-trodden path for the more obscure alleys quite precisely. There was no doubt so far, and no doubt at all until a small church was reached which brought puzzlement to his face. On this occasion, they turned back and found only one alternative, an alley which was both narrow and foul-smelling, at which Alphonse shrugged. Eugène was patient. It had to be done, and this was as sharp as the memory would be, albeit at the space of several days. Alphonse pointed with some conviction at an oddly carved doorpost, but the grim alley came abruptly to a halt, and they emerged into a curious, cramped square, with a small graveyard to one side.

They stood in the shadows to catch their breath. They had seen few people: a young woman with a child who had held out her frail hand more by habit than in any great hope, and a man already sleeping on a wide doorstep chosen for the purpose. Eugène looked at Alphonse inquiringly, but then turned to look at one side of the square as Alphonse seemed to shrink into the wall. They both stood stock-still.

Loic crossed the square in no great hurry in front of the graveyard. He was dressed respectably, but even without the baggy shirt and the tell-tale neckerchief his figure was distinctive to one who had gazed down at him longingly in the half-light of the street. Eugène saw the recognition, and grinned in relief. He raised his finger to his lips, and whispered to his ear in a tone that left no room for questioning: 'Wait here.'

He slipped off slowly. If he had been expecting a long trail, then he was pleasantly surprised. One or two twists, and then he came to the entrance to the small court that Alphonse had mentioned earlier. There was indeed a dim light at the far corner — enough to show up the face of the young *gars*, and the earring that glittered briefly. The young man disappeared, undoubtedly up the staircase that Alphonse had recalled.

There was no need to wait. They still had a day or two. Enough to work out a plan, and enough for Eugène to ponder what Loic, and so undoubtedly Coline, who had both been agents for the British government in France with him earlier in the summer, were now doing in London, at work in such a dirty trade.

CHAPTER VIII: A WOMAN OF MEANS

There had been no word about a companion for Héloïse on the journey or indeed during her stay at the Guèvremont house in Pontivy, and Babette began to prepare herself to go with her. But after a long discussion she accepted that Héloïse would prefer to travel on her own, and would take what she found in Pontivy in good spirit. It was only for a month — they had fixed on that, resolutely — and in a way Héloïse was excited. So when the coach finally appeared along the avenue, they were both already waiting side by side in the salon of the manor at Kergohan. Héloïse was wearing her cotton dress with the vertical red stripes for the journey, and the white bodice over it laced at the front.

Daniel had found a trunk buried away somewhere in the house, and cleaned it up for her, and the rest of her clothes were stowed in there, along with a few precious possessions and her small collection of books. The trunk stood by the front door, and as the carriage drew near Daniel and Babette carried it out into the turning circle in front of the house. Héloïse stood for a while at the window in the empty room, looking not just at the coach but also at Daniel and Babette, dutiful as always. There was grey in Daniel's hair, but none yet in Babette's.

At the moment of parting, tears came from them all. There was no one in the carriage, but the coachman was Guèvremont's man, Robert, and he was friendly enough as well as civil. Babette gave Héloïse some well-water in a corked bottle for the journey, and some of the cold chicken left over from their parting feast — as Héloïse had called it — of the evening before, with rolls and two of the figs she had found in Auray market. No basket, just a wrap of cloth; no butter either, but Héloïse did not say anything about that.

In the evening that followed Daniel and Babette contrived to be quite merry, although it was obvious that if they stopped talking everything went eerily quiet. While Babette was clearing away, Daniel left the room, and she could hear him going along the corridor to his office. He came back in carrying what looked like a leather pouch tied up with black ribbon, and Babette vaguely recognised it as belonging to Héloïse. He needs to be sentimental, she thought. There was the ceremonious untying of the ribbons, maybe once used for her hair as a child, which he laid carefully aside. He then opened the pouch. Babette came round to look, and he put his arm affectionately round her waist.

'Small treasures?' she asked kindly.

'Small? Well, no, not small. Come, sit with me.'

He opened the pouch, and pulled out a thick bunch of folded papers, all more or less the same size, and spread them out.

'You'll forgive me telling you the story, but it is necessary to understand. You know Héloïse's history. Her father Octave Argoubet was the owner, the planter, not just of Galouane where they all lived but of other plantations, what you would call domains. Well, he gave some of them to Héloïse when her mother died. We had all been freed before then. He did more or less the same for his other children: freedom, and gifts. There were not many of them; one of them settled in Cap-Français. It is a harbour there in Saint-Domingue, a port. Héloïse calls this woman her sister, which is right in a way: a half-sister, perhaps, is more accurate. Her name is Félice. She trades in coffee and other things, but mostly in coffee.'

Babette found this a strange world to imagine. There was an image of a palm she had seen in a book at some point, an incident in the life of Christ. That was what came to her when she thought of Saint-Domingue. The other cruelties she shut out; Daniel had told her, she had listened, and held him in her arms. He had no marks on his body, apart from his foot, where he had slipped near the boiling sugar. He had been lucky.

'You see, we were close to Félice. She is a good woman. Independent, strong, kind, to her sister above all. She is respected in the Cap, she played her part strongly after much of it burnt down some years ago. And that was before the fighting. The revolution. She has survived because she can hold her own with the men: white, black, slaves and soldiers.'

'And so?' Babette stroked his cheek with her finger, and her voice was gentle.

Daniel swallowed, and caught her hand in his. 'I made a decision. Her father had trusted me, as his daughter's uncle. He gave them into my hands as a trustee.'

Babette looked puzzled. 'Gave what?'

'His gifts. Of plantations. Mostly coffee, some indigo, but not many. Two, I think were indigo. They were all quite small, but the land was good. He kept the income while he was alive and before she came of age, but if he died it was hers.'

'And this is the record of all of that? Is that what you are showing me?'

'Not quite. These are copies. I had them made before I left, and handed the originals over to Félice. They are the deeds to the land, the proof of ownership.'

Babette worried for him now. It may have been a world away, but she knew what must come next, and that it would trouble him. She spoke quietly.

'And what of the people on the plantations? You know, your people?'

'There were lists. I threw them all away, burnt them, in fact. One evening, in front of the old house. They were meaningless anyway, after the revolts, and the declarations of freedom by the French Republic.'

Babette felt relief for him.

'So, is that it?'

He kept hold of her hand. 'No, that is not it. There is more.' It was always like this with property, she thought, as it is with Kergohan. There is never an end to it, nothing was ever properly resolved.

'I told Félice to sell the properties. The land, at least. She said she would wait, until things settled down. There would be buyers, probably people like her. They had money, they stayed out of the tumult as far as they could. It is likely they will end up in charge there, I would guess.'

'Have you heard back from Félice? Is that what is worrying you? Or —' as the thought struck her — 'have you not heard? Is that the worrying thing?'

He smiled at her. Thank God he had Babette with him. Where would he be in all this chaos they called life without her?

'Yes, and no. She wrote to me at Lorient, through the woman called Jacinthe there, who sent the letter on. The bills of sale have arrived with the letter. Félice found buyers. Some of the new generals under Toussaint, who have confidence, and some of the people in the town. Some finding the money for others, much as Laurent Guèvremont provided money for the Galouane plantation and Héloïse's father. Which *Monsieur* Guèvremont must now own, what with the mortgage having been so heavy, and the lapsed payments. But that is another story.'

'Is that good? Surely the sales will be good for Héloïse? Does she know what you have been doing?'

'She was told, but I don't think it means much to her. There was so much that came first. But it will change her life now. She will have money.'

Babette shifted on the bench they used in the kitchen, and put her hands together on the table. It was still and quiet in the house.

'Does that man Guèvremont know? That she had this property? And that other brute, who came here? Surely he knew?'

Daniel shook his head, unsure. 'Lafargue was what you would call the steward of Galouane, that plantation, which was the largest and the most profitable. He may have known something about the gifts made to the children, but I don't think he knew which properties, or where the deeds to them were. No, I think he made a gamble. He may have believed Héloïse would be a good bargaining counter. But I fear it was just…'

'That he felt she was his property, that she belonged to the plantation. That she was his, possibly, in the same way…'

'As my sister had been to the owner. So he hoped, perhaps. It was a gamble that failed, but not really a plan.'

'And Guèvremont?'

'I believe he is fulfilling what he believes is an obligation. That is what he said. I think Guèvremont does not suspect that she has any money. In fact, it is my belief that he may be intending to provide for her himself in some way, at least enough to make her attractive to a suitor from the town.'

'But he does not know her, Daniel. She is a lovely child, but she will not be bent to anyone's will, or their convenience.'

For the first time, Daniel smiled.

'Perhaps when she has her own money, she will be able to do what she pleases.'

Babette saw Daniel off. He was to be driven to Auray in the cart by Youenn, and would then take the *diligence* from Auray to Lorient, where he would collect the bills of sale from Jacinthe. He was aware that he would be stared at in Auray and in the coach itself by some of the other passengers; but he had lived with white people all his life, and knew how to shut them out when he had to do so. He had packed his bag, and was about to prepare some food before Babette pushed him aside and insisted on doing it for him. He accepted her help with a good grace, and wondered quietly what the coming days would be like without her. He had grown so close to her she was a necessity; there could be no other word for how he felt. You did not realise that you were parched until you found fresh water. She was like water from a spring.

He sat on the motionless cart in the yard alongside Youenn, and tried to look at ease and cheerful. But there was a sorrow in Babette's eyes that had not been there before, and although she smiled and waved to him, he remained haunted. She had said she would visit in the village, take up some of the eggs now there were fewer people to eat them at the manor, probably risk baking bread, or content herself with the usual biscuits made from the buckwheat. She would want to spend some time with Yaelle, and he could picture her wide-eyed at the stories of pregnancy that he was not allowed to hear, and with that mixture of wonder and sadness with which she always came back, silently tracing the path through the forest.

He rolled with the cart. Was it him? Was it his fault? It must be so. He blamed himself. He recalled Jacob from the plantation. He had put aside his wife of many years, who had no child, for a slip of a girl, but she had been beautiful, the envy of all the young men. He was so proud, boastful, made them feel it, risked their resentment. But the long months went by, and the boasts began to falter, and the talk behind his back began to smoulder. He heard them saying what he knew they would, openly now, saw them turn to each other as he passed, while his young wife became sullen, pushed him away, even in public, and went to the old woman, came away from her crying.

He began to speak angrily to the girl, sat in the sun with the flies on his head, cut less cane, and the overseers became so furious with him that they beat him, more than once. Months became a year, and then one day he was missing. The overseers cursed, word went out, and they searched for him. His young wife sat in the shadows on her own, waiting, pushed away anyone who came to speak to her. Word was sent out again that he was a runaway; but they gave up looking for him themselves after only a few days, and left it to fate, or to hunger. In fact, it did not take more than a week: when they found him, he was dead.

The *diligence* was nearly empty. Just an old woman and her grandson, and a man who might have been a clerk. They ignored him, and each other. The hot weather and the time of year may have put people off making their journeys. As they pulled out of Auray, it started to rain.

CHAPTER IX: LOVE FOR A SOLDIER

Lieutenant Vernier pushed back his chair and cursed at the heat. He had been shuffling papers, as he called it, all morning, and although he had cleared his desk to a tolerable degree after weeks of putting it off, he would really have liked to swim in a cool river. That was the sum of it. But it was difficult. Dignity demanded that none should see him, or at least recognise him, and his duties meant that he was rarely out of uniform. Something needed to be done about that, but he had not yet worked it out. There were other little bodily matters of a similar sort on his mind, some of which had a distinctly feminine aspect. He liked, where possible, to get what he regarded as his simple and natural satisfactions without the obligation of paying for them, although he was not averse to that so long as it was combined with merriment. For some strange reason, his habitual source in the desperate wives or sisters of prisoners had mostly dried up, partly because there were now fewer Breton rebels being held, and partly by the strange chance that most of those females within his reach were dampeningly plain.

The church clock rang contentedly through the quarters. Vernier did not stir from his reverie. The first hour struck, and a persistent fly paused on his desk to scratch its head with its legs. Vernier raised the fly whisk and hovered patiently above it. There was a scraping noise at the cabinet door just as the whisk struck the desk, slapping down furiously in the spot where the fly had been an instant before.

Martineau saluted. Vernier retained his composure.

'To what do I owe this pleasure, Corporal?'

'It is eleven, sir. You asked me to knock at eleven and remind me of your appointment in the town at thirty minutes past the hour. That is all, sir.'

'Yes, yes. I had not forgotten. You may go, Corporal.' Vernier wiped his forehead on an initialled linen cloth that was hanging over the back of his chair, and took his coat down from the set of hooks which he had had installed. He had grown up in favourable circumstances in Amiens, and disliked slovenly habits.

Joséphine Guèvremont listened as the eleventh hour struck on the church clock. She counted the bells with some anticipation, and most attentively. She was standing in one of those establishments which she frequented in Auray, that of the dressmaker *Madame* Cloennec, which was a little way from her father's house. She had calculated the necessary timing very carefully, and was quite ready to bring to a close her discussion with the dressmaker about the new, classical gowns that were in fashion. She summoned her maid Marguerite from gazing at an extravagant bridal dress, bid good day to the dressmaker, who after an encouraging conversation did not need reassurance that her young patron would be back, and walked in a determined way towards the street that ran across the top of the narrow alley she had been visiting.

The centre of Auray was not imposing, and it had remained relatively small, altered only when an individual plot was rebuilt, and with grandeur largely reserved for the marketplace. The church of Saint-Gildas presided over the upper end of the town, with smaller and curved streets and lanes spreading down from it. Joséphine resolutely directed her steps to join the narrow Rue Gachotte, all the while chatting lightly to her maid, who was flattered by the attention and honoured by the promise of a pretty bonnet which she had secretly envied, and for which her mistress apparently no longer had any use.

They emerged on to the Rue de Belzic just as the church clock was striking the first quarter, and Joséphine suddenly ceased her unaccustomed chatter with Marguerite, and strangely took her arm as she pulled aside to look at the wares on display at a milliner's. Sensing the nervousness in her mistress, Marguerite became aware of approaching footsteps that faltered, momentarily, and then almost marched forwards towards them. Out of the corner of her eye she saw an extremely handsome young officer of the Republic, and had just enough time to pull back out of the way as he came up to her mistress.

'*Mademoiselle* Guèvremont, enchanted, what a lucky chance to have the opportunity of greeting you on this fine, if regrettably hot, morning.'

'Lieutenant Vernier. Indeed, very hot. We are just returning home to seek some cool rooms, or perhaps shade in our garden. But you are no doubt embarked on business or duties, from which we must not detain you.'

Vernier smiled. '*Mademoiselle*, you find me by coincidence on a mission to your father, whom I make sure I never disappoint by a lack of punctuality. Your father is most particular. This accounts for my presence so close to your house.'

'I see. How fortuitous. It is not far.'

'Certainly not. In which case, I wonder if you will do me the honour of allowing me to escort you the last few steps to your door?' And, since she seemed to hesitate: 'Politeness would insist that at least the offer should be made. But forgive me if you find this impertinent. It was not so intended.'

His face and tone were all innocence. For her part, she was too intent on her purpose to pretend to take offence; but she knew better than to appear to be anything other than suitably reserved in front of her maid.

'Why, I thank you.'

'May I offer you my arm?'

She accepted it without more words, and only one or two of the more curious, including a neighbour who looked down from an upper casement, took any notice. They walked on in silence, each in their own way pleased with how this was going, each with a very different construction of how this opening might be exploited. Marguerite followed behind, loyally scowling at two girls who whispered to each other and giggled. Vernier stopped a few paces from the front door, and released Joséphine's arm. He bowed, for all to see.

'*Mademoiselle*, you must let me know if I can be of service to you.' He bowed again, and replaced his hat on his head. She did not hesitate, but spoke very quickly and quietly to him. It was the moment for which she had carefully planned this supposedly chance meeting, and despite her nervousness she kept the tremor out of her voice.

'Lieutenant Vernier, may I ask you if any word of Captain Leroux has come through to you, or to your superiors? He became so attentive to our household, to my father's enterprises, that it is difficult to see him go into danger on behalf of his country and then to ask no more of him.'

Lieutenant Vernier shook his head. 'Sadly not, *mademoiselle*. I might wish that we did have news, and that it was good. But sadly not.'

Her heart sank, and the animation that had come over her face vanished again.

He leaned forward. 'But leave it with me, *mademoiselle*. I shall make enquiries. And be sure that I shall communicate whatever I may find directly to you. It may, of course, be a little awkward to…'

She looked worried. Then she found her solution.

'It has become my habit to make an evening prayer in the church. I shall do so on Fridays. At six o'clock. Let us pray for him.'

Vernier happily avoided saying that a prayer was probably the last thing that stiff-necked atheist and rationalist Nicolas Leroux would choose, congratulating himself instead on a completely unexpected rendezvous that might be nurtured, with care, into an interesting possibility. He had always found churches helpfully intimate places.

'Shall I knock at your father's door for us both?' he said in a loud voice for all to hear. The maid Marguerite could see that he glanced quickly at her and gave her just the flash of a smile. He was, on first appearances, far more charming than the last officer they had received in the house.

The horizon was just about discernible now, the long line of darker grey marking the forest, lighter ground stretching out in front of it, then the dip that had allowed them to be caught by surprise. Not him, perhaps, if he was fair to himself, but the carabiniers had been stationed just back from the brow and they should have known. The truth was they were barely awake and stirring, and disastrously they had mounted only to ride away in flight before the rampaging Austrians, who were relishing their furious pursuit in the palest light of dawn.

Leroux had been awake. He rarely slept much on campaign, and the little experience he had gathered told him that an attack at dawn was far more likely than evening or night. What sleep he had he took early, and he arose to go round with his adjutants and his senior sergeants, greeting the lieutenants as they got their men in order, watching how observant his staff were. They sergeants took back his watchword, which was 'preparation': powder, cartridges, flints, mechanism. Those who were unprepared were noted and punished after any engagement. This brought him gradually to the attention of General Lambert, who approved of him, and Taponier, who thought he was an upstart. One commander above another, until you reached those who were out of sight.

The carabinier officer and three of his men were sitting on powder boxes that were due to be taken away, their horses cropping the grass. The officer, the *chef d'escadron*, had turned back when the others had fled, trying to rally the light cavalry to hold their position alongside the infantry, but to no avail. The Austrians had swept them away, and would have swept all away had it not been for the infantry line, which held the brow against them, inflicting casualties until they withdrew.

But only for the time being. Leroux disliked these pauses, breaks in the action that always seemed to be accompanied by an uncanny silence, in which you might hear the birds or even see a rabbit. Sergeant Robineau told him that the ones with long ears were hares, but he could only grunt at him: he would never be able to tell them apart. Townsman and city-boy he was, and no amount of mud and rain would make any difference to that.

Leroux saw the lookout running first, and Robineau turned with him. He was waving, uselessly, trying to run and also indicate a direction, but Leroux knew where they would be coming from. He saw a puff of smoke from a copse to the left, on that isolated hill, and then another. The *chef d'escadron* and his men mounted their horses. He could see the Austrians riding along the side of the dip, and then saw movement further round. His men were on their feet, the *chef d'escadron* with a tight rein beside him. Lambert's battalions were behind him, hopefully alert, perhaps even now retreating.

The sound of the cannon thudded into the hills, much as the shot would soon do once they got their distance. It was away to the left. The lines were forming, in good order. He wanted them just off the brow of the hill. To defend, he would go forward, off the skyline. Do not let the cavalry gain the ridge. He turned to Robineau.

'They must sing.'

'What would you have, sir?'

'What do they know?'

'The drummer knows the *Carmagnole*, he can beat it out.'

Leroux and the *chef d'escadron* looked at each other. The *chef d'escadron* put his hands on his thighs, reins held lightly in one hand, and shrugged. Leroux made up his mind.

'The *Carmagnole* is a dance-song, Sergeant. We're here to die, not to dance. Let us hear what we are dying for.'

The sergeant saluted.

'The *Marseillaise* it is, sir. Some of the boys are from Narbonne, they know it well.'

'Let's have the song as we march down to take up position. That will confuse them. Then it's silence. We wait for them to come up the slope — if they do — like fools, and we shall give the first volley. We can retire behind cover further up. The lieutenants on the left and right know this.'

'Yes, sir. Understood. The centre is yours, sir, as instructed. Duport, Pecqueux, to me!'

With a few words, the corporals ran off to the ranks, where others ran on along the line. There was a cheer as the news spread. Leroux made sure his bicorne was firmly placed, his sword loose in his scabbard.

The line began to move, and as it did the now-familiar words of the *War Song of the Army of the Rhine* rolled out and down the slope, in the pale light of the dawn. Leroux stiffened as a small portion of the left flank was flung up and back by a shot landing; another shot flew across and landed harmlessly. The horse next to him stirred nervously, its rider running his hand over its neck to calm it.

'Aux armes, citoyens
Formez vos bataillons
Marchons, marchons!'

The next shot landed underneath the horse, hurling its rider backwards as it collapsed sideways in its death agony. Leroux crushed underneath it. The *chef d'escadron*, dazed but miraculously unhurt, staggered to his feet and called to others, and frantically they did all that they could to pull the lifeless, inert animal off him.

Lieutenant Vernier sat in the study at Guèvremont's house listening to the clerk, Fourrier, droning on and shifted in his seat to maintain his attention, or at least to appear not to be losing attention, which he was. He had inherited this role, as military liaison, from Captain Leroux, who had seen it as a good opportunity to impress Guèvremont, and so part of his grand strategy to win the hand of the lovely Joséphine. That had not gone well, as Vernier had warned him it would not; and Leroux was now sweating in the dust and blood of campaigning with the French armies beyond the Rhine, disappointed in love and without the promotion he had been hoping would come his way.

Uniforms, uniforms, uniforms — taken from dead men or captives, red uniforms dyed black, for heaven's sake, a seemingly endless process. But what little Vernier picked up from Fourrier's tedious report suggested that progress was finally being made, and he might have something to do himself, making some of the arrangements to get the damn things into Brest, although much of that journey was by sea. It was always secrecy, covers over the carts, sometimes even a night journey rumbling down to Lorient from Pontivy when the small barges were not available.

Speaking of uniforms, he felt he was quite well turned out today. He had found a new man, a fussy old fellow, but he was a dab hand at starching and whitening, and provided you did not listen to him he was worth the pittance that Vernier paid. Looking his best had a purpose of a kind. The visits to the house offered a chance — not much more than that, regrettably — to come across the delectable young Joséphine in the hallway, even on the steps: who could say? Her impressionable maid was, admittedly, a more distinct possibility. Yet the whole scheme was almost certain to prove a fantasy, as it had been for Leroux: Guèvremont was self-important and influential, and Vernier was not even remotely suitable for matrimony in the father's eyes. So, he did not know quite what it was that he wanted; but that would not hold him back from trying to get it.

The meeting was over. He drank his coffee in haste, and took his leave, pulling the study door to behind him. In the hallway, the house seemed completely still: no sound or movement from any quarter. Bernard had been serving the coffee, but he now came out quietly and with a softly spoken 'Pardon' went to the front door, which he opened. There was nothing for it. Vernier was all politeness, and ran lightly down the steps as the door closed. He had hardly turned the corner when he ran straight into Gilles, who was drifting along and daydreaming. Vernier was prompt in his greeting.

'Well, I should wish you good day, *monsieur*. My apologies for almost knocking you down. No offence meant, needless to say.'

Gilles looked up, and his face brightened with recognition.

'Ah, Vernier, isn't it? Have I got that right? You are deputising for Leroux in some way. We have seen you at the house.'

A thought came to Vernier, which was to combine purpose with pleasure. A clever thought, or so it seemed to him.

'Well, I do my best. Deputising. But not in all respects, of course, if you take my meaning.'

Gilles did not take his meaning. He had no idea what the officer was talking about, and cared even less, were that possible. Still, he had learnt to be able to reply no matter what he did or did not understand about a conversation.

'Yes, indeed. Why not?'

'I tell you what, why don't we have a beer? Or a glass of something? I've got a thirst on me.'

Gilles thrust his hands in the pockets of his coat. He had been told it was slovenly, by none other than Guèvremont himself, and that he should not do it; but he found it invaluable when he was weighing something up, as now. He also pinched his nose with his finger and his thumb, a mannerism he had adopted because it gave an onlooker the impression of thought, and so was useful whether you were or were not actually thinking.

'Yes, why not? I could manage a glass. It will be hot again later, no doubt.'

They began to walk off. Vernier began to direct their steps towards the Lion d'Or, a place he had heard about from a chance comment by Leroux, and one that was quite close to the house. The landlord there kept a reasonable white wine, according to Leroux, and they sat at a table inside to avoid the heat. The walls were thick, and the room relatively cool, but the table was greasy. No sign of any help, just the same old men still as death on a bench in the corner.

'A pitcher of white, please, Roic. Can we have it from the cellar? Cooler, which is preferable.'

Vernier stretched his legs, and look at the boy, just emerging into a man, in fact. That fair hair was striking, and he had heard that the fair-haired Guèvremont had taken him as his ward: it did not take much to guess at what was going on there. He wondered how Joséphine was taking to it, and the best way was to ask.

'How is *Mademoiselle* Guèvremont? I rarely see her in the house…'

Gilles looked at him strangely. Roic brought the wine, but left them to pour it. He could tell the boy was a local, but the other could fend for himself. Gilles drank, and enjoyed it.

'Well, Lieutenant, *Mademoiselle* Guèvremont does not spend much of her time in the hallway, or in meetings. She is not often in the kitchen either. I don't quite see why you would expect to see her, if I may say so.'

So, the boy was protective. That was perhaps to be expected, but not so good for Vernier.

'I think you may misunderstand me. I have some reason to believe that she may be regretting the departure of Captain Leroux, who I know was at times privileged to be her dancing partner. He was very proud of that, as you might expect.'

'Your meaning, sir?'

Vernier drank from his glass. Roic always provided glasses, and Vernier would not know that it was a sign that he was not local.

'Nothing. Nothing at all.' He pulled his chair up to the table. 'Look, I think I owe you an apology. We may have got off to a bad start. That rebellion last year, and all that. A series of mistakes, I think, and it may be that I was as culpable as anyone else, including Leroux. You were a lad at that time, caught up in it, anyone might have done the same…'

Gilles stared at him. He was beginning to regret coming here. But Vernier would not stop.

'I think we should let bygones be bygones. I dare say that you might have been involved in some way in the escape of that baron character, too, later on, but one baron more or less hardly matters to either of us. It was a dirty business, through and through, and I can't say I approved of the line taken by the authorities. It was lucky he got away, and I don't want to know where he is, if you're thinking that. Am I being clear?'

'Possibly.'

'Come, let's drink to it. Water under the bridge.' Vernier grinned. 'I know a little place…'

'What place?' Gilles was sincerely puzzled.

'Just round the corner here. Could be very convenient for you — very clean and comfortable, and not too pricey. You must meet *Madame* Vaillancourt. Come now,' and he pushed his chair back and stood up, 'I'll introduce you myself. Some very lovely Breton girls, small but full of fun…'

Gilles had gone red in the face. It might be the wine, but he was sweating, and fighting angry.

'I know of no such place, sir. We should take our leave of each other. I am expected back at the house.' It was a vision that had him shaking. Vernier saw the signs, and was completely at a loss: what had he said? The young man was on his feet now and walking to the door, incidentally leaving Vernier to pay, which he did.

Roic swept the coins off the counter, and watched the *bleu* out of his tavern. He had seen and heard how it went. He understood. The boy was a Breton. He would not like a Frenchman talking about his women like that, even women who sold themselves. He went to his door, and watched as they went their separate ways. No, the boy was a Breton, and all the better for it. He spat on the ground, in the direction Vernier was taking, and went back inside.

CHAPTER X: LIFE IN PONTIVY

First impressions of Pontivy were indistinct, just a town with men and women on the streets, narrow or slightly wider, and the odd variety of clothing that they wore. Héloïse could hear the shouts and cries, but most were drowned out by the racket that the carriage made, its wheels grinding over the cobbles in the middle of the town. Then there was a lurch, and they seemed to be climbing back out, but they turned off abruptly. As the coach swung into a yard she caught a glimpse of a massive building with towers, quite unlike those on the churches she had seen. The carriage came to a halt, and the coachman, Robert, came to help her down, took up her trunk, and began to carry it in. She followed him.

Just inside was the kitchen, with two young women leaving off what they were doing and looking over at her, their faces blank. Through the wide door at the far end came a woman of middle years, her hair tied and pinned up, dressed in a kind of dull green with a buttoned bodice, plain and simple; she was immediately in charge.

'The two of you will say "Good day" to *Mademoiselle* Argoubet now politely, if you don't mind, and then you will get back to your work, if you please. *Mademoiselle*, please step this way with me, and Robert follow along, if you will, and try not to let that dust from the road fly off you all around my rooms. You may leave the chest at the foot of the backstairs, Robert, and Tudual will see it goes up to the chamber. Then take some refreshment with Nanette here in the kitchen, by all means, although I dare say you will want to see your horses stabled first, if old habits stick fast. This way, please, *mademoiselle*.'

The interior of the house smelt of wax and a kind of incense, nothing like the manor, and still less like the big, creaking house in Saint-Domingue. The wood was dark, with shiny hinges just visible on doors; the floor was even. They came through into a hallway, and the woman stopped for a moment and turned to look closely at Héloïse, who was embarrassed at the scrutiny.

'Forgive me, my dear,' she said, pulling out Héloïse's sleeves where they had been compressed by the journey, and taking her dress, and shaking it a little.

'There, you'll do,' she said. She led her to a door and tapped on it. There was no reply, and so she tapped lightly again. 'Enter,' came a woman's voice, low, almost musical. Héloïse was motioned quickly into the room; the housekeeper dipped in a curtsey, shut the door and left Héloïse to face the occupant alone.

'Good morning. You will be *Mademoiselle* Argoubet. You will have heard of me from *Monsieur* Guèvremont, who will have explained my function in this house, which is to provide you with — what shall we say? — tutelage.'

'I am very pleased to meet you, *Madame*. Please call me Héloïse; I have rarely used my father's name.' Héloïse had forgotten the name of this woman: was she Lalande, or was that the cook? It was a simple confusion, but deeply embarrassing. Yet her mind was racing: had the Guèvremont man ever actually told her? She did remember something about the widow of a cousin who would be in the house at Pontivy, but the name?

'*Mademoiselle*, please be seated. Here, by me. Never mind the dust of the journey. It will do no harm to the fabric just for now. There. Now let me explain. My cousin tells me that you have become used, shall we say, to a rural living, with its casual familiarity. But you are now in town, which is a different world altogether. Let me assure you that you should be very wary of any familiarity here. Let none, especially young gentlemen should you ever meet them, presume to make use of your first name. Should they attempt to do so, you must correct them, and not suffer any repetition. Do you understand me?'

'I do.' But what if they used your first name and then kissed you, as Gilles had done, in the woods and with the breeze lightly waving the leaves about your heads? And your head swam? Yet that was long ago, weeks, maybe a month, at least.

'Good. So, *Mademoiselle* Argoubet it is. And so it must be in front of servants. I do not know what your arrangements were at the farm…'

'Manor, *Madame.*'

The woman looked at Héloïse for the first time with some displeasure. 'Manor, then, if you will. But here we have servants, and there must be respect. And the preservation of a degree of distance. Let me assure you that they prefer it like that, and this new order we have still prefers it to be like that. But enough of that. You must change out of those things and refresh yourself after your journey. I shall send my woman Adelaide to you. She will serve for both of us for the time being. It will do her good to be busy. She will fetch something from the kitchen for you. I believe they have lemonade. I would not recommend wine in this heat, even chilled, if such a thing were possible in this household.'

She stood up, and held out her hand. Héloïse was unsure whether she should kiss it or shake it. So she held out her own hand, and the woman lightly touched her fingers.

'There, we are started. Let us go on as tidily together, and we shall do very well. You will come down when you are ready, and then I think we shall review your garments together and think of any other requirements you may have. We shall dress for dinner, but there will be no guests. Adelaide will be waiting for you out in the hall. I shall be here, when you are ready. And then we shall discuss what you will be doing. One should always have an occupation to hand.'

In the Guèvremont house at Pontivy they did not start early on the following day because consideration was given to the effects of a long journey. Héloïse was impressed by the bath she took, which had ample warm water, although she drew the line at Adelaide standing over her, to pour in more water or — more horrendously still — to wash her. She had been able to slip down in the tub until her chin was level with the water, and move the herbs and small flowers around the surface with her fingers, occasionally blowing them. She refused to have Adelaide dry her, but she was at least now sure of all the names. Adelaide had referred to her mistress as *Madame* Lalande, without Héloïse having to ask, and added that in company her preference was to be called *Madame* de Lalande; the woman she had first met was the cook, *Madame* Perrée.

When Héloïse finally came down to breakfast, it was quickly decided that they would walk out to the market this morning. Héloïse was unsure when and how her 'tutelage' would begin, let alone what form it would take, so a trip to the market was a relief. It was mid-morning by the time they stepped across the threshold, greeted by a wave of heat and direct sunshine, and by the sounds of voices swirling up the gentle slope from the marketplace. Adelaide followed discreetly behind them both, and Héloïse partly envied her for that, although it could hardly be called independence. Adelaide carried the parasols, which could be inconvenient while threading through the throng of traders and citizens.

The unusual heat, and then the heavy smell of meat, fruit, rye bread and cakes with preserve in them swept over Héloïse like a sudden visitation of moments from the past. It reminded her of her childhood and early youth, on those rare occasions when she had been taken by her father in the *chaise* on exciting trips to the markets at Gondaïve in Saint-Domingue. So many people, moving about freely, well-dressed, on some occasions holding up fabric, looking at lengths of it, laughing. And the colours, at times overwhelming. As here, there was food for sale, some live animals too, but her senses were sharpest in bringing back to her the luscious array of fruit that filled the air with its scent.

In truth it was not like that here. There was no colour in the clothing, and with the clogs, the brimmed hats, the bonnets that wrapped up faces, it was all so different. Here the meat smelled strongest, the milder part of it preserved and inoffensive, but the rank odour of offal hung over everything, the fresh vegetables and the fruit unable to fight it off. They passed on, along a short street which was still crowded into what was obviously a different market, one noticeably without strong smells. *Madame* Lalande had acknowledged one or two thoroughly respectable people that they had passed, and even greeted one couple briefly, but without breaking step. Without warning, *Madame* Lalande stopped and called to Adelaide for her parasol.

'Come now, *Mademoiselle* Argoubet, take your parasol from the maid. You must protect your complexion from the sun, which can give the most frightful headaches after only a short exposure. And, of course, we are walking out far too late in the day for good sense.'

Madame Lalande retrieved a parasol with a flower-pattern and a short fringe around it, while Héloïse was furnished with one in an attractive pale blue. She was happy with that, and started to twirl it until she caught Lalande's eye and adopted a more sober profile, holding it almost upright, as she saw her preceptress doing.

A cat ran quickly across the street and jumped on to a ledge, and as Héloïse turned to watch it her parasol caught in another. It was held by a young woman of about her own age, perhaps a year or two older, who was wearing a walking dress of almost precisely the same hue as Héloïse's parasol, with the addition of lace at the neck and sleeves. Her hair was taken up prettily, while the ribbon and the scarf tied loosely around her neck were of a darker blue. They both apologised at once. *Madame* Lalande came quickly and told Adelaide to take the parasol and fold it again, which she did. But most of all she expressed pleasure and surprise in her greeting to the young woman.

'Why, *Mademoiselle* Floch, how delightful it is to meet you on such a fine morning! We ourselves are about late. You must allow me to introduce my guest, indeed to introduce you to each other. *Mademoiselle* Héloïse Argoubet, who is staying with us here, and *Mademoiselle* Katell Floch. *Monsieur* Floch, our dear Mademoiselle's father, is a firm friend of *Monsieur* Guèvremont.'

The young women smiled at each other, and laughed again, in a little, rippling noise that lasted a few seconds. Katell then stood aside, and a young man who was older than her and had been hanging back took a few steps forward. He had finely cut features and dark, waving black hair that swept over his forehead and down the sides of his face, and he was dressed all in black. His demeanour seemed shy, but he looked frankly at Héloïse, and pushed his hair back from his eyes.

'Come forward, Roparzh, and greet *Madame* de Lalande properly now, if you please.' The young man made something of a flourish, and brushed his lips over the hand that *Madame* Lalande offered him. 'Now, *Mademoiselle* Héloïse, this is my brother, Roparzh.' Héloïse was unsure what to do, so she held out her hand limply, and he took it lightly in his fingers, released it, and stood back, his gaze drifting out over the crowd but then back to Héloïse, at whom he suddenly smiled. *Madame* Lalande took charge once again.

'There, we are now all introduced to each other, and it remains for me, Katell, to propose sending you an invitation to call on us, perhaps one morning later in the week. I do hope you will be able to consider a visit. *Mademoiselle* Héloïse is but lately arrived in the town, and I am sure she would be delighted to make your further acquaintance, should you be so kind. Where do you walk today?'

Katell was as lively as her brother was still, and she was delighted. At Adelaide's warning, they all stepped aside for a handcart to pass, and Katell responded enthusiastically to the prospect of an invitation.

'Yes, how lovely, how much we should enjoy speaking more together, should we not, Héloïse? You do not mind if I call you Héloïse, do you? I do so dislike too much formality. Please do send out the invitation. Ah, where are we walking? Well, *Madame*, we thought we would walk this way and up to the chateau for a little while. Some shade may be found up there, if we are fortunate, and my brother has some little seats. You see, Héloïse, my brother is an artist, and he sketches when he is not painting in the little studio we have at home. That is what he is carrying in his canvas bag, which you will have noticed. I have brought my book with me…'

Madame Lalande felt that they had been standing far too long in an open street, and that propriety should set a limit to their remaining there.

'Oh, do you not think that we are a little in the way here, *Mademoiselle* Katell? The livestock may be coming through at any time soon. So, with your leave, we shall carry on our tour for a short while before retreating into the cool of the house. I bid you good day, *Monsieur* Floch. Come now, *Mademoiselle* Argoubet, we may just pass through this next square, and see if we might catch one or two shops before the afternoon closure.'

Farewells were given and taken, in a mixture of enthusiasm from Katell, moodiness from Roparzh, and not a little wonder from Héloïse. For the most part, she was lost in thought, and *Madame* Lalande's continuing comments on what they passed drifted over her into the air, mixed up with the snatches of chat and bargaining that flew up all around.

The dressmaker had already closed her shop, or perhaps did not open it on a market day. They walked back and around by another, shady lane, past a baker who had nearly sold out. Héloïse noticed an odd little court with a strange carving above a door, and decided that towns could offer some intriguing curiosities if you gave them a chance. As they drew close to the Guèvremont house, she puzzled over what Katell Floch had meant by 'an artist'. Her brother, though older than her, admittedly, was surely too young to be an artist? She realised that she knew nothing about painting or sketching, how it was done, or who did it. She wondered if she would meet him again. If she did so, she could ask him, and perhaps he would show her. She was certain that she liked his hair.

CHAPTER XI: LETTERS FOR ARABELLA

Eugène sat quietly on a chair in an upstairs corridor at Dick's, out of the way, and contemplated what lay in front of him in less than an hour. For Coline and Loic to be found in London and involved in a sordid game like this had shocked him, but he dismissed it from his mind. He put his head back against the wall and trailed the hair out of his eyes with his fingers: other people's scheming was enough to give anyone a headache. He was completely sure of what he would do: he would confront Coline by himself, without Alphonse, at the time that had been fixed, and that was that.

A suave, older politician whom Eugène dimly recognised squeezed past him; it was best to avert the eyes in some cases, so as not to offer any encouragement. Downstairs, he could hear the young Frenchman's tinny laugh. A barber had first introduced Alphonse to Dick's, where his feeble grasp of English had kept him isolated for a while. Very few indeed of London's new French population had been invited into its welcoming rooms; only one, a leery Huguenot, outwardly a strictly old-school Calvinist, had kept his eyes on the boy, but not in order to look after him.

The politician made a point of edging past Eugène again, brushing his knees and looking round to offer his apologies, exhaling wine fumes and anchovy canapés as he bent down to offer his approval of Eugène's opal pin, which his mother had given him. Eugène got up from his chair, smiled politely, pushed past the man and made his way down the corridor towards the small landing, where Dick had for once stationed a clock in preference to his beloved mirrors. It was a beautiful longcase, by Charles Howe, an object which Eugène had coveted since he first saw it: one could stand there idly, look at the minutes always on the move, and yet be going nowhere. Was that philosophy or just comfort?

Dick touched him on the shoulder. 'I think you are right, my boy. From what you have said, the time has come. Are you sufficiently prepared? We have no wish to lose you, you know.'

'Yes, you are right. And I am — prepared, that is.'

'Well, we knew you would be; we have every confidence in you, of course. I shall keep dear Alphonse entertained below. You need not be concerned. He won't follow you, and if he tries to do so Samuel will see to it that he is very gently dissuaded. You may trust to that.'

'Thank you, Dick. You think of everything.'

'And far too much of you, my boy. Now, be gone, or Madeleine will be looking for you and get in your way. You know what she is like whenever there is something important to do which does not concern her.'

Which Eugène did, although he could forgive her for it.

He left the house in reasonably good spirits. The important difference was that it would not be dark this time. It proved to be no trouble to retrace his steps, and find the cramped little square. He arrived there in good time, and took a seat on the low wall of the graveyard. He had no precise idea of what he would say when he confronted Coline, but he was confident that he could turn her patrons against her. The Abbé Carron need not know the precise details; but a vague description of extortion practised on a young *émigré* would not help Coline's standing with the Abbé or with the community of exiles.

A young lad crossed the square, whistling; it was not Loic. Eugène sat still for a few more minutes in the silence: then two women's voices shouting at each other, a man shouting back, some footsteps running, a door banging. There were the usual dogs barking, but in the distance. It was surely time by now. He trod lightly and evenly over the cobbles and the broken paving down the alleys, walked quickly past the court, and then back again, glancing in to fix his eye on the door. It was all as it should be. He spun into the yard, crossed to the door, ran swiftly up the stairs, knocked on the door and stepped in, all in one movement.

The room was empty. Completely empty — not just of people but of things. Stripped down to essentials. The air was still and stale. He opened the adjoining door. Not an item left there either. It was as if they had never been. And yet he knew they had. Alphonse was not imagining anything, and they had both seen Loic, and followed him.

He felt some relief. It would surely now be hard for them to go after Alphonse again. But it was very odd indeed that they had not stayed for this rendezvous, and the money they were hoping to extort. Fifty guineas was a very tidy sum, and they could have been in and out in a matter of minutes. Had they left London, perhaps? For even larger takings? A shipment of *émigrés*, down to the coast? Or left the country altogether? One thing was certain. There would be no point in searching round for a clue to any of that: Coline would never be so careless.

So, that was it. Eugène blew out his cheeks, and sighed: so much for his sense of adventure. He left the door open and ran nimbly down the stairs, paused, shrugged, and climbed quickly back up to shut it. On the corner of the second step was a small ball of paper. He spread it out. It was, incongruously, a page from an abolitionist pamphlet. He had read such stuff while with Amelia Wentworth, idly, without giving it the attention it probably deserved, because he was distracted by her. But where was she now? And with whom? Distressed by these intrusive, jealous thoughts, and his inability to answer them, he screwed the paper up again and dropped it in an exaggerated gesture, to indulge his self-pity. So much for the love of a woman, too.

But something nagged at him; he picked it up again, spread it open, and turned it over. Scribbled on the other side was the beginning of an address, hardly legible. He put it in his pocket. Whatever else this strange removal meant, it called for a celebratory bottle, and he hoped fervently that Dick had taken his advice and ordered in a better white. A Saumur would do: a glass or two of that, and he would pack the boy off home.

Amelia Wentworth was writing a letter to her sister-in-law and friend, Arabella Wentworth.

My dearest Bella,

I have just completed reading your last letter, and must thank you for news of the village at home in Devon and of your growing impatience with casino and all forms of card games in our manor at Chittesleigh there. Since you forbid me any mention of your condition, I am bound to content myself with a description of Brighton, or Brighthelmston, where I am now. Both names are used and, as you will perceive, the one is shorter and more convenient, the other by far more romantic. It is the oddest of places. There are but a few streets, and none of those broad, and more remarkable is that its centre is placed to one side, if you can follow my meaning. This centre is surprisingly just a stretch of open ground known as the Steyne, and I am looking out on it now from the small library conveniently located at its limit …

There was a burst of music from outside the library, followed by loud laughter. Amelia laid down her pen, and continued to wait as the band playing just on the edge of the Steyne started into another tune, only to break off, to yet more laughter. The noise died down, and she was keen to resume her letter.

The Steyne slopes some little distance inland up from the sea and the shingle, offering a broad and attractive promenade for those who are visiting. Here you may see high society, they say, from the Prince of Wales when he is in residence to earls and dukes and gentlemen of all ranks and to be sure of all shapes and sizes. Indeed, the Prince has a house here on one side of this stretch of land as do others, of some magnificence, newly built in the finest style and facing out, for all the world as if this bare stretch of land were their park. I can see them now, from where I am sitting in this comfortable library.

But enough. You ask me about my health, which I think is in return for my asking after yours. I must tell you it remains frail, but is steadily improving. To that end, I am determined to brave Caroline North's disapproval and take myself into a bathing engine, to be plunged unceremoniously into the sea. How could one come to Brighton and not indulge in bathing, recommended as it is for all ailments, including those of the nerves? This town is a veritable shrine to the virtues of sea-bathing, as much as it is at night dedicated to the all too familiar vices of drinking and cards. There are also sea-water baths…

The band suddenly began playing again, and a crowd of young gentlemen came storming in through the doors, transforming the quiet of what was supposed to be a library into what would be more like a club. Amelia put down her pen, and began to gather her things. Then, without rhyme or reason, the young men all rushed out again. Amelia placed a full-stop after 'baths', hovered over the paper, and continued:

And yet, weeks after his failed plans to abduct me, in conjunction with the dreadful imprisonment he inflicted on you, it is evident, although nothing is said, that they have still not apprehended Tregothen as the guilty man...

There was suddenly the sound of feet outside, and the same group of young men came bursting in with one of the musicians in their midst, grasping his violin to his chest as he was lavishly feted. Amelia ceased writing, swept her belongings together into a small bag, including her unfinished letter, and walked out under the portico and on to the green of the Steyne.

Arabella Wentworth sighed and wriggled her toes, one foot at a time. She wondered idly if she would have liked to go to Brighton, where Amelia now was staying, but could hardly envisage how it might have been brought about. Her father would never have dreamed of such a place, full of Whigs and reprobates as he would have had it. Besides, the only chaperone that might be found would have been her aunt, who was as stern as a granite headstone on a dark day in February. Arabella burst into loud laughter at the thought of Aunt Sophia dipping her toes into the water from a bathing machine, or whatever it was that they had there. Yet all she got was a small kick for her pains, and then another, and she placed her hands on her womb to feel the little feet even if she could not see them under her gown.

Grace had looked up from her sewing with a smile on her face at the laughter from her mistress. Arabella sensed that she was being watched, and immediately responded.

'A glass of madeira, if you please, Grace. Call Thomas for it. He is used to my ways, and the baby may be used to it too by now. Perhaps he will sleep. I know I do.'

Grace left the room, rather than summon Thomas, and Arabella sank into reflection. It was odd that while her husband Justin was away, and she was free from the endless concern over every little thing, she had begun to feel lonely. For all that he was dear, he had begun to be too much, and the terrible events from which she had only just emerged unscathed had made his doting on her far, far worse. She was endlessly grateful for his wonderfully prompt actions then, even if — by chance and in sheer desperation — she had extricated herself from Tregothen's libidinous grasp. But as her time approached, she felt that she would need Justin's mother, Sempronie to be at hand to deflect her husband's endless worrying. An invitation had already been sent to Sempronie, who had declared that she would be with her by the end of the week, willing to stay at Chittesleigh until it was absolutely clear she was no longer needed.

The madeira came in with Thomas. With a slight wave of her hand in acknowledgement, she picked up the other letter. Justin's was far shorter than that of his sister Amelia, who was in any case a far more regular correspondent. She puzzled over it again. While allowing for male brevity, it was so short it resembled a note rather than a letter. She ran her eyes over it once more:

My dearest &c... I am afraid that a further matter which I had not anticipated will require my absence for another short period of time. I must journey out of London to this end, but shall return forthwith, and then continue to Devon with expedition.

A little flush of anger came with the second sip of the madeira. Something about his language troubled her, even if she might not put her finger on it. The tone was distant, and she found it excessively formal, as if he were writing to his butler or his steward. And yet she was the one who had wanted him to take himself away to London, at least temporarily. Now she was beginning to act like those women she despised, the jealous wives who suspected everything when there was nothing, who wished to keep their husbands forever in sight and in hand.

With a little difficulty, and her complexion heightened by the wine, she moved across to the writing desk she had had installed in the drawing room for convenience, took up a pen and paper. She would not let herself sorrow; it was too much to bear. There must be a sensible, practical reason for this unexplained absence. She sat down. She would write to Eugène; Justin had no closer friend. He would not object. She knew where Eugène resided when in London, and knew his father's address as well, since Justin kept a full address book in his desk in the library. She knew where Justin was staying, too, or had been staying. It was not much to ask of a friend, just to check up, to let her know there was nothing amiss.

Grace looked in at the door, almost without a sound, and saw her mistress writing. All seemed calm. She shut the door quietly behind her.

CHAPTER XII: AMELIA TAKES A DIP

When they had called in at Awsiter's Baths the day before, Caroline North and Amelia had been informed that in the matter of sea-bathing a lady would benefit from the close attendance of a person known as a dipper, that experienced women of this sort were invaluable, and their services much in demand. In response, the spectacled clerk at Awsiter's proposed a Mrs Jenner, on whom they might most securely rely, who was most delicate and proper in her manner with gentlewomen, as far as the clerk had report. If the ladies agreed, he would take it that the arrangement would be made for just on two o'clock, when he was reliably informed that the tide would be at its best. He was to make sure that the charges would be delivered to their residence, payable, as he trusted would be acceptable to them, by the end of the month.

For the rest, they were reliant on Mrs Gibb, their host in East Street. Mrs Gibb was fully acquainted with the proprieties of sea-bathing, which was not for her as she freely admitted, with her knee in the condition that it was. But she believed it to be well within her duties as a host to offer sound advice to guests. This she insisted on doing in closet with Amelia, and yet all that came from this private conversation was that it was customary to wear a shift of some suitably light material under one's gown, and that the machines permitted the removal of the gown in seclusion. After drying, which was a matter she would leave to the hired woman to introduce to Miss Wentworth in due time, one might then clothe oneself again, and she would from the experience of her patrons suggest the inclusion of a small mirror in a reticule so that suitable attention might be paid to concerns about appearance.

As with many new undertakings, there was much to be thought about, and while Caroline quietly reviewed how she might engage her woman Dawson at the vital hour to remove her from any possible involvement, Amelia allowed herself to become excited. She determined to take a light bag that she occasionally carried herself when visiting shops at home, and to place in it a folded undergarment. Caroline had a small hand-mirror, which was ideal for the purposes described by Mrs Gibb, and once dressing was completed in the morning Caroline quietly slipped it into Amelia's bag while Dawson was down in the kitchen.

The morning was bright and breezy, but after a leisurely breakfast it soon gave way to an increasing heat, which made Caroline declare that she must seek a straw hat to guard against the sun. Dawson went with her, and they departed in good order, with Caroline placing her hand on Amelia's arm discreetly and whispering encouragement. Amelia was left to slip into the lightest and simplest gown that she had, replacing the more substantial walking dress in which Dawson had earlier clothed her. The shoes she chose were both old and firm, and if the combination was hardly elegant it would serve. She tied up her hair with ribbons in a practical spirit and decided to forego a sunhat.

Besides, any caution about the damage the sun might do to a complexion was cast aside in five minutes of joyful freedom, glancing back from the shimmering horizon to gaze into the eyes of passers-by, looking away again modestly, observing a strange hat, a crooked nose, a fine leg, brilliant boots — your ears full of the screams of the gulls, your nostrils picking up the scent of the baskets that had held todays catch, a glimpse of the leathery, wrinkled face of that fisherman, with those fascinating, gnarled, broad hands. All she had to find amongst the vehicles standing at the top of the beach was a piebald pony. How easy that proved to be! There it was, its head down in the sun, its driver capped above a mop of wild hair, a ring in his ear, salt-caked boots, short, stocky, a hand to his forehead and a gesture to the back of the wagon to a woman emerging from behind it, who would be Mrs Jenner. She was dressed in charcoal black and wore an equally dark hat that most resembled a large pie. It was tied on tightly under the chin.

'How do, Miss. It's Miss Wentworth, isn't it? Water's warm 'n lovely. Your first time?'

Amelia smiled back. 'Yes, my first time, Mrs Jenner. Pleased to meet you.'

'Mary 'tis, Miss, if you don't mind. Just plain Mary. Mrs Jenner to the menfolk, for respect. Here, up you go, don't mind if I take your hand, there you go.'

Mary Jenner, the dipper, followed Amelia smartly up into the hot cabin of the machine, which had just one small window at the top on one side. There was a rough bench running along its short length, and a small cupboard set up above.

'Best take off your gown and stow it here in this box. Up here, Miss.' She pulled open the door of the cupboard to show Amelia. 'Your bag too. Shoes best off, or they'll wash away. When you're ready, bang on the side, and sit down tight. Horse will pull us out, and Tim'll turn him round. See this here?'

Mary pulled open the door in the front of the wagon, and put her hand on the canvas of a gathered, hooped awning that was tied up to hooks either side of the door.

'I'll be letting this down after we turn round, and then you'll be nice and private. I'll be dippin' you, as much as you like,

Miss, then I'll dry you off with my cloths, hangin' up there. Just like a maid, I am.'

'Will you leave me a cloth when…?'

Mary Jenner nodded. 'When you want dry clothing? I'll be pullin' up the hoops, Miss, and you get on with your dressing. Jus' bang on the side again when you're feelin' right, and Tim and his pony'll pull us back up.'

Lewes was a grand place, no doubt about it. Jowan Tregothen had discovered that he had a taste for history, and could easily fancy himself as something of an antiquary. The priory, now, that was a fine thing, monstrous walls leaning this way and that, the thickness of a man's outstretched arms, no doubt signifying buildings of one use or another. It would be satisfying to be an authority, although he doubted if he would want to publish papers, still less undertake the painstaking digging that was required. Yes, there again, it might be possible to get labourers to do most of that, just content oneself with picking over the findings, a bit of bone here, a shard of pottery there. Then one could be a thoroughly special kind of dinner guest, fascinating to maidens and matrons alike, irritating to their stupid husbands with their endless appetite for shooting and hounds, who boasted they were never happier than when unseated on a windy afternoon, no bones broken, all that kind of nonsense. Yes, Lewes was a grand place, that eagle's eyrie of a castle, sat on a hill like a pimple amongst the sweep of the Downs, disdainful of the pettiness at its foot, traders and thieves and washerwomen, the filth of the streets, the sublime height of embattled towers brought down to the earth below where men wrestled in the mud for a copper penny.

Keep out of the mud. If there was Latin for that, it would be his motto. Squalid little people, with their squalid lives, their abject hopes and wretched fears. At times he had dreamt that people such as that went down on their knees praying to him, begging him to save them, to give them bounty, or some such thing. It was enough to disgust him. Had he not shown how much he despised them? He had never thrown a farthing to a beggar, and never would.

He would ride up to the Downs today, to take a look. He was here for the races, like so many of his good breeding. A horse race was another fine thing, and one might mingle there with the best blood in England. At Lewes, or in Brighton, or whatever they called the place. August was a grand month.

Amelia was in her shift, which felt strange enough, and could see more or less nothing out of the small window except the sky, even if she stood on tiptoe, but she could hear voices all around. Sitting was best. There was a slightly sour smell in the wagon, grinding over the stones, and lurching a little. But it was hardly a journey. The machine soon began to turn around, slowly and deliberately, with words and clicks of encouragement to the pony drifting back to her; then it stopped. There were still sounds — bumps and creaks — although the vehicle was quite motionless, and that would be Mary Jenner clambering about and lowering the awning. Amelia sat in the stillness, with just that lapping sound and the voices, one an excited scream.

There was a tap on the door, and as Amelia said 'Yes' it swung back to reveal the dipper with a dim backcloth behind her. She was smiling.

'We're all ready now, Miss, if you are? Now, I'll back down the steps, and you come here to the top. You'll give me your hand, if you please. There. That's it. Steady now, let your feet get in, and then down a bit, there, steady as you go.'

It was surprisingly cold, but not, as she quickly corrected herself, as cold as the stream by the Norths' cottage in Cornwall, and she had plunged in that, admittedly not by design. She worried that she would slip on the worn steps, but went further down, gingerly. The sea caught her shift now, and she realised she would rather be without it, but not in the company of this woman. Her hand was still held firmly, that was good. Like a grotto, the dark canvas of the awning arching over them both, with sharp bright beams through the cracks, the sea swelling back and forth, warmer now for an instant, then cold again.

'Now I'm going to take you in my arms, like a babe, Miss, and like a babe I won't be droppin' you, don't you fret. That's the easiest way. Just step down one more, there, that's right, and hold on to my left hand, like that, and I'll put my arm around you, and then let my left hand go and I'll tuck it under your legs as they swing.'

It was astonishing. How could the woman be so strong? Her mind slipped back to Eugène by the stream, but he had put her down quickly, although she had wished he had not. She could smell the salt on Mrs Jenner's face and in her hair.

'That's it, there, here we go.'

She was in the water, the shock made her gasp, the cold running up her legs and on to her stomach and upwards. She felt an involuntary shiver, and the salt splashed in her face momentarily; Mary lifted her in her arms up above the water again.

'There, that's it. Best to dip again, there ain't no wind in here to chill … yes, splash the salt on your face, here we go, and up again, you can stand too, if you like.'

The water came up to her chest. Amelia held Mary's hand, to steady herself. Then it suddenly swelled up and over her shoulders, just below her chin, touching the back of her hair that she had tied up so carefully. There was nothing like it. Nothing at all. It was as if the sea were alive, and playing with her.

'There, we best be goin', Miss, as the tide may be turnin', comin' in like. You take my hand and put t'other on the step in front of you, that's it, easy does it. See that strap there — hold on to that, that's it, up you go, and here I come.'

They were inside, and dripping. Mary reached for cloths, and patted them over Amelia's neck and shoulders, asked her to put her feet one by one up on the bench, and dried them too. She pointed to the other cloths in the cupboard.

'They'll be yours. I'm goin' now to put up the hoops. You just shut the door and don't mind the banging. We'll be ready when you are, right as rain. But just remember to sit down afore we move, and hold on to the bench. Tim's as good as gold, but it can be a bit bumpy.'

Mary Jenner shut the door behind her. Amelia stood in a daze. No maid to help her this time. She reached down, and resolutely removed her dripping shift.

CHAPTER XIII: REUNION

The Steyne, the Steyne! The Duke had forbidden Thirza Farley to walk on it unless she was on his arm, citing the need to keep her safe after her dangerous misadventure in Plymouth. But privately she thought that he was possessive, that she was his prize to flaunt in front of those he knew and those he did not, provoking the envy that he coveted. So she might be seen *only* with him, might *only* be approached when his suzerainty over her had to be acknowledged, be greeted *only* through him, and not because a man was drawn to her.

The Steyne, the Steyne! The day was really too hot, but the chance of freedom was too rare and precious to be passed over, and she thanked the stars for the presence of the races, to which men were drawn like moths to the proverbial candle, leaving their womenfolk free to indulge their tastes and pleasures. In her case, one of those was memory, bitter-sweet memory. There was less built then than there was now, but they had walked over and back again, standing out of a shower in the portico of the circulating library, like colonists on the veranda of some villa — where would that be? India, the Americas? She did not know.

Will was a sentimentalist, the sweet boy, but Thirza could not leave her profession as an actress, so recently commenced, with such early success, so much flattery and attention, not all of it decent when compared with his absolute purity. His hands trembled when he held her arm, and she would have given herself body and soul but for the fact that he was penniless, and it would have meant their ruin. So she had resisted him, been cruel. Young, darling Will. She sighed and fought back a sentimental tear of her own. Had it been now, she would have had him, and damn the cost. But Will was long gone, and his beautiful innocence might now have hesitated in front of her, unsure, and dismayed.

Few admirers troubled her now. She had been gone for a good six months, was less known, and eyes were searching for those who were the talk of the town, not for one whose fame had dimmed. Or whose bloom had faded, she jibed at herself. Her hand went to her mouth and fingered the scar by her lip, then moved to her brow, a reminder of the assault she had suffered from Tregothen. Both of them now healed and pale, but as such etched on her face. Still, she would not be daunted. Was she ever? She had refused to give in to the new fashion of the clinging, columnar gown, which conveniently was not to the Duke's taste either, and had gathered her curled, raven-black hair under a crowned hat decorated with violet ribbons. Her walking dress was a lawn-green robe, with an extravagantly large breast knot, her shoes laced and heeled, and holly green. The Duke had money to spend, or so he claimed, and it was her idea of a gorgeous summer costume.

Amelia came up lightly from the beach with a spring in her step, carrying her bag with the wet smock in it almost like a schoolgirl. She was laughing as she stepped on to the path, and found herself confronted by a small, beautifully dressed woman who was not afraid to stare at her. More to the point, the young woman — for so she proved to be — twirled her parasol around in front of her, folded it in a neat gesture, and posed pertly with it pointing to the ground like a walking stick.

Amelia wished to apologise; she had come too quickly on to the path, absorbed in her own thoughts. The sun was hot.

'So, you would cut me dead, my young Miss Wentworth, and yet it is only a matter of months since we were thick as thieves.

And what are months if not a few weeks, and weeks if not a few paltry days! Why, if I am allowed to calculate as my sentiments would wish, 'twas indeed only yesterday that we were together.' And without hesitation, this imp in shades of green curtsied theatrically, lifted her head, and grinned.

Amelia stood stock still, and with embarrassment became painfully aware that her mouth was open, because her companion ruthlessly gave a mocking imitation of it. At length she found her voice.

'Thirza Farley. Why, it is you, Miss Farley! How wonderful to meet you here, and in Brighton!'

'None other, my dear Miss Wentworth, and you see our stars must be well-placed, or is it the planets, or whatever else the poets tell us in their fancies, so here we are.' Here Miss Farley cast a glance aside at nothing in particular, and said mischievously with a rueful air: 'Well, there are those that might risk an embrace with me on meeting, and not be repulsed.'

Amelia stepped forward impulsively, and leaned in to kiss the cheek that was daintily offer to her.

'Why, I believe that is better. Yes, indeed, I feel more myself after a peck on the gills. And, so, what do you do here on the edge of the shingle, in the beached margent, Miss Amelia? Would you have been after bathing yourself, and the sea so broiling and tempestuous?'

It was ridiculous, of course, stage language mixed to her own amusement, but she missed very little and had no doubt noticed the simple garments, a few strands of damp hair. Amelia became conscious of her appearance, and blushed, and Thirza stepped in quickly.

'There, I have caused you embarrassment, and must chastise myself. We shall take tea, and you shall walk with me. I shall hear no objection. The young man can wait…'

'There is no young man,' Amelia said rather sharply, and then wondered why she had. There was Eugène. She must tell Thirza about Eugène.

'Ah, well, sometimes we ourselves do not quite know if there is such a fellow. Come, we shall walk, I am not situated so very far away, and I shall tell you all as we progress arm in arm.'

Which she did not, although they did progress as she suggested, because telling all was not her custom, and could not be since there was always something more than might be openly declared. But as they walked — and it was really not far to the New Inn in North Street — she told Amelia about the Duke, or rather mentioned the rank but not the man, since it was perhaps better that way. He was her patron while she was resting from her labours, as at present, and how generous he was too, so that he had installed her in good, furnished rooms in one of the best of the inns in Brighton, where she found herself most comfortable. When Amelia exclaimed how fortuitous as well as fortunate this was, Thirza warmly agreed and informed her that she was also furnished with a maid by the Duke, who was attentive almost to a fault, when he was not in amongst horseflesh as he was today.

At the New Inn, the staff showed Thirza the greatest respect as she came in with her guest, and she took a moment to order tea to be delivered to her rooms.

'So you see, I am like one of those cleverly designed things that always ends the right way up no matter how hard … you throw them.' She had not seen the sting in the tail of her own phrase coming before it was too late. Amelia looked at her, and tears sprang into her eyes at the memory of the beginning of it all, the assault her companion had suffered from that libertine Tregothen while they had all been residing in Plymouth. Thirza lifted her chin, and raised her finger.

'No, you must not, I am such a foolish chit to let that slip out, there is no help for me… There, you have me playing the fountain too.' She came forward to Amelia, and brought her into her arms. She ran her fingers through Amelia's soft hair.

'There, there,' she said. 'The words come out…'

There was a knock at the door. 'That will be tea,' said Thirza. They disengaged themselves. A neatly dressed serving maid brought them some silver pots and china cups and saucers on a square, wooden tray.

'Yes, you may put them there. That will do splendidly. Thank you kindly.' The door closed.

Thirza pointed out to her two, upholstered chairs standing by the small, slightly shabby side-table on which the maid had placed the tray.

'Come now, you must sit after your endeavours. Tell me, how do you find the world after Plymouth and Cornwall?'

It was a long walk to Patcham and the cottage, but walking was like work, it never hurt anyone. The worst part of it was the sun and the heat, but the lane had trees and so there was shade on part of it. She had best be back by evening so that she could be up early tomorrow and in at the New Inn in good time for Miss Farley. Elisabeth had not ever puzzled out why some women who had menfolk were called Missus and others called Miss. Nan had told her not to trouble herself with how other folk lived, but they were all Missus in her family and always had been, thank you very much.

Her feet would be sore, but she would soak them and they would be as right as rain. Always got a blister or two, but at least there was no mud. Too much dust in place of it, that gets in a body's face and hair, no matter how her bonnet sits tight. Miss Farley was a good'un, cheerful always, kind to her, though she herself lived out just down from the New Inn and across in the alley with Missus Bowles, in a little room which did well enough. The Duke's man had found that for her, found her to serve Miss Farley too, to be honest, the ostler at the stables at the inn being a friend of her father's, him now dead and gone, rest his soul. The room was neat, and Missus Bowles gave a bit of dinner too, not bad.

Miss Farley had sent her away today because she fancied walking, she had told her. The Duke was up at the races on the Downs, she had heard them say, Whitehawk, and Miss Farley never went out without him. He did not let her. But Miss Farley was stepping out today, and she knew that was why she had sent her off to visit the cot at Patcham and old Nan. It was only a walk on the Steyne or beach, but the Duke would not let her do it. So Miss Farley did it when his back was turned. That was how it was: when the cat's away.

'You'll do, Lisa,' the Duke's man had said when he saw her. Lisa indeed! The cheek of it: her name was Elisabeth, to him and others. She had dressed her mother's hair before she had passed a year back Michaelmas, and clothed her too, when her legs gave out and she did not rise much. Miss Farley did much of hers herself, but she could help her, as with other things. Always had been a help. Used to it. The Duke gave her coins, but she thought the ostler had taken more for finding her in the first place. Still, it was enough, and she could take care of herself, although her brother Ned at the inn in Lewes said he looked out for her; probably lied his way to Lewes and back about looking out for her — as if he did! No one did that. But she always got by, even if her legs were tired now.

The tea was rather thin, and Amelia was unsure in any case if tea was precisely the refreshment that she wanted after bathing. But she was, she found, quite thirsty and so it was welcome in its own way. Thirza duly served, and her expression and ridiculous manner and one or two silly phrases made Amelia laugh, until Thirza excused herself and went into a neighbouring room for a short while.

Amelia looked around for the first time. The drawing room was dominated by a large window, which looked out across some rooftops lying at odd angles, higgledy-piggledy until the view was obstructed by the wall of another tall building. The sun came in aslant, and lit the room brightly, and in truth it was not large, although it had a small dresser, the two embroidered chairs on which they had been sitting, three assorted side-tables, and an armchair of reasonable fashion but on which the fabric had begun to fade.

It was a grand drawing-room crossed with a small parlour, and Amelia surmised that there was more, a bedchamber into which Thirza had withdrawn briefly, and perhaps a closet or dressing room within that. The panelling was the grander part, but it was unadorned by paintings or portraits, the colours a faded blue and white, the curtains a deeper blue. Amelia reckoned that she had no dukes within her acquaintance, but had heard of measureless wealth and bottomless debts, and she wondered most actively why this man had chosen an inn rather than lodgings for his … for Miss Farley.

'What do you think? Your judgment of my burrow?' Thirza came to the table, and lifted her cup again. 'Why, I think a lady should be grateful for attention, and for being granted the use of what is, after all, a *dear* set of rooms. There, I have answered for you, and were your opinion adverse, you now have no call to air it. Come, another sup, Miss Wentworth?'

Amelia stood up, protesting. 'You must not serve me, but be seated yourself. There, I was thirsty, and perhaps tea is right after all.' She poured, and sat down again. 'You asked after me, and I shall reply that I am here with my dear friend from Plymouth and Cornwall, Caroline North, with whom I visited in London.'

'Ah ha, and where in London was that?'

'It was at Hampstead, a pretty village. We spent some time taking the waters, and at other times called in at acquaintances, met some new friends, looked in at shops, and … and then withdrew.'

Thirza looked across at her, and scrutinised her face while delicately holding her cup in front of her mouth, poised, with three fingers and a thumb.

'Withdrew?'

'Yes, withdrew, from London, briefly to home and to Cornwall, and then here to Brighton. Once again Miss North accompanies me to this place, and we are lodged in East Street, comfortably and conveniently.' Her eyelid was fluttering, she could not control it, but otherwise she had managed her account well, edited as it was. Nay, be honest, censored not edited. She could not, would not tell Thirza of what had happened in London, burden her with that too, and the name of Tregothen again.

Thirza stifled a small belch, which in male company she would not have troubled to do, and attended to the half-moons of her nails with an abstract air.

'It is my fault, and I accept full responsibility for it.'

Shocked at hearing this assertion, Amelia protested vehemently, but Thirza continued without pause, raising her voice just a gradation or two within its wide range. 'I refer, of course, to the breach in our relations after Plymouth. I should have replied to your letters, but I failed to do so. I believe I gave you an address in London, but even there my memory fails me. I am a poor correspondent, there is no excuse for it.'

'It is of no consequence. You owed me nothing, and how you could think of another when your own condition was such … when recovery and a return to full health were of the greatest importance.'

Amelia stood up and crossed over to the window. It had become certain that Thirza had no knowledge at all of what had happened to Amelia in London, or still worse to Arabella in Devon, nor indeed of Tregothen's involvement in both. She looked out: there was an alley below, with a dog curled up asleep in it. She thought idly that it might lead around to the stables. Her fingers picked at the edge of the curtain. Thirza came across, and Amelia felt her pulse rise. She looked down at her face, noticing the scar by her eye for the first time. Her finger traced its outline. And then down to her mouth, and then away.

The actress said sombrely: 'In a certain light, you cannot see them.' She pulled away. 'I shall dress for dinner. My maid Elisabeth is away into the country today, so it will take me longer. With your permission…'

Amelia felt enthusiastic. 'No, you must allow me to help! I insist. You shall call me when you are ready. I shall dress your hair, tighten stays, adjust your bonnet, that sort of thing. It will be a pleasure. I never had a sister.'

Thirza smiled. 'So be it. Me neither. No sister. Three brothers, too many by half. No, that doesn't count out, does it? When we are acting, some of the ladies do for each other if the dresser is already taken. I must choose my gown.'

She drifted across to the door to the chamber, and disappeared. Amelia looked around for a book. There were several stacked on one of the small tables. A tap came at the door to the corridor. Amelia crossed to the door and opened it. The maid who had brought the tea to them stared at her for a moment, and then asked to take away 'the cups': Amelia stepped back and closed the door behind the girl when she left. A small mantle-clock was placed above the empty fireplace; Amelia stood and looked at it, without taking note of the time.

Sounds came from the bedchamber. Amelia walked over and stole a glance through the half-open door. A crimson gown was laid out on the bed. Amelia sat back down in the parlour and opened a copy of Shakespeare's comedies: she particularly liked the scene between Orsino and Cesario, but could not find the page. She put the book down, and crossed once again to the door of the bedchamber. It had closed a little, perhaps with the breeze coming in from the window, and so she pushed it back ajar, to where it had been.

Thirza was standing next to the bed, looking down at the crimson gown and a shift that now lay on top of it. She had been wiping herself with a cloth. She was completely naked, and the damp cloth hung down loosely from her right hand. Amelia did not know where to look. But her gaze chanced on a mole on Thirza's left breast, and she became possessed by the idea that it needed to be kissed.

It was not a large room. Amelia stepped forward, and it seemed as if Thirza moved almost imperceptibly towards her, her own eyes following the direction of Amelia's glance. They both stopped, just inches short of each other. Amelia's fingers were trembling, and there was moisture above Thirza's lip. She reached out with both hands and lightly drew Amelia's simple gown up over her head.

CHAPTER XIV: TO BE A GENTLEMAN

Laurent Guèvremont was determined that his new ward, Gilles of Kergohan, should be tutored in the arts of a gentleman. Since the boy was an orphan, as far as anyone knew, then he had undertaken to look after him and see him settled in life, and it was evident that acquiring some of the traditional accomplishments of a gentleman would be to his advantage. His manners were, not to put too fine a point on it, a little rough. Sadly there was no *école d'armes* in Auray, nor was there in Pontivy, but there was a *maître* in Rennes. Laurent Guèvremont wrote to him, and agreement was reached that he would, for an enlarged fee, come to Auray and offer what he called an *épreuve* of *Monsieur* Gilles in a short set of lessons. It would have to be seen if a period of lodging in Rennes might be subsequently required, for attendance at the *école* itself. There might be other advantages to that, but Laurent preferred to have Gilles where he could keep an eye on him. He was convinced that young blood had its ways, and that Rennes and independence might be a combination that proved to be too much.

Monsieur Laubadière arrived one morning at the Guèvremont residence, dressed all in black with a tight little waistcoat over tight black breeches, and a scarf tied loosely above. He was of moderate height, but he was accompanied by a tall young man dressed in a similar fashion, but in brown and without the scarf, and with an impeccable shirt that ended at the wrists in little flourishes of lace. Both bowed elegantly to Guèvremont, who marked them down without a second look as vain, and so to be indulged in nothing or they would attempt to negotiate everything. Indeed, Laubadière almost immediately launched into a set of provisos and caveats which only confirmed Laurent's first impression, at which he nodded only once and then brought to an abrupt end with a 'Yes, yes, quite, quite, I am sure we understand each other'.

There was an outbuilding behind the house, which Bernard had been set to clear and clean in advance. The floor was of beaten earth, and the light came through a pair of shuttered windows. Bernard undertook to introduce the *salle* to the guests, who walked about in it, tried their tight, unadorned shoes out on it, and professed it to be satisfactory. Gilles came in moments later to introduce himself, which Laurent had considered to be the right thing for him to do. There was bowing on all sides, and Gilles was introduced to the *fleuret*, the foil tipped with its soft cap and displaying a slightly worn and tarnished pommel, grip and guard.

Gilles had handled swords before, but only in a kind of admiration, although he would know what to do with a knife or a dagger if he had to use one. He flexed the blade of the *fleuret*, inspected the end, whipped it back and forth once or twice, and then grinned at his companion, standing motionless with the point to the ground.

'Strange-looking thing, isn't it? Not good for much.'

Richard de la Motte-Baillot said not a word and moved not a muscle, while *Monsieur* Laubadière scanned his potential pupil up and down. He was overdressed; the coat would have to come off. His hands were too big; he stood like a carthorse. He would have him in bare feet, or at least in stockings; those were ridiculous heels, they would break his ankle on the first retreat. The pupil proved obedient, and they were ready.

'*Monsieur*, shall we begin?'

Gilles was unimpressed. When it came to it, fencing was all about prancing and flouncing around waving a useless bit of steel like a parasol — not about sword-fighting, your life or his. And there was no way he was going to be quick enough. Sure enough, he could run like a hound when the need was there, and his arm was strong for delivering a blow; but there was no moment for slashing here, just poke, poke, prick, prick, back, poke again.

'The palm up, *Monsieur* Guèvremont, yes, right round — you know the phrase, in the palm of your hand — the fingers and thumb extended, yes, and the rear arm raised, if you please. Richard, demonstrate, if you will. We must not grip it like a cudgel, either, so it is lightly but firmly, if you please.'

Lightly but firmly. What on earth did that mean? And damn *Monsieur* Richard de la Motte-Baillot: only a Norman could look like that.

Lunch was welcome, something on which Gilles insisted and which the house had been willing to adopt for him, a hunk of bread and rough cheese, and a small glass of the white that Bernard locked away. But there they were waiting for him, like the slaughterers for the pig, lean and mean. He tried to behave, swallowed hard, smiled at them both, and asked himself why he always reacted like this.

The afternoon wore on, and he learnt *la garde* to their satisfaction, apparently, and felt pleased with himself. They disbanded for the day, but he asked to keep the foil, and in the evening practised in front of the cheval mirror, thinking to strike a pose at least. Yet he remained convinced that the face of the person he would most like to impress would probably fold up in laughter at the sight of him. He indulged himself with a carefree swipe or two, the last of which caught the handle of his hairbrush and sent it flying against the inkstand on his open *escritoire*. Fortunately, it was empty and dry; there were evidently benefits in not writing many letters.

The next day he found that various parts of his body were aching, and he decided it was because he was constantly being led back to the position required for *la garde*. In a rush of blood to the head he asked for a taste of combat, at which Laubadière seemed incredulous, and assumed his most patient and long-suffering voice.

'*Monsieur*, the art of *escrime* does not engage in combat. We exercise the body and the mind, recalling that wise principle of the ancients, namely that of *mens sana in corpore sano* — a healthy mind in a healthy body — with which you are no doubt familiar. Exercise is a fine word, or we might otherwise talk about an *essai* or an *étude*, perhaps. You see —' and he tolerantly called Gilles over, to sit next to him on a long coffer that stood to one side, patting the top of it — 'if we look in this book by the remarkable Domenico Angelo, with the title *L'École des armes*, you will see the wonderful engravings that establish the outlines of our art so vividly. It is a work written in French, of course, which is quite as it should be. But there, you are impatient to progress, and this we should understand. Come, Richard, and I will show you what follows. You sit here.'

Laubadière took up his own foil, and walked in an easy gait, lightly, on the balls of his feet, into the middle of the *salle*. Richard watched him approach, and then suddenly raised his foil and assumed *la garde*, as did his *maître*. All was momentarily still, and Gilles did not know which of them to watch, or what to be looking for. Suddenly, Laubadière began to shuffle forwards, then backwards, then forwards once, forwards twice, and then he lunged with one leg bent at the knee, and back up again, while Richard, who had been backing and edging forwards again himself, attempted to push his master's foil to one side but became caught in a game of twist-the-sword, as Gilles later described it, and was almost touched on his chest as Laubadière broke free for a vital second. It was exhilarating, exciting, and the two men drew apart and bowed to each other.

Gilles picked up the book, and quietly thumbed the pages, fixing on some of the positions, for a moment fascinated, intrigued, and also bewildered. Laubadière stood next to him, wiping his face on a soft cloth. Gilles made up his mind, closed the book, and stood up.

'You will forgive me, *monsieur*. I have watched, listened, and learned, with your great indulgence. It is not for me. It is beyond me. I shall bid you good day, and thank you once again for coming all this way to try me. You have been the embodiment of patience itself.'

He bowed to the agile, nimble *maître* and then strolled over to the young Norman, who was by now leaning once again on his foil, impassive as ever. Gilles stretched out his hand, and was almost surprised when it was grasped, with the foil tossed carelessly from one hand into the other. He was completely sure about it all, and walked out of the *salle* and the building, determined to tell Laurent himself of his decision. It was a good thing when you admiringly shook the hand of a man you would gladly have had by the throat only one day earlier.

Monsieur Duchesne was another thing altogether, although it was noticeable that he and Laubadière were of a very similar stature, one which Gilles was all the more ready to respect now that he had seen the *maître d'armes* in action. The speed of fencing had impressed him, with the agility, and he found that he liked the manners too, if that was the right word for the way in which the whole thing was conducted. It was something in which he was woefully lacking, he had to acknowledge, and he resolved to learn from it. He already knew Duchesne by sight, and had heard one or two reports of him, mostly from the kitchen back-chat of Gaëlle and Marguerite, which was more in the way of gleeful slander, although he had also heard one or two passing comments made by Joséphine Guèvremont over the table at breakfast which were favourable. He had formed his own judgments, in the casual way that he did, and there remained surprises in store for him.

These came quickly, in the choice of necessary dancing partner. Duchesne declared himself willing to take *Monsieur* Gilles through the preliminaries, and to rehearse him in some simple steps, those for the minuet for example. But he was adamant that little progress would be made in independent study, which was another way of saying that partners would be required. Gilles quickly wrote with an invitation to Clémence de Moire, but her reply did not hesitate to remind him of those occasions when his conduct had been insufficiently courteous. It was not greatly to his credit that for a while he could not even recall when or in what way he had fallen short of her standards. When he did, it was obviously to no purpose feeling aggrieved about the tone of the reply, nor indulging in embarrassment about how thoroughly he had ignored and offended her at the disastrous tea-party.

Subsequently, it came as no great surprise when the would-be *incroyable* Théodore Bérard offered his profound regrets that he was on the point of departing for Paris, since society there was very lively at present. But the upshot was that Gilles could only blame himself, and for the time being he could not hold out any prospects for a wider acquaintance, not until he had acquired the very skills which he was experiencing such difficulty in acquiring. It was easy to get despondent.

So backwards and forwards it was, strangely like the fencing, across the polished wooden floor of the *salon*, which Joséphine had yielded to him for three mornings a week but for one month only, and that with disdain, adding that it would take an eternity in any case to find a female who would stand up with him. Backwards and forwards on his own, with Duchesne first shouting out the steps, then showing them, then explaining them, then going through them in slow motion, then moving in parallel, so that Gilles in watching Duchesne did not look at the movement of his legs as he had been doing, and attained the remarkable distinction of actually treading on his own feet, notably on a little toe that objected with a stab of pain, and then in an extended protest refused to heal.

Nevertheless, the minuet was finally mastered, and the sounds of Duchesne's violin and his shouts of approval began to filter out into the hall, where Bernard smiled to himself as he took in the coffee to Guèvremont, who looked up from his desk and also seemed satisfied at what he heard. Yet it was not more than two days later that Bernard opened the door to the unexpected sight — granted the known disappointments about partners — of *Monsieur* Duchesne accompanied by an unknown young woman. This diminutive and dimpled personality was clad respectably in one of those light dresses of the latest fashion, her hair held back from her forehead by what Bernard, with limited knowledge, would call a riband.

Since the lady was accompanied, Bernard chose not to announce them, but opened the door to the *salon* with some satisfaction, the young lady herself having the unusual courtesy to thank him for it. Gilles stood up from the sofa at the side of the room, put down his newspaper, and gave his waistcoat a tug to get it in good order.

'Now, *Monsieur* Gilles, may I present to you *Mademoiselle* Duchesne.'

'*Mademoiselle* Clotilde Duchesne, Papa, if you please.'

'*Enchanté, mademoiselle*.' Gilles felt a bow was the right choice, to which *Mademoiselle* Clotilde curtsied in a manner that was more like a bounce, short, quick, and in good order. She appeared to be caught in some kind of reflection while her father tuned his violin, and came to a resolution.

'*Mon Père, Monsieur* Gilles will fall out of step if he has to run all the way through "*Mademoiselle* Clotilde Duchesne" every time he wishes to address me.'

Her father looked up from his violin, which he had on his knee, his leg on a stool. 'But that is precisely why I suggested *Mademoiselle* Duchesne to be used. It is both proper and fit for our purposes.'

'But Papa, if I permit *Monsieur* Gilles to address me as Clotilde, that will be very convenient, and you will not disapprove of it?'

Her father looked doubtful, but went back to tending to his instrument. 'It is as *Monsieur* Gilles wishes, my little bird. If he is happy, then we are happy; but only within these four walls, mind, and for the purposes of ready instruction. I am sure we shall understand each other.'

'But of course, *maître*.' It was the first time that Gilles had used this title to the dancing master, who lifted his head that instant, and swung his leg down.

'Now, if the formalities are over, to work, *mes enfants*...' Then, quickly correcting himself, 'Forgive me, *monsieur*, I was forgetting myself.'

'Not at all. I am honoured to have such a charming partner.'

'Hola, *Monsieur* Gilles, you must not flatter me! That will not do at all. For all that you know, I may be a creature of great impatience.' And with that teasing statement, the young lady twirled herself around in a few, lightning-fast steps, and then broke into a dance with her father enthusiastically playing what Gilles took to be a popular tune with a joyful beat. She and he came to an end simultaneously, and Gilles spontaneously applauded, at which father and daughter held hands and bowed to him together.

'Since she was five, *Monsieur* Gilles. In Burgundy, where we were, the nobility took great pleasure in dances of the people.'

'Perhaps you may teach me one of those?'

'Perhaps I will. There is one that is gaining favour even now, and we may try it. *Mademoiselle* Joséphine was most enthusiastic about it until she lost her dancing partner, Captain Leroux. A sad loss, of a quite accomplished dancer. I wonder if we shall see him again.' He tapped the back of his violin with his knuckle. 'But for now, it is the minuet *à deux*, *monsieur*, and enough of my idle chatter. Come, my heart, you must stand to the assistance of your partner, who is far newer to this art than you are yourself.'

'That is so, Papa. And I shall aid him most happily.'

CHAPTER XV: HÉLOÏSE AND ROPARZH

Héloïse had never looked at pots and pans like that before. The housekeeper, *Madame* Perrée, had laid them all out on the massive worksurface, partly like a table but mostly like a carpenter's bench, which sat in the middle of the kitchen. There was the skillet, the *rondeau* and the *fait-tout*, the broiler and the stewing-pan, and a whole list of other pots and utensils whose names she nodded at but could not retain. Then there were all the different spoons, and heaven help you if the wrong spoon was used and the taste carried over. There was a story about that which was supposed to make her shocked, and *Madame* Perrée clearly could not get enough of it, because she tutted and shook her head as she told it. Then the knives, quite unlike the two pitiful things they had at the manor, one with the blade broken at the tip and the other with its handle missing a piece. No missing pieces here, more like a regiment of weapons on parade, the racks impressive and indeed very practical, which Héloïse admired, and similarly with the array of plates and dishes; but once they were mentioned it started all over again, with names for everything which she would never remember.

All the while Nanette and Lise bent over their work, but by the mid-morning they had gone, with Héloïse left guessing that the preparation for the evening had been completed as far as it might be. She went compliantly with *Madame* Perrée into her little office, which was the size of a carriage without the seating in it, with just a solid table and one plain wooden chair. On one wall hung an embroidery of Christ showing his heart, and a simple, wooden cross on the other. Being the woman she was, the housekeeper told Héloïse to sit while she bustled out and came back with another chair from somewhere.

On a shelf *Madame* Perrée had her lists in two boxes with clasps, one inlaid. The first contained all the bills from the merchants and tradesmen, which were covered by an accounting ledger of sorts, with ruled pages and dates and figures. The second box contained two types of sheet, handwritten. The first pile proved to be of menus, drawn up carefully to provide a full meal, with quantities given below for different numbers of diners. The second pile was of recipes, from patisserie to desserts and sauces, with the ingredients and quantities, but also with some spidery instructions.

It was strange to be thinking about all this food and drink but to be tasting nothing. Héloïse found that she was not only hungry and thirsty by now, but also that her head had begun to ache. Without any warning she yawned right over the instructions for creating a *velouté* sauce, which was unfair because it sounded delicious; but it was a sauce too far, and the thought of the right pan for it let alone the right spoon proved too much for her. *Madame* Perrée paused in her lively account of the process, and stared almost in incomprehension at a young slip of a thing who could be fatigued with the busy affairs of the kitchen by this stage of the mid-morning.

Adelaide appeared at the door of the cabinet. She dipped in a curtsey.

'If you please, *Madame*, we are now approaching the time that *Mademoiselle* Argoubet is to visit in the town with *Madame* de Lalande to the Floch household. You will forgive me.' And she curtsied again but left before a reply was given. *Madame* Perrée gathered her papers together, including that containing the magical spell for the *velouté* sauce, and folded them neatly down into their box.

'Well, *mademoiselle*, our time this morning is now at an end, as you see. Our next task will be to visit the shopkeepers and tradesmen, and the markets, to see about supervising the purchase of foodstuffs. *Madame* de Lalande herself will be instructing you in the keeping of accounts, although I am sure I can say that I have been accounting to great satisfaction in this household by myself for a good many years. But *Monsieur* Guèvremont knows what it is that he has planned, and there will be purpose in it, we may not doubt. A very good morning to you, *mademoiselle*.'

Héloïse pleaded the headache. Only by doing so was she able to put a stop to any more demands being made on her, and also to create a situation in which she could request food and drink in the proportions and of the kind that would do her most good. Word was sent round quickly to the Floch household cancelling the visit. Adelaide was to convey this message, and while she was gone Héloïse retired to her bedchamber, which the combined skills and care of *Mesdames* Lalande and Perrée had made attractive, cool and comfortable in equal measure. The patisserie which had escaped her all morning now lay on a tray at her side, or at least the remaining part of it, and Héloïse had already drunk one glass of lemonade, while a second stood half-finished on the side table that Lise had placed next to her bed. Her head was still throbbing, but the food and drink were having a good effect. There was a light knock at the door, and Adelaide put her head round it: Héloïse gazed at her blankly.

'*Mademoiselle*, forgive me for disturbing you, but *Mademoiselle* Floch insisted on accompanying me back to the house, she was

125

so concerned to hear about your *maladie*. She is waiting downstairs at this moment.'

'Oh. How kind. I am feeling a little better, it is true, but…'

Adelaide came a little closer to the bed. 'Would you care for me to show her up to you, *mademoiselle*? It seems a pity…'

'Well, yes, why not? Bring another glass, Adelaide, if you will, and perhaps a small plate. *Mademoiselle* Katell can share my refreshments. It will be fun. Thank you.' Then a thought occurred to her that brought a finger to her lip: 'But will *Madame* Lalande…?'

'*Madame* Lalande is out, visiting.'

'Ah. A napkin too, then if you please. For *Mademoiselle* Katell.'

The door was not completely closed. Héloïse could hear an excited voice, and then one or two sounds downstairs and on the stairs. Katell's lively face peeped momentarily around the door, then disappeared again. There was a loud whisper.

'You say she is not sleeping? I shall not be disturbing her?'

It was a cue for Héloïse to slump further down in the bed, and turn her head away. She could hear the footsteps creeping slowly and quietly towards her, and when she judged it was right she turned suddenly and sat bolt upright. Katell jumped and gasped, and then as Héloïse held out her arms she laughed and embraced her.

'So, you are not so bad? I was so worried that I just had to come and see you. It is not… I mean, have you been vomiting and … worse?'

'No, it is not, and no, I have not. And now, Doctor Floch, will you blood me, and set me on a diet of that disgusting Breton porridge — what do they call it?'

'*Yod.* No, I shall do no such thing, but I may with your permission…'

A tap at the door, and Adelaide appeared with the plate and glass, and the napkin. Katell sprang up and went to fetch a chair.

'*Mademoiselle*, you must let me do that.'

'Nonsense, how can you, Adelaide, when your hands are already full with things for me? There, it is all done. How wonderful! Just what was wanted. We shall turn a sickroom into a salon!'

'But with no music to entertain us, I am afraid.'

'Why, we should have my brother with us. He might bring his violin. He is so talented, he could serenade us, although it might perhaps be a little improper. Shall I send for him?'

'No, I think perhaps not, Katell, although it is a kind thought. I'm not sure *Madame* de Lalande would approve, nor perhaps would your brother. We shall hear him another time. Besides, he may be bound up with his sketching or painting.'

'He is not. No, he is preparing to go to the church.'

'To the church? Why?'

'Oh, I cannot say. Perhaps he will tell you himself. But let us not talk about him. What have you been doing? Do you see, I have these gloves which papa bought for me, and I have been reading *Candide* again, which makes me laugh. What do you like to read, Héloïse?'

'Let me see those gloves? They are of leather, are they not? Very smooth.'

'Yes, they are of kid. But tell me, what have you been doing?'

'Oh, I have been looking at pans… I have been under instruction. Yes, that's it.'

'Do you have a governess, then? How exciting! Or perhaps not. Is she very severe? I did not know…'

'No, not like that. *Madame* de Lalande and *Madame* Perrée have been instructing me.'

'But what can she show you? *Madame* Perrée is your cook, is she not? Are you going to be baking biscuits?'

'Not exactly. No, but… Look, the butler Tudual has been teaching me to play cards. *Madame* Lalande has approved it, since she would rather not do that herself. Adelaide sits with us and sews, while we play. *Madame* Lalande will let me learn piquet.'

'Then we must play together. Would you like me to lend you my copy of *Candide*?'

Dear Katell had bubbled her way out of the room after a while, since she had to go for a dancing lesson, and Héloïse had felt a growing conviction that she should go to the church. Her headache had eased, and what she wanted to do was to settle a time for confession with the priest for a weekday, since she wished to avoid Sunday with its crowds. It was not far from the house to the church. Inside the porch it was already blessedly cool, and Héloïse made her way to a bench towards the side, where she sat and pressed her forehead and then her temples against the cold stone of a pillar.

Then she saw him. She had been expecting to see the priest, but she saw Roparzh Floch instead. He was sitting bent forwards, and it seemed as if he must be praying. It was the hair that gave him away, beautiful as it was, and as he sat up he brushed it from his eyes and face. Then, miraculously, he turned his head and saw her against her pillar. She was certain that he had seen and recognised her; but he turned slowly back and resumed the same posture.

She knew that she should not interrupt him. But she decided to move across to the centre of the nave, where she could gain a better view of the glorious, carved altarpiece of the holy family, earthly mother and father, the divine son, and the divine father above, with the wings of the holy spirit. Out of the corner of her eye, she saw Roparzh rise from his meditations. He walked quietly down the side of the church, and she noticed how elegantly he moved. It was evident that the priest was not to be found, so she left her new seat, crossed herself again, and trod lightly and quickly back towards the main door in the west end.

Roparzh was standing obscurely in a corner, looking up at a small statue and reading an inscription. He turned before she passed and his sombre face smiled a greeting. She took it that she should wait for him, which she did while he knelt and faced the altar, bowed his head, and crossed himself. Such devotion! Perhaps he was destined for the priesthood? Or it might be that he was in an agony of doubt about that decision, which accounted for his presence here, struggling with earthly desires in the midst of an attempt to cast the snares and enticements of the world from his body. When he spoke, his voice was low, resonant and mystical.

'*Mademoiselle* Argoubet. Have you visited the *chapelle* Saint-Ivy? It is no more than a step from here. Then I feel that we should take our separate ways.'

He had not questioned her presence here. He understood implicitly her true belief, which was like his own.

'No, *Monsieur* Floch, it is unknown to me, but I should truly like to visit it.' Especially with such a guide, she might have added, but did not. It might be misunderstood, and disturb his feelings further. They went out into the light and crossed the square. Two small boys watched them, and their mother shaded her eyes against the sun, and then called them away to her. Héloïse was unsure why the chapel should have its doors open but be completely empty. There was a small entrance-hall from the street, and she realised that the building seemed familiar because it was a similar size to some on Saint-Domingue, and quite simple as they often were. Roparzh went quietly ahead of her, showing reverence in his way of walking and his obeisance, and when he spoke it was in soft tones.

'I do so love this building. The spirit of God infuses it, so you are never alone. The church is grander, but it overwhelms the senses.'

'Hmm.' It was a response, but not much of one. She did not know what to say to him, and doubted in any case if he really wanted her to talk about his feelings. Roparzh wandered, as if in a dream, up the central aisle. He turned to look back at the building as a whole, and spread his arms suddenly.

'What it must be to give a homily to the faithful? What inspiration for one's own faith must one take from that?'

She stared at him. She was probably not enough just by herself to be a congregation, but he might appreciate her attention. She sat down in order to concentrate better, but he had finished his moment of ecstasy: he dropped his arms, brushed his hair back from his face, smiled, and came towards her. He sat down almost in front of her, and spoke back over his shoulder to her.

'And as for you, *Mademoiselle* Argoubet, do you come to the church to pray, or to meditate on human folly? Or do you … have a personal sorrow?'

Héloïse was made uncomfortable by these probing questions, so before she could became annoyed she said: 'Why … do you?'

She could see his body stiffen, and immediately felt that she had said the wrong thing. It was hard and unjust if he could ask her, and she could not ask him. But, still, she wished she had said something else. She crossed her legs under her gown, and placed her hands in her lap. Let him play aloof if he chose.

He rose, and she thought for a moment that he would leave her there, after bringing her into the place. The blood came into her cheeks at the thought of such arrogance. But instead he turned sharply and came to sit by her, not close, but at a short distance away, enough for modesty but permitting a kind of intimate conversation. She kept her hands folded firmly on her lap.

'You are right to put the question back to me, *Mademoiselle* Argoubet, more right than you could possibly have known. My tone was insolent, that I must acknowledge, but it perhaps proceeds from a hurt I have taken on my own feelings, that makes me seek for a similar hurt in others. Yet I could not wish it on another...'

Once again, she felt that she could say nothing. She pursed her lips, but otherwise stayed still. He sensed her willingness to listen, but also was aware that there were limits to what he himself was willing to communicate. Yet he had her interested. When he spoke, his voice was solemn.

'I do not solely bring my miseries into the presence of the Lord; I would not have you think me selfish in such a way. But you know his compassion too, I have no doubt, I sensed it in you when first we met. I pray for forgiveness, for my sin of attachment to another, and my resentment when she was taken from me. There, I have said it all, and no doubt you will think poorly of me for it.'

There was, inevitably, a silence in the chapel. Héloïse cleared her throat, and moistened her lips.

'That I do not, and would not. Your humility does you credit, *Monsieur* Floch. I respect you for it. Furthermore —' and here she cast a sideways glance at him — 'you have my compassion too.' Here he looked up. 'A little thing beside a great thing, no doubt.' It was emotional, rather more than she had expected, and her voice broke a little. Without moving his head or body further, his hand reached out for hers. She relaxed her grasp on her own hands, and slipped her fingers slowly across to his. They touched.

He stood up abruptly, leaving her hand where it was, and using his to brush back his hair.

'Come, *mademoiselle*, we must step out into the light, and return to our homes before we are missed. Allow me to take your arm for the moment. I shall release you at the door of the church.' He stood back to allow her to make her way into the aisle, and then smiled.

'You must come to see me paint. I should like that very much. My sister Katell will make up a party for us. The summer allows me to paint in the open air.'

CHAPTER XVI: PICNIC BY THE CHATEAU

'Do come in, *Herr* Wiesemeyer, come, come, we shall not lose ourselves in ceremony or formalities. Please, step forward. There we are. Now, allow me to introduce to you my daughter, *Mademoiselle* Floch, and this young lady is *Mademoiselle* Argoubet. I trust this room will be suitable.'

'*Madame* Floch, I must thank you with all my heart. It is true that I have worked in larger, but I have lived in smaller! There, you see we Austrians always laugh when we may.'

'Well, I do suppose that we might search for a more capacious venue...'

'No, no, *Madame* Floch, you misunderstand me. We shall make do, make do very well. So, these are our young ladies, and our first task must be to ask you if you have been dancing.'

'Well, *Monsieur* Wiesemeyer,' began Katell, '*Mademoiselle* Argoubet and I love to dance, between ourselves, that is, but I am not sure our figures would please you... Our dance figures I mean, of course. Why, I believe I have had lessons on several occasions in the past...'

'That is wonderful, *mademoiselle*. And *Mademoiselle* Argoubet, perhaps?'

'If you will excuse me, *Monsieur* Wiesemeyer,' *Madame* Floch cut in, 'other duties now require my presence. Should you need anything, then my daughter will ring on your behalf, I am sure.'

'Of course, *Maman*.'

'So, let us resume. *Mademoiselle* Argoubet? How is your dancing?'

'I enjoy dancing, *monsieur*, I have always done so, since I was a little girl.'

'And do you dance a great deal, where you come from?'

'There is much dancing, but perhaps not...'

'My friend and I have played a little with the minuet, *monsieur*, and she is so light on her feet, are you not, Héloïse?'

'Ah, now you interest me, *Mademoiselle* Floch. Light on the feet, you say? "Dancing is like the flight of a bird". Do you know who said that? You do not? It was Mozart. Wolfgang Mozart. None other. You have not heard speak of Mozart? Well, times are difficult. So, we must start with the minuet. All dancing begins with the minuet. All noble dancing, that is. We do not need an instrument; I shall clap with my hands. But first, I must show you myself. The better part of instruction is demonstration. So, you will please stand back...'

'You ask me about my history, and you are right, even we Austrians have a history. But the good *Monsieur* Floch does not pay me to talk to you about my history. We must dance. It must be the *cotillon*, I think, and we shall have to make do as we are. You say that your brother does not dance, is that so?'

'No, Roparzh believes dancing to be frivolous. But, *Monsieur* Wiesemeyer, we are tired, or should I say a little fatigued from the minuet. We have learnt *so* much from you this morning, and we hear so little of other places...'

'Well, I shall sit then on this stool, so that if anyone comes into the room I can stand up immediately, and you will take a rest. What do you wish to know? *Also*, I can guess, it is why I am able to speak French to you? It is because I have lived in Trier, which in your language is Trèves, and before that in Koblenz, and then before that in Wien. You see, your armies of the Republic have captured where I was living, not Wien, god forbid, no, but these other towns. And, in fact, I have been annexed. You have no idea what that means. It means I am now a French citizen, no less. You know nothing of this? No, why should you? There you have it. I am a Frenchman, you see, not an Austrian! We must laugh when we may. That will do; the *cotillon*…'

'Do they dance in Trèves?'

'Trier is a serious town. Koblenz is different. And Wien different again. They have palaces, and dancing, and wonderful balls, some with masks; you would see hundreds of noble people, thousands of candles in the *Grosser Redoutensaal* in the Hofburg in Wien, the musicians, gold everywhere…'

'Was your Mozart there?'

'Yes, he was there, or his music was there. He laughed, but it was a sad end. Very sad.'

'We are sorry you are sad, *Herr* Wiesemeyer. Would you like *Mademoiselle* Argoubet to dance for you? You said you would like to see her dances?'

'No, no, Katell,' protested Héloïse, 'I cannot do that. I said I could not before. I… I do not have the drum. It…'

'Héloïse, you may clap your hands! Why, *Herr* Wiesemeyer claps his hands for us if he does not play his violin. The *cotillon* is so dull…'

'I cannot clap my hands and lift my gown. You see, it is improper.'

'Héloïse, please! Ah, I knew you would! It is so lively, there… Oh, you have finished.'

'It is lively, *Mademoiselle* Argoubet. We have such dances where I come from, in the villages, and I have danced them myself. We call it the *ländler*. The music has an interesting rhythm, you see … like this … or this. There is also a dance which is beginning to have some favour in better society, which is for couples, and that is unusual…'

'Show us, please show us! We are a couple, it will be perfect! No more tiresome *cotillon*…'

'It is most simple. You see, one, two, three, one, two, three — and there, it could not be simpler, but you may dance to one side of each other, or dance facing each other. You may hold each other's arms like this, and stand together.'

'What do they call it?'

'Alas, it is only in German, *mademoiselle*. They call it *der Walzer*.'

Gilles made up his mind that he would ride to Pontivy. He could not expect that Héloïse would write to him, and he did not know what to write to her, and was afraid in any case that she would not be impressed. They were bound by old rules of propriety, and by those timeless laws of uncertainty, diffidence, and confusion. That had been true for most of the time they had spent together, which was not much more than a year, and now they were apart. He did know where she was staying, at the Guèvremont house in Pontivy, where his only real acquaintance was with the Floch family, since the father had helped him a little. The daughter, Katell, was a pretty and lively person and far too sophisticated for him. The son, Roparzh was betrothed — he had gathered — to the daughter of a wealthy lawyer in Rennes. He might visit them while in Pontivy, if he had time.

Gilles had no manservant as yet, making do at home in Auray with Laurent Guèvremont's valet, François, who was amused by his youth and enjoyed turning him out well. François wrapped up a good set of clothes carefully, and stowed them in a saddlebag, since he knew his employer would want his ward to give a good impression. François would not be travelling with him, and he could only trust that Gilles would lay everything out to lose its creases once he reached Pontivy.

The distance proved to be greater than Gilles had originally imagined, so he stopped to rest overnight at Baud, where he found courtesy of the ostler that his horse was almost trailing a shoe. There was that to contend with, in addition to the worry that the horse might have begun to go lame, which was settled in the horse's favour once the farrier had done his job. The food was passable in Baud, the company appalling, what there was of it, and he even got bored of walking aimlessly around the small town, where the children stared at him with their fingers in their mouths.

On the next day it rained, and he had only a coat not a cape or collars, while one of his strange pet aversions was to wet saddle-leather, which he was sure would leave a stain on his breeches. And it kept raining. Whenever he thought it had finally blown over, it started again, and sheltering under a stand of trees became impossible, or he would have made no progress at all. The previous day his thoughts had drifted to his aunt Jeanne Cariou, and to the village of Brandivy where she lived which lay over to the right of the road he was taking. He realised he had not asked if her parents were still alive, which they might well be, and whether they had cast Jeanne aside too, as they had her sister, his mother. He knew so very little at all, and had not even known he had an aunt until a short time ago.

As the horse ambled along contentedly, despite the rain, he pondered on what kind of hold it was that Guèvremont's ominous steward Le Guinec had over Jeanne Cariou. After a short spell in Auray, staying with Bernard's family, when Gilles had talked to her about his mother, Jeanne had insisted on going back home to Brandivy. Unfortunately, Le Guinec was all too close to Brandivy, because he had been given the responsibility by Guèvremont of supervising a new timber-mill on the River Blavet. In an idle moment, Gilles found himself hoping that with luck Le Guinec might get one of his shapeless cravats caught in the machinery, and then that would be the end of him. But as for his own grandparents ... well, it might be best anyway if they were dead, since they had done so little for his mother or for him.

Soaking wet and yet hot, he drew near to Pontivy, smelling the tannery below the town, thinking of why he had come and what he would say to Héloïse, of a kiss in the woods and perfume on a warm neck, of how to be casual when there was always that disturbing impulse of something else that should be done, even if you could never be sure of what precisely it was.

On the day that Katell Floch and Héloïse had planned their promenade and picnic, it rained, and the arrangement was postponed to the following day. *Mesdemoiselles* Floch and Argoubet had themselves proposed that the party should walk a little way past the chateau, and then settle down at a suitable spot on the embankment surrounding it and proceed with their sketching. Since *Mademoiselle* Katell was further advanced in this art than her companion, *Madame* Lalande was satisfied that she would be able to advise and help her charge, which would obviate the danger of too much interference from young *Monsieur* Roparzh, whose talent lay in watercolours. His presence was acceptable, but as the young people wished to be modern, and eschew the antique custom of chaperoning in the light of the changed times, *Mesdames* de Lalande and Floch agreed that the party should be accompanied by the maids Marie and Adelaide, who would be needed to carry the picnic and the sketching materials in loose bags.

The following day was bright and sunny from the start, and they set out soon after breakfasting on their walk through the upper part of the town. By some kind of gentlemanly instinct, Roparzh led the way, with his easel strapped to his back, his materials in a bag over his shoulder, a black bonnet wrapping much of his hair. The two young sketchers followed behind, chatting and laughing, conspicuously dressed in broad-brimmed straw hats and gloves to give them protection from the sun. Marie and Adelaide came only a discreet distance behind, and only ceased to chat when their feet began to be sore and their collars a little damp from the exertion. The party started to climb up on to the embankment, and Katell still had breath for her limitless curiosity.

'Pray tell me, Héloïse, how do you go on with *Madame* Lalande? *Maman* calls her de Lalande, but I am not convinced. Tell me, is she strict?'

Héloïse took a moment to consider these questions.

'No, I would not say strict. She is very polite. And I find her kind.'

'This path is quite steep. Come, we must take the bags from Marie and Adelaide. I think they are quite tired. Marie, you must let us take our sketching bags now. No, no objections, please. It is quite steep. There, now you go on ahead, follow *Monsieur* Floch, he knows the way.' And then, in a capricious aside to Héloïse: 'After all, it is only a chateau with massive towers! Anyone might miss that!'

'Why do you ask?'

'About *Madame* Lalande? Because … well, I mean, it must feel very different from … how you were living before. To be frank, Héloïse, my tongue leads me into questions before I know why I am asking them! It happens all the time. *Maman* is for ever telling me off about it, while Papa just laughs.'

'And Roparzh?'

'Oh, him. He is away in the clouds. He doesn't listen to me. Come, now mind that root. But look, we are nearly there. Do you see the view? No, it is better from here.' She took Héloïse's hand and almost pulled her along a pace or two. 'See, not just the river and the town, but the fields beyond too!'

Héloïse looked along the embankment to where Roparzh was setting up his easel, freeing it from the straps by which he had carried it. He looked over, smiled, and waved to them. Héloïse waved briefly back, and then thought better of it: Marie and Adelaide were sitting close to them, and not so absorbed in their own world to miss gestures like that.

'I do so love the countryside, but I live in the town. Don't you find that strange? Let us sit here. Marie has left us a soft blanket. The ground can be very rough. I do hope those soldiers do not come any closer. *Maman* would be very displeased —' she leaned in to whisper in Héloïse's ear — 'even if we might not. But Roparzh will ask them to move away. There, they have gone.'

But not very far, Héloïse thought. Had not the butler Tudual talked of a garrison in the chateau? She could hardly remember; so much had been said to her.

'You are right,' she said.

Katell looked puzzled. 'About what?'

'That how I have lived before has been different.'

Katell seemed very excited. 'Have you lived in a big city? Nantes is very large, but Rennes not so large. Or maybe I have that wrong. No, what a fool I am, you were living on a farm.' Katell then put her gloved hand to her mouth. 'I am so sorry.

On a manor, of course. There is all the difference in the world…'

Héloïse laughed. 'Not at all. The manor is a farm; you are in the right of it. Cattle, chicken, goats, wheat and rye, barley too, buckwheat, harvesting, apples.'

Katell leaned back, and looked at the sky. 'How I should love to live on a farm, especially in a manor. A wonderful old house full of the smell of smoke, the scent of hay and straw, the cattle lowing…'

'It is hard work, of course.'

Katell looked reflectively at her. 'Were you a lady of the manor? I don't really know…'

Héloïse crossed her legs on the ground, under her dress; Adelaide glanced over at her, and then looked away, and carried on talking to Marie. Héloïse tucked her hair behind one ear.

'No, it is not like that. It is complicated.'

'But what about…?' Katell bent forwards, in order to speak softly again, and then broke off. 'But here I am asking you all these questions. How rude of me. I am so simple myself. You see, I was born here, and have grown up here, and have only been away to Rennes and to Nantes, and that not very often, with Father and Mother and Roparzh. What do I know of the world?'

Héloïse gazed at her with affection, and then her eyes narrowed. 'Do not ask to know more. You are happy here.'

'Yes, I suppose I am. But we must have our picnic.'

Roparzh was standing at his easel, an odd little folding-stool between his feet. Katell crossed to Marie and Adelaide, who stood up and began to lay out their picnic under her delighted supervision. Héloïse walked over to Roparzh, and stood a little back.

'It is no good you looking at this,' he said suddenly. 'I am not happy with it. There is too much of the town, and too little of the landscape. I must put it aside, if not destroy it.'

He was a little flushed, and clearly rather angry: the artist, not the priest.

'I know! I should turn to the sister art. Will you sit for me?'

Despite herself, Héloïse blushed fiercely. She could not grasp what he meant. Sit where? How could that be a proper thing to say? She turned to leave. He reached out and put a restraining hand on her shoulder. She swung round, fiercely indignant.

'What do you mean by this, *monsieur*?'

He dropped his hand immediately. For an instant, his eyes searched hers intently, and then his face relaxed. 'I see. Forgive me. You do not understand my meaning. No, you must forgive me! It is what we say when we wish to draw someone, to take their likeness, to make a portrait. We ask them "to sit" for us.'

'Oh,' she said. They stood in silence for a moment.

Katell had looked up and seen them standing together, and she sensed some awkwardness, or offence given. She did not want the maids to notice it too, and so she tripped across to the young couple, picking up her dress and calling out to them.

'You must be in need of refreshment. Roparzh, pay attention to *Mademoiselle* Argoubet, and not just to your painting. We have laid out the food. You really must come.'

'Of course, sister. But we shall also come back. I am to draw *Mademoiselle* Argoubet, with her permission, of course.' He bowed. Héloïse said nothing, and Katell took her arm and talked quietly with her as they strolled back together.

The inn was just down the street from the Guèvremont house in Pontivy, and Gilles lodged himself and his horse there. He would make out that he was just passing through. That would do, and no one would think to remark on it. It was a bright day, ridiculously, after all that rain, and he hoped that they would put his saddle out in the air, if not in the sun, to dry out a little. In the saddlebags he had found a new shirt, one of those with lace at the cuffs, an open neck despite the fashion, a satin waistcoat, no less, his new, dark coat — what did they call the colour? — decent knee breeches, good stockings, and none of it particularly damp from the rain. That was François: the whole wrapped up meticulously in a kind of oilskin and then canvas. What more could anyone want? He dressed himself, left the inn, and walked up the road.

Tudual's face at the door showed no recognition, just good manners, and he bowed respectfully.

'Good day, *monsieur*. Allow me to observe that this is the house of *Monsieur* Laurent Guèvremont. Alas, *Monsieur* Guèvremont…'

Gilles put on a quizzical expression, and waited.

'*Mon dieu*! Why, it is *Monsieur* Gilles! Of course it is! Please forgive me, *Monsieur* Gilles, for my complete foolishness and impoliteness. You will be pleased to step right in, *monsieur*…'

Gilles raised his hand to cut him off.

'It is a pleasure to see you, Tudual. No impoliteness, none at all. But may I ask you discreetly, before we go further, if *Mademoiselle* Argoubet is indeed in residence? That I was led to believe, but one knows how…'

'*Mademoiselle* Argoubet, in your own chosen words, *monsieur*, is happily in residence.' Here Tudual bowed again, because he was unsure how to proceed. Gilles detected that the butler was uncomfortable, but could not understand why. With a slight hint of irritation creeping into his tone of voice, he chose to make the obvious request.

'Well, perhaps you might announce me?'

Tudual quickly looked round into the hall, stepped forward and pulled the door gently to behind him. He leaned forward, in a confidential way.

'Since it is you, *Monsieur* Gilles, let me just say that *Mademoiselle* Argoubet is taking a promenade this morning with friends.'

That did not sound too bad. In the open air. He could meet her by accident. In a way it was a godsend; indoors would be far more constrained.

'Thank you, Tudual. That is most helpful.' He waved a hand vaguely around: 'Would you by any chance know where...'

'You will think I am spying, *monsieur*, which I am not. But I did hear it said that there would be a picnic by the chateau. I do know that such a picnic was prepared. This morning. In the kitchen,' he added, rather redundantly.

'Tudual, I am grateful to you. I shall trouble you no further.'

With that, Gilles skipped down the steps, and headed for the chateau, which lay directly ahead of him, at the end of the slight rise of the street. He did not know the environs well, and he made the mistake at first of heading down from the gate, believing that there would be grounds below it. There were one or two young ladies down by the river, but they were with their mothers and maids, as far as he could see. There was no point in getting caught up in the narrow streets around the bridge; it was no place for a promenade, and surely too far away from the house.

The search was becoming frustrating and annoying. Added to that he was getting hot, but he realised he must not allow himself to get truly angry, that his impatience was — as always — his greatest enemy. He climbed up the embankment again, but there was still no sign of Héloïse. Damn Tudual and his wretched picnic! Those two maids were staring at him, probably at his waistcoat, while the other young woman was intent on her sketching pad. He stalked past them, ignoring the snigger of the maids, stared again at the sketcher, but nothing could make her into the person he was seeking, and then...

He strolled quietly but purposefully along the embankment, and took a sloping path down its side a short way. There was very little cover here, so he tried to face away from where the couple were sitting. He was absolutely sure it was Héloïse because she was partly turned towards him, perched ridiculously on some kind of stool, which was so low that she had to sweep her legs to the side as she sat there. She was wearing one of her white dresses from Saint-Domingue, with the laced bodice, and he noticed that the lacing was loosely tied at the top. He looked away before she saw him, and pretended with as much effort as he could muster to be looking over at the chateau walls, cursing that he had not thought to bring a hat.

But who was she with? A fellow with black hair, and dressed in black. What kind of party was this? The young man had his back to him. The whole must surely add up, so that would mean that the other three women on the embankment were of the party, and would account for the food and baskets. A promenade and a picnic.

He could not bring himself to approach. What to do? He kept up his pretence of scanning the walls and towers, hands deep in his coat pockets, and as he swung around to catch another glimpse, a memory came to him. It was actually of the maid's face, the one with the dark hair. He was completely sure she was the maid at the Floch's house. In which case surely...

His confidence was subsiding rapidly. He hesitated, but then sauntered slowly back along the path. He peered this time. The artist chose that moment to lean forward, away from his sketch, reaching out to brush a lock of her hair gently away from one side of her face. He then took her chin in one hand and turned it slightly, letting his hand stay on her cheek. All the while, Héloïse kept her eyes fixed on the artist's face. Reluctantly, as it seemed, he turned back to his sketch and easel.

Gilles confirmed his suspicions. He was seized by fury, not so much that Roparzh Floch — for that was who it was — was taking liberties, but that Héloïse was letting him. The whole scene disgusted him. A pair of soldiers had come together on the ramparts, and seemed to be looking over at him, staring. He turned back. The maids had wandered off somewhere, the young woman — who must surely be Katell Floch, Roparzh's sister — was still absorbed in her sketching. He would not interrupt any of them. He turned up the collars of his coat and sank his head into them; he felt like a beaten dog.

When he got back to the inn, he asked for his horse to be made ready. The weather was fine, and he was determined that he would make it back to Baud well before nightfall.

CHAPTER XVII: A MOTHER'S INTUITION

Arabella heard a scratching, down by the bedpost, under the bulging plaster with its fattened, cherub face. She pulled the curtains aside, peered through them, but her foot was caught. She tugged at it, but then the other was caught.

She drank from the vast green bottle he had left, but it was empty: no, it was wine, it had a wide mouth and fat neck, but it tasted foul and she threw it at him. Missed. There was a scratching at the window now, and she dragged the bedclothes behind her — there was a pit outside and a dead animal in it; perhaps that had been the scratching... Then the face at the window, thin and mean, blood running down from the eyes, an open cut through the cheek, but gone again, just a bony hand reaching for her, not stopping...

She heard the bedroom door creak open now, footsteps running, and she fought the hands, choking her as she sat bolt upright in bed, gasping.

Grace's face, her nightcap round it, and Mrs Willan with a candle, the light on Grace's face. Arabella looked blankly at the familiar features of her woman.

'Now where have you got yourself to? Come, let's sort you out, you're all tangled up. Thank you, Mrs Willan, a lemonade from the pantry would be just the thing. And the door to, if you please.'

Arabella listened, urgently. The room was quiet. No scratching. None.

'Thank you, Grace. I...'

'You're a little hot and pothered. I'll just wipe your forehead and you'll be right as rain. 'Tis a hot night. We have the casement open, shall we pull the curtain back? Just for an instant. Thank you, Mrs Willan, that will be all, we are settled here now. Goodnight to you.'

'Thank you, Grace. Did I shriek?'

'You cried out, yes. Just a bad dream, nothing to worry about. We all have them. Now shall I bring a pallet in? We'll sleep sound. Now sip at that lemonade. It'll cool you down.'

Arabella sat half-upright, holding the glass, and stared out in front of her. The baby prodded, once or twice, and then kicked more vigorously. Her throat felt sore.

It was Andrew who collected what post there was at nine o'clock. The groom rode her chestnuts regularly now, the mare and the nervous gelding, to keep them exercised, and Arabella wished ridiculously that she could ride down to the village and back with him instead of waddling around like a goose being fattened for Michaelmas. Confinement, they called it, and although the rigour of that was still some months away, she felt like Elizabeth kept imprisoned at Hatfield House. When she was young, her father had idolised the old queen and read whatever he could find about her, and she wondered if she had disappointed him by not learning six languages by the age of fourteen, or whatever it was. One was her limit, and she rarely used even that, although Justin would tease her by speaking too quickly in French every now and then, a trick he had learned from his sister.

There were times, recently, when she had wondered what she was good for, and why he had married her, apart from this round belly and what went with it, or rather before it, to be accurate. Was it enough? She had thought so, and they had

148

laughed a lot, and she had visited in the village and around the tenancies, and the word was that she was well-received. But now? She had tried early on in the marriage to interest him in dancing, with some success, but that would have to wait. She would ask Sempronie to lead her in sewing; they could order some linen, make him shirts. And she would play. The piano was there, and she would play and sing more often, and they would have guests. There, that was it.

There was a man in the garden. He nodded respectfully to her as she stood by the window, and the gardener himself came up with a wheelbarrow and they moved away. She made up her mind to take a walk in the garden. She would like to go back to the rose arbour, and sit on that bench, and think again about him bending the knee to her. Foolishly, a tear came into her eye at the memory, and then more than one: she cried quite openly. The man's name was John Scott, and he had been selected by Justin and her father, very carefully. He was a former excise man, and used to 'rough work', as her father had said. But he also liked gardening. She knew he was a guard for her after all that had happened with the abduction by Tregothen.

She would supervise the preparation of rooms for Sempronie and her maid Betty. That would do for this morning. Sempronie should be with her later today. Amelia was in Brighton; another letter should come soon. It had been a little while since the last, but Amelia seemed happy and amused. Justin's curt letter to her was in her pocket, where it would stay. There had been no other word. That odd little man Richard, the Quaker, had not come again; perhaps he knew where Amelia was. He seemed to follow her around, but that was guided by the principle of the abolitionist cause as much as loyalty, let alone love, she thought. There was nothing from

Eugène either, in receipt of her letter, but he would be in London, no doubt, where he had family. She could rely on that.

When Sempronie arrived at Chittesleigh, it was already the afternoon, and her first thought was of the orchard. But, of course, there was her host. Betty supervised placing her things in her room, and she went into the drawing room to greet Arabella. Justin's wife was rounded now, but she had had the good taste not to invite her mother-in-law to place her hand on her belly, as the younger people might now do, apparently. The pleasantries over the journey, its length and the warmth of the day and the dust and the comforts of the new carriage, were soon exchanged between them, in a kind of shuttlecock of manners. She was relieved once more that little had been altered in the room. The piano was still in its place, an instrument acquired by her son for the present incumbent, although his current absence was as yet unexplained. They sat opposite each other, comfortably, on soft chairs.

'I expect you have been feeling a little isolated, my dear Arabella. Perhaps your father has visited from Alverscombe?'

'He is bound up in the affairs of state, madam. He remains in love with his newspapers and his pamphlets. I can smell the dust from the library on his occasional letters.'

Arabella's tone was sharper than she had intended, and she felt embarrassed by it, so she hurried on: 'My father has only recently expressed a desire to go shooting with Justin; but he will insist on riding over, and of late his knee is giving him some trouble.'

Sempronie inwardly marvelled that Justin could be induced to go shooting, but a man such as Sir Francis Wollaston had to be actively entertained or his only talk would be of politics of a certain hue. She risked asking the question that had been on her mind.

'So, we are expecting your husband in a few days?'

Arabella turned her head to one side, and revealed a flushed cheek. Sempronie began immediately to regret the directness of her question, but it was already too late.

'Yes, I believe we may expect him.' Arabella stood up and walked over to the door. 'Shall I ask for refreshment? My own preference is still for madeira. Will you take some with me? We are to dine soon.'

Sempronie also chose to stand, but remained by her chair out of deference to her host.

'That is most considerate, Arabella. No, I believe I shall take a pass or two through the garden.' And she added, almost apologetically, with a smile: 'It is an old friend.'

Sempronie wanted to see the small, green fruits on the trees. There was no mature orchard at the dowager house at Endacott, and in general the grounds were in their infancy, moderate in scale though they were. The orchard here at Chittesleigh had been her pride and joy. Yet she could not stay there for long; it proved to be too hot outside for comfort, even in the relative shade of the trees. She took her easiest path back to the house through the stables, and slipped past the kitchen into the empty hallway, which was pleasantly cool.

There was something magical in climbing those stairs once more. Before the marriage, Justin's chamber had been along the landing to the left. She had scrupulously avoided this room even more so than his library; now she was drawn to see it, perhaps for the last time, and without giving offence. The door was unlocked, and the hinges were noiseless; but she was immediately disappointed, because it had been stripped of his belongings. All that was left were a chair and his old desk.

She sat down, and with a strange determination pulled open a small drawer on the left at the back of the desk, which yielded nothing. Without resisting the further impulse, she reached across to the right-hand side. There were papers here in this one, and she saw immediately that they were written in Breton. Her eyes were drawn to the signature: it was unmistakably that of Mael Sarzou, the family's steward at Kergohan. He wrote to Justin in Breton, and Justin replied in Breton: it was a habit they had established.

She put the top letter back on its pile and closed the drawer, then after a pause opened it again. Below the letters lay a small ledger. She lifted the letters, put them to one side, and drew out the little black book. It was a register of grain, the quantities and the prices fetched in sales. There was more paper beneath it: smaller sheets, folded, but only two of them. They were addressed from Quebec; just that. No year, just the months, April and May. The letters were in French. She could have sworn that they were written in a woman's hand, clear and open, but she did not need to do so: the signature below was plain enough, Marie-Rose Heaume.

She could not bring herself to read them, to spy on her son in that way, for all that she craved to know what had come to pass on what was surely his second posting overseas, with Lieutenant Governor Simcoe in Canada, not so many years back. As an excuse for her prying, she began to be convinced that something had warned her: it might have been the tone of Arabella's letter to her, her son's unexplained absence, or his wife's evasiveness under innocent questioning. It could be that there was another woman. They said that men became rovers when their wives were with child. Yet this would have been well before that.

There was a movement at the door behind her. She stood up and turned to face the intruder, her gown spread to cover the face of the bureau, in consternation at the face she might see.

'Excuse me, ma'am, I came to look for you, and they said you were not downstairs. Begging your pardon, but dinner will be served soon, ma'am.'

'Yes, indeed, Betty. Thank you for your concern. You will be good enough to wait for me in my chamber, and I shall be there without delay to dress.'

'Yes, ma'am.'

It was an easy matter to replace the folded letters, then the ledger, and then the correspondence from Mael. That had been as close to an unwanted disturbance as she would wish to be. They said freely that daughters were difficult, and that might well be the case; but sons were inscrutable.

CHAPTER XVIII: THE ABBÉ CARRON

My dear Mr Picaud,

Propriety suggests that I should not presume to address you by the name — that is, Eugène — under which you are most familiar to my husband, and so to myself, because in his absence I cannot without presumption lay claim to his acquaintance. I do so hope that I find you in health and good spirits, and indeed at the address to which we have sent an invitation to you in the past. I know that my husband regards you with great tenderness and affection, as a friend of many years and of his youth, who has also seen distinguished service alongside him in recent combats, no doubt helping to preserve him…

Which I did not, Eugène thought to himself, *because I could not find the damn fellow, who had tried to jump over a piece of Republican shot and been nearly buried for his pains. But be that as it may. We did look for him before we withdrew to the ships with our tails between our legs. I thought the fellow was truly dead and gone until he popped up again. Oh, Quiberon, Quiberon, remember me in your orisons! Now, to resume…*

It is in that capacity as a friend and companion that I wish to approach you with a request which you may at your discretion decline, since it does not come in the garb of a duty or obligation that you might with honour recognise. Here you must forgive me mention of honour, in the case that you should imagine that anything of what I may ask you would risk any infringement of that great principle.

'Hello,' said Eugène to himself, 'what have we here? I hope I do not detect...? Justin, you scoundrel, what have you been doing? These deep chaps will hide their secrets.'

There was a tap at the door, and a woman with her hair tied back entered, in a spotless apron no doubt donned for this very purpose, carrying a square bamboo tray which fascinated Eugène. His dinner was on it.

'Ah, Mrs Temple, thank you. Just put it there, as usual. And how is little Matty?'

'Oh, loud, Mr Picaud.' And she laughed.

'Well, a good pair of lungs, as they say. She's a dear little soul.'

'That's her father in her, and God be praised. Thank you, sir,' and she retired.

Dinner would wait for a while, but not too long. So, where was he? Yes, yes, blah, blah, and lo!, here we have it...

I would be most greatly relieved if you would, as a token of your friendship, be willing to pay a visit to Mr Wentworth at his customary lodgings in London, and assure yourself that he has suffered no misadventure. He must surely return from his business out of town within a few days of you receiving this letter, and then I may hope to hear further of him, which will restore me from any apprehensions that I have on his behalf.

Eugène was unsure whether to smile or to feel sympathy for the young Mrs Arabella Wentworth. Her writing style was, he freely admitted, not what he would have expected from the frank and seemingly carefree wife he had first met. Nor indeed from the insulted and abused woman who had been subjected to the gross attentions of the same villain who had intended to blight the life of the sweetest... So, sympathy must be extended to her. She had been abominably treated. But in what kind of to-do had Justin entangled himself now? Or was his wife prey to wild imaginings about matters with the most mundane of explanations?

He pulled the small table over to himself, sniffed the wine, wrinkled his nose and shrugged, and began to eat the meat pie hot from the baker's oven. A visit to Justin's London address could do no harm, and one might winkle out some hints about where he had gone, or at least the approximate direction he had taken, if not precisely what he was about. Then he must return to his own father, unpleasant as that thought was. The old rogue must find him something. His need was great. So, Wentworth's address in London was... He glanced at the letter.

Something akin to a shiver ran down his back. He dropped his knife, reached for his coat and fumbled through the pockets, coming out with the ball of paper he had found at Coline's rooms, which he unwrapped urgently and spread out on his knee. Not the print from the abolitionist pamphlet, but the scribble on the back. There could be no question about it at all: it was without any doubt the first half of the address that Arabella Wentworth had given for her husband's lodgings in London.

Eugène reached for the only bottle he had, which was a Cognac from one of his father's warehouses, a rare gift he had taken reluctantly. He ignored his glass, pulled the cork on the bottle and took a large swig, and stared fixedly out of the window at the meagre tree across the street.

Fitzroy Square was grand and imposing, but the Abbé Carron was not at home. Everyone Eugène met had a good word for him, and he soon came to know how much the Abbé had done for the French children and for the faith, but not where he was today. As always it was a little old lady who let drop the secret, which was no secret, because *tout le monde* knew that the Abbé was off looking for a new home for his charities today over the road, just over there, and her friend who was curious about the young man knew the name they gave to the place: it was Somers Town.

The carriages and carts ground along on the big new road, raising the dust and managing somehow not to block each other, as he stepped between them and ran the last stretch to the other side. If this was Somers Town it was a building site, with scaffold and stone and brick, hammers, handcarts, dust and shouting, shacks and hovels over to one side and beyond, but some good rows of new houses already standing. He lifted his hat to two or three black-clad master craftsmen, who were manifestly not the Abbé, and who to his mind did not look as if they knew where the Abbé was. He wandered on, and soon came up against a set of houses angled around in the middle of what would surely become a square. It was a peculiar arrangement, and another man in a dusty black hat, seeing his surprise, lifted it and said, 'Polygon'.

'Polygon?'

'Yes, Polygon.'

'Ah,' said Eugène.

'Fine building,' said the man. 'Name of Mather. I may be of assistance to you, Mr …?'

'Walsh,' lied Eugène.

'Ah, Mr Walsh, I should shake your hand, sir. No business without formalities, and no formalities with a greeting, I am sure you will agree, sir. You have an interest, I can see, and where there is an interest then an agent such as myself can make the connection. It is connections that matter in business,

Mr Walsh, and I like making them. Gives me great satisfaction to be of use to a gentleman of your substance, sir.'

Eugène began to bid him good-day, but Mather would not be discouraged.

'Now the Polygon is one of our finest, and ...'

Eugène decided to make the best of a bad thing.

'Indeed, Mr Mather, I shall take your word for it, and I wonder if you have by any chance been speaking with a gentleman of the cloth this morning, indeed a gentleman from France, displaced by the sad events of which we are all too aware.'

Mr Mather looked grave, took off his hat again and placed it against his chest in a solemn gesture.

'The king, sir, *and* the queen. A machine contrived in hell, and to hell they shall surely go who would dare to do such an ungodly thing. Mrs Mather and I speak of it Sundays to the children, as a warning, and it so impresses on their gentle minds that it is with difficulty we get them into their beds, they are so afeared of the mob.'

'Yes, absolutely. A French gentleman, this morning? Looking for houses?'

Mr Mather replaced his hat, and a note of displeasure entered his voice.

'Yes, I believe there may have been. With Shuttleworth. A rather short man. You may find him a little off to the right, in the rather plainer lots.'

Eugène queried the description. 'Short, you say. Would you mean Shuttleworth? Or the clergyman?'

'Shuttleworth. There is the back of him, d'you see?'

'Ah, I am most grateful to you.' The short back of Shuttleworth was disappearing around the corner, and Eugène began to run after it.

'And good morning to you.' Mr Mather turned on his heel, unimpressed, ever a believer in the formalities.

From beyond the Polygon the acrid smell of brick furnaces came drifting down and hung in the street into which Mr Shuttleworth had gone. Eugène slowed, and as he turned the corner the agent looked up at him hopefully; Eugène raised his hat and passed by. There was a small group of men and one woman talking enthusiastically a little way on, loudly and unashamedly in French. The group suddenly parted, leaving a man in the garb of an Abbé walking with one remaining companion in Eugène's direction. The priest smiled at him considerately, and would have passed on, but before he could do so Eugène raised his hat again, and bowed.

'Do I have the honour of addressing the Abbé Carron?'

The man's face was benign. His companion fell back a pace or two, and waited patiently.

'You do.'

'I wonder if I may have a word or two with you, Abbé.'

'You may indeed, if you will walk. I am afraid I have an appointment, and it is across the new road, near my lodgings. Will you walk with me, or shall we determine another time?'

'No, I shall walk with you. Happily.' He hesitated only for a moment. 'Only, what I have to say, to ask you about, might be considered rather personal, perhaps one might say confidential *but not —*' as the Abbé was about to interject — 'such as would need to be spoken in the confessional.'

The Abbé nodded in understanding. He turned to the man behind him:

'Mathieu, would you be so kind as to meet me back in Fitzroy? Thank you.'

They started to stroll together, at an even pace.

'I am enquiring after a young woman from Jersey, *Mademoiselle* Heaume. I was led to believe you might be acquainted with her, *Monsieur l'abbé.*'

The Abbé was a strong walker, but he slowed as he listened to the young man at his side, smiling and nodding slightly, his head tilted to one side, like an intelligent bird. He made no sign of acknowledging the acquaintance that had been suggested, but none of denying it either.

'Well, I think we should be introduced before we go much further. You know of me, but not I of you, as yet. Would you be so kind?'

'Yes, of course. *Monsieur* Picaud, *Monsieur* Eugène Picaud.'

'Ah. From which province?'

'Touraine.'

They were now approaching the dust and din of the new road. The Abbé paused in his stride.

'And what would be your interest in *Mademoiselle* Heaume?'

There was nothing unexpected in the question, and Eugène had anticipated this moment, deciding on sincerity. After all, who could be sure what this gentle but resolute man knew?

'She is a person of my acquaintance, Abbé. We were … placed together in Brittany, quite recently, and I heard that she had come to London.'

The Abbé nodded again. 'Quite so. You said "placed together"?'

Eugène looked him directly in the eyes. 'Yes, I did. I believe the phrase describes our situation well.'

'We must cross this road.'

The Abbé was nimble, and they avoided the usual curses from carters for anyone crossing their path. Eugène decided to dig a little deeper.

'It was my impression, *Monsieur l'abbé*, that you first met *Mademoiselle* Heaume during your time in Jersey not so very long ago, and that she was of assistance to you in your Christian projects there? There is much talk in Marylebone of your charity.'

'Yes, that is so. She was a great help with the orphan children. Her father had been a most successful fur-trader in Quebec, but he died suddenly, and she left. Yet something far more pressing must surely be on your mind?'

'Not necessarily pressing. More of … a sentimental matter. You may perhaps understand. I wonder if you would be aware of an address for the young lady in London? Or is that unlikely?'

The Abbé paused again. '*Mademoiselle* Heaume came to see me here in London, not long ago, and has since sent me money, for my charitable activities. It arrives, but regrettably I do not know of an address.'

'And unless I am mistaken, it has been brought by a *gars*, who answers to the name of Loic, I should imagine?'

'I see you are well-informed. No doubt an orphan, like those in Jersey. There were so many that came to us, and *Mademoiselle* Heaume was a devoted teacher, and patient with the children, as one must be. When we were forced to leave the island, we had no choice but to leave so many behind. I have not been able to return.'

The Abbé began to walk briskly. There was little time left. Eugène remained insistently curious: after all, why not know more rather than less? He probed a little deeper, in what he hoped was a casual manner.

'Others will surely have cared for them. Did *Mademoiselle* Heaume ever mention somewhere in England that was known to her, a kind of safe-haven? Perhaps somewhere on the coast?'

They were in Fitzroy Square. The Abbé stood with his foot on a step, looked up at a window, and briefly waved to a figure inside.

'I believe she did, now you mention the coast. Sainte Hélène, or was it perhaps Sainte Catherine? I do not know the province. Would that be right? Now, if you will forgive me...'

Eugène had forgotten that the English still had their saints, not just in the names of churches. By the time he thought to reply, the Abbé had gone, up the steps and into the house. He was a busy man.

CHAPTER XIX: ST HELEN'S

Justin and Marie-Rose sat opposite each other in the front of the boat, not as far forward as the bows, that would have brought them too close together. It was a fair day, as yet only warm, with the clouds pushing along from the south-west, large and lazy. She was wearing blue, her hair bound up behind her head, and his eyes rested on her small ear, the lobe less dependent than many. He looked away sharply. He knew that she felt her nose was too snub, or had done so, but it was he who could recall the shape of her ear. The breeze did him no good, nor the spray which came over the bow. But he could bend round and gaze down into the water, sinking his troublesome thoughts into it, and avoiding his broken reflection.

Loic and the old woman they called Françoise — if those were their real names — were in the stern, huddled together, perhaps not enjoying the short crossing from Portsmouth to the Isle of Wight. He imagined they were less sea-hardy than their mistress. The breeze became a wind that whipped suddenly across, and the boat yawed as the small sail bellied, the little waves sending their spray into his eyes. Marie-Rose merely stared out at the line of the island.

Bembridge harbour was their destination, close to Saint Helen's, and that must be it, opening up before them as no more than a crack in the shoreline, a church tower to the right of it along some dunes, but no church attached. There was a tiny village visible up to the left, and the harbour was hidden at first, with a muddy estuary stretching out into the distance. The sail flapped and cracked, and the boatman pulled it down and stowed it behind, reaching for the oars. He pulled them in steadily, with the wind cut out by the headland. The tide was high and the creaking jetty low, slapped from time to time by a more boisterous wave.

Marie-Rose slipped just slightly as they climbed ashore, but pushed his arm away angrily, and turned to help pull the old woman and the boy out of the boat and up on to the sodden planks. The sun was growing sharper, and he felt the salt tighten his cheeks. They walked off the end and on to the land.

She lost no time: 'The boatman will take you over to the other side, to Bembridge. You will find an inn at the top of the rise. There will be room enough, I imagine. I shall send Loic to fetch you to see your daughter tomorrow, and you must do what I say, and leave when I say, or you will never see her again. Do you understand?'

He glanced at her without warmth, and then cast his eyes over the harbour and out to sea, where they had just come. He could see the outline of Portsmouth, he was sure.

'I said, do you understand?'

'Yes.'

She turned on her heel, and the others followed, walking along the edge of the dunes. The wind caught her dress, and revealed her fair ankle, and to his rueful shame he realised that he remembered that too.

Loic came late, far later than Justin had imagined. The inn was not much more than a tavern, and there was nothing much upstairs for sleeping, but the host was civil, which surprised him. In the morning, he went for a stroll up to a windmill and then back again. Its reliable motion soothed him a little. Loic found him in the tap-room, drinking a draught from the barrel, and it was passable, too. There was a small boat waiting on the shore to ferry them across the harbour mouth, and then their path took them down to the foreshore and along it.

Justin waited until they were out of sight of the few dwellings, and then stepped forward, grabbing Loic round the neck, and seized his wrist, twisting it up and behind his back. The boy cried out, but Justin pushed him down to the breaking sea, a knee in his back, ducking him in and holding him below the surface, squirming. He let him up spluttering, put his mouth right up against the lad's ear, and churned out words in the closest he could to a snarl.

'Now you little bastard, if you think to trick me ever again like you did in London I shall have great pleasure in twisting your arm out of its socket for you. Then you might find reason to call for help from an innocent passer-by. Do you understand me?'

The lad looked stunned. Justin shoved his head under again, and Loic's legs kicked. He pulled him up.

'I said, do you understand me?'

'Yes, yes, let me go!'

Justin threw him down on the beach, and stepped away from the water's edge.

Loic stood up; he was drenched, and sore, but he had been worse. What he really did not like was that the man had spoken in Breton, fluent Breton, and Breton as they spoke it in the south, which was where he came from himself. What did Coline think she was playing at? It could prove to be a dangerous game.

The two walked on silently, but now side-by-side, as the path rose up a slope overlooking a mill building of some kind, with large ponds that were vaguely reminiscent of the salt pans of Brittany. A little further on and Justin could see the gates and sluices. A tidal mill: wind on the hill above Bembridge, where Justin had been, water down by the sea here.

Their path became a lane that led up between cottages and then out on to a wide-open space, a green. Justin could not recall ever seeing a village green so large, or so bare. There were farm buildings at the edge, cottages above, perhaps a small tavern. The road to the left must lead down to the sea somewhere, perhaps to the tidal mill. A cat stared at them and slunk away. It was not a featureless stretch of grass; there were wells, a number of them, and donkey carts with barrels. The Isle of Wight fed and watered the ships of the line; it was a good trade, or so he had heard — perhaps almost as profitable as smuggling.

'This way.'

Loic trudged off, and Justin flexed his wrists, not feeling a strain in either. The warning he had delivered might be useful: who could know what else Marie-Rose might have up her sleeve? He realised he was nervous. Would the child look up at him with his mother's eyes? Would she have her hair? He could not recall what he himself looked like when he was that age, but another Amelia would disturb him quite as much. What scant words the child had would surely be French.

They walked around the top of the farm, and seemed to be heading out of the village, which they were. A lane curved round, and a small cottage stood on its own, rough and old. There was no sign of a child. The door opened as they approached. A goat was tethered to one side on a small patch of ground, munching grass. It lifted its head, stopped and stared, and then went back to munching. Justin entered first, and Loic followed. Marie-Rose was in the tiny parlour, standing by the hearth, her hands behind her back.

'You will never come here without invitation. If you do…'

Justin took in the neat room, and the little seat by the small front window, the deal dresser.

'That's enough of those threats and prohibitions. I, too, can walk away from here, as you well know…'

'What happened to you?' She spoke sharply in French to Loic, not sympathetically, but with some concern.

'Oh, I slipped on the beach. It was stupid.'

'Then go and stand outside in the sun and dry off. I do not want that muck in here. And brush yourself down when it's dry. But don't wander off.'

'As if I would,' he said.

The parlour door closed behind him; he could be seen through the window. Justin adopted a more conciliatory tone. But he would not speak French to her.

'So, how do we proceed? Here I am, and for that matter, here you are too. You wanted me here, or you wouldn't have gone to such lengths to find me and draw me in.' He took a deep breath. 'Where is the child? Or is there no child? Is that another trick of yours?'

She looked at him, and wondered if she still loved him. It was only a few years, but he was older, more stolid. There were lines on his face, the grey in his hair had increased, his voice seemed heavier. It would never come back again, unless… But he could be made to pay. Her voice was low when she spoke.

'So, everything is a trick to you, you who has never deceived anyone in your life. Still, we both know how easily you walk away, so I must take care to behave properly. Your daughter is coming back here with her nurse, who will entertain her in the garden, since the weather is fine. You may step up the stairs, and see her through the small round window you will find there. She will not notice, since the nurse will amuse her. We shall allow only a few minutes, and then you must leave. You can find your own way back across the harbour. There is always a boat.'

Justin listened, motionless. He could see that she held all the cards. The child did not know him, could not recognise him, could only be frightened by him until she became at least a little familiar with him. Perhaps then he might be able to talk to her, explain who he was, gain her trust. Without that, there was nothing. He had to go along with this.

Marie-Rose led him up the stairs to the landing and showed him where to stand. She went down and he stood there, prey to mixed feelings. He did not feel paternal, but he did feel shame. He heard her voice below, raised in greeting, and peered furtively out of the window. He breathed shallowly. A little girl was there in the garden, a young woman with her, in a bonnet and apron. He leaned forward and looked again. The child had dark hair, but he could hardly glimpse her face as she ran between Marie-Rose and her nurse. She shouted some words that he could not hear properly, but they were in French accents. The two women swung the little girl up by her arms, and then back, facing away from his vantage-point, and as they did so Marie-Rose glanced sideways up at his window.

It was enough for the moment. He slipped down the stairs and out through the front door. There was no sign of Loic. He had not felt this kind of emotion before. It lay heavily on him, along with a strange kind of delight that he feared to recognise or acknowledge. He stopped at one of the wells to watch the drawers. He realised he could not remember the colour of the child's dress.

In Eugène's lodgings in London, a wasp was crawling round the edge of the bowl which contained the remains of his rice pudding, while another was buzzing about up towards the ceiling. They did not distract him. Eugène stared at the piece of paper in front of him; he had written his address, but no more. He could not afford to scratch anything out, and he had precious little writing paper with him, so it must be right from the start. If he waited any longer the ink would be dry in its well. So he picked up his pen and continued.

My dear Miss Wentworth,

It is with some trepidation that I choose to write to you, knowing full well that your displeasure may rule that you do not read on. I must first convey my best wishes for your health and strength, and trust that your — what was the damned word? *— composure is now fully restored. One who wishes you all that good fortune can bestow —* now that was better *— must admit to having his thoughts turn towards that part of the country in Devon in which you so —* felicitously, not fortunately, surely? *— felicitously reside. Yet it may be said that a certain corner of Cornwall is dearer to me for your sake, and the hope remains warm in me —* did the English say that? *— that your memory of those days which now seem so distant will not be dismissed as being too faint to be still cherished.*

It was too late now, but that was surely nonsense. So, a good way to appear not only inept in his manners, but also illiterate. Glorious! There was sweat on his forehead, and in his palms. Eugène put the pen down in frustration. There was a knock at his door.

'Come in.'

The door opened slowly, and instead of Mrs Temple a young lad filled the opening, dressed in a tightly buttoned jacket and rather tired breeches. Eugène stared at him, and he stood where he was, with his hands behind his back. Something vaguely military about him entered Eugène's mind. The boy started speaking, and instantly Eugène recognised who he was.

'Mr Picaud? I am bringing to you a message from Major Houghton…'

Eugène stood up promptly. 'Ah, yes, it's James, isn't it? How are you, James? Come in, please, and forgive my bad manners.'

Before he could answer, there was the sound of footsteps thumping rhythmically up the stairs, with a rich baritone ringing out above them: 'Damn you for living in a garret, Mr Picaud! Worse than the forecastle on the old *Perseverance*.'

Major Francis Houghton heaved himself into the room, and took a breath. Eugène came forward, shook his hand heartily, and then took the lad's hand too, who seemed very pleased by that.

'Now, off downstairs with you, James, and I dare say that Mrs Temple who seems a good woman will find you a morsel. And, James — take that bowl down with you. Mr Picaud has surely finished with it.'

'Yes, I have. Thank you, James.'

The door shut behind him.

'Well, Francis, it is good to see you. Unexpected.'

The major took a turn about the room, which did not take long, and sat down without an invitation on the bed, stretching one of his long legs out in front of him.

'A neat cubbyhole you have here, my boy. We'll make a sailor of you yet.'

Eugène placed a book over his letter, as he hoped surreptitiously; but little escaped the major's notice, although he betrayed nothing at all.

'Dammit, Francis, I should offer you something. Mrs Temple…'

'No, never mind that. We'll be gone in a jiffy. How are you going along? Used to being ashore, so to speak?'

'Oh, that. Yes, London is easy enough. But what brings you here?'

'Something to do in Whitehall, stupid fuss, all probably nonsense. Brought the boy with me.'

'Ah, James. As I recall, you said he was only with you for a week or so in Chatham.'

Houghton wrinkled up his face in disapproval, crossed one leg over the other, and then with a wince of pain thought better of it.

'Yes, that was how it was meant to be. But the father's a bad apple — dumped the boy and ran. No one knows where he is. I am to visit the mother today. Best thing seems to keep him on, but we'll see what she thinks. There's no money for him, I'll be bound. We shall have to think of something.'

'And what are his feelings about it, Francis?'

'He seems keen enough. Quiet boy, though. We can find something for him down at Chatham, but it may not suit in the long run. What about you? Still going about as Picaud, if I have that right? Your father got a name as long as my arm, don't he?'

Eugène swatted idly at the wasp as he felt the old embarrassment raise its head again. The other intent intruder crawled round the neck of the cognac bottle.

'Look, Francis, you may be right about the marine commission. No, don't protest, I picked up what you felt, you were good enough to listen. It was a bad moment. I'm not sure if I can truly see myself staring at bivouacs on a river-bank in Canada.'

'Well, I shan't aim to lean on you one way or the other, but we'd have to reckon on getting you out there in one piece and back again. Marines, *Monsieur* Picaud: the clue's in the name. You'd not ever have much time with your feet on firm land, excepting being stuck in barracks.'

'I know, Francis. And I also know that you came here to see if my sentiments had changed.'

Houghton stood up, and wrapped an arm around his friend's shoulders.

'You'll work through it, mark my words. Something will turn up. Squeeze that old man of yours. There must be a way. Well, I must be off, or I'll find that boy downstairs playing with the baby.'

'To be sure, Francis.' The tall man went to the door. 'Ah, yes, I meant to ask you. Naval and military, you hear a lot. Ever heard talk of Saint Helen or Saint Catherine by any chance? A long shot, I suppose.'

Houghton stooped by the door: 'Saints or places?'

'Not sure. Could be both. Church names, or…'

'Well, they've had me down at Portsmouth before now, and we'd take on fresh water and stock up from the Isle of Wight. Regular it was, and probably still is. There was a place there on the northern side facing called Saint Helen's, not Saint Helen. Any use to you?'

'It could be, Francis. Thank you.'

Houghton grinned. 'Woman involved, eh? My advice, income comes first. But I'll be off. I'll hope to see your face again at Chatham, one of these days.'

They shook hands. The footsteps clumped back down the stairs. Eugène sat down again, and picked up the pen, removing the book from on top of his letter, and began to write intensely, but this time in French:

If I have offended, then I must seek forgiveness, but the most precious memories have taken residence in my heart, nourished by my gratitude in being happily allowed to be of some service to you...

CHAPTER XX: BRIGHTON RACES

Amelia folded the letter and put it into her pocket, and walked over to the window, which looked out on to the road. The street outside was noisy; it had been all morning. Carriages, chariots, phaetons and curricles, brimmed hats and high collars, and a great deal of calling and shouting. Brighton was certainly unusual: one might see a prince, a duke, and gentlemen of different figures and degree mixed in with sharper or careworn faces in an equal variety of plainer clothing. Her growing suspicion was that the business of Brighton was gambling, and behind gambling, drink. She thought of her friend Richard Bevington, who had promised to visit down from his sojourn in Lewes, and how like a fish out of water he would be here. Quakers were always the same wherever they went: that was their merit, and perhaps their impediment too.

'Ah, there you are my dear. Are we quite ready, do you think? I am told that the coachman Benjamin has the horses harnessed to the chaise, and will bring them round to the front.'

Caroline came over from the door to join Amelia by the window. 'That is, if he can find space for us to get through. Why, I confess I have never seen such a throng. Oh, there he is, I believe. From the look of it, it seems a commodious and comfortable carriage. You are very silent, Melia.'

'I suppose I am. You must forgive me. I am feeling excited, I assure you. I have never seen a horse-race. Nor such an assembly milling about. Do you not think it is as if the court had been turned out of the palaces and sent down to the

174

seaside to drive around and then gather madly on the hills?' She laughed. 'Then let us be giddy things too. The coachman will doubtless know where to place us so that we may have the best views of the racing. What a gay time we shall have!'

Which proved to be true. How could it be otherwise? From the moment that they stepped out of the door, they were overwhelmed by hurry and confusion, and once safely inside the chaise they were swept along in a tide of vehicles and horsemen, with the occasional intrepid female willing to take the risk of riding in the midst of them. Neither Caroline nor Amelia had any idea of where they were going, except that it must be uphill and away from the sea. The road chosen by the coachman took many twists and turns as it climbed, and at moments they found they could glance down.

'Why, there is the sea, and does it not look fine above the buildings? I wish I could identify something, but I fear I cannot. There must be churches, but I do not know their names.'

'We are fortunate in a sunny day, and one blessed with a breeze. Good lord, would you believe that? These young bloods in their curricles! He was close enough to scrape us and force us off the road. Well done, Benjamin!'

Amelia leaned back on the cushions, in teasing mood. 'Why, Caroline, it must be acknowledged that it is not just the madcaps who sport a curricle. You will remember that your brother, Colonel North, drives his own.'

'Well, that is true, but I should have words for him if I thought he was racing like that! You must hold on to that strap, Melia. There it is, just above you. Why, I do believe that we are emerging on to the Downs! The track will surely be more uneven. But, thank heaven, it will not be slippery. They say that chalked earth is the very devil with a touch of rain on it.'

Caroline had envisaged an orderly procession as they approached the gathering, such as they had in Plymouth for the assemblies, where the situation of the Long Room, perched out on a headland with an even and regular driveway, made for a kind of discipline in the delivery of ticket-holders. They had been amply forewarned that the races were a rout, but Caroline had taken this to apply to those attending at the course, and not to the carriages that took them there. Perhaps it applied equally to both. She sighed. Dawson would have disapproved mightily, and not for the first time she was relieved that she had left her behind, engrossed in mending her blue satin slippers. Since Dawson was meticulous, this would occupy her handsomely until they returned to dine.

They heard Benjamin's voice raised, but from the tone it was not for them. Caroline put her head gingerly out of the window, and brought it back in quickly.

'It is to do with backing up. There is an altercation.' She looked out briefly again. 'There, I do believe Benjamin is down from the box and at the horses' heads.' She sniffed. 'If you care for my opinion, all this is the result of horse-racing being a gentlemen's affair. There is only a secondary place for ladies, and gentlemen thrown together may all too readily lose control of their behaviour. Thus it has always been.'

'But we are told that it is a spectacle, Caroline, and to be fair it is for the present just the coachmen and drivers who are in contention.'

'That may be,' as the coach lurched forwards again, 'but I dare say there are gentlemen here distinguished as such only by their dress, and not in their manners. Accept my word for it.'

Which Amelia did, because she was content to take in the view beyond the struggling vehicles, which gave out to a panorama of sea and sky, the Downs themselves stretching off like a set of velvet pillows, needing only a beautiful goddess to stretch out her ivory limbs on their divan. She laughed to herself at this sudden fantasy and felt herself blushing.

'Amelia, are you quite well? You have a flush, my dear. Is it the jolting? We must descend and walk, but where?'

'Did you not mention a stand, Caroline?'

'I did indeed. Or, rather, it was mentioned to me.'

'Well, I see it, and Benjamin is taking us to it, and ably. A few minutes, perhaps less, and we shall be up alongside it. What is more, I see many dresses and parasols in addition to the gentlemen. We may have found your polite gathering!'

'I do hope so. I shall not bend across you to look, Melia. Now, you have your parasol, and I am, I think, in good order. Yes, all is as it should be. I shall content myself with my hat, although I must sit forward for the last few paces so I do not crush the brim. What think you of the ribbon? Is the purple too deep a hue?'

There was no time to answer, because the carriage came to a halt. They heard the coachman calling to a boy to hold the heads of the horses, and he himself came round to the door and lowered the step.

'Thank you, Benjamin. I shall ask you to wait behind the stand, and be ready to take us away should we become fatigued by the crush here. Now, Amelia, your arm, I think.'

They were surprised by the breeze, and Caroline briefly put her hand to her head to secure her hat. In a few steps they were swallowed up in a dance without music, where a parasol had to avoid the press of high beaver hats or the challenge of another parasol carelessly swung from one fair shoulder to the other. The men were loud, the ladies both refined and painted, their fashions elaborate or classically simple, the colours of dresses and hats magnificent, the gentlemen's breeches and boots all that could be desired, and their waistcoats vying with each other in stripes, buttons and lapels, often in satin or silk, and with one or two lavishly embroidered.

Caroline whispered to Amelia: 'It is as I said, my dear, one might expect to see anyone here. The Prince himself, perhaps, but here there is society at its highest even without his presence. There will be those who will know whether to expect him. I am not counting on it.'

Some had already clambered into the tiered stand, which looked a precarious kind of thing, but was a place to be seen as well as to see. Oddly, there was no sign whatsoever of a horse, apart from those more wearied beasts attached to the carriages that passed. Amelia decided that she did not understand racing, but she did wish to keep looking for Thirza, who must be here with her Duke. Amelia was still inclined to wonder if this was truly the kind of Duke who had lands and titles to his name. Thirza had remained unforthcoming on the subject, and there had been little time for questions.

'Ah, Mrs North, I do believe. Why, it is a pleasure once again.'

The speaker was an older man of some six or seven decades, dressed in a more sober style that might make him a resident of Sussex rather than a visitor. He spoke to Caroline, but his eyes drifted over to Amelia.

'I shall answer to Miss North, Lord Pelham.'

He bowed slightly. 'Yes, indeed. Your servant, ma'am. And this lady? Allow me to introduce myself — Thomas Pelham.'

'Then may I present to you Miss Wentworth, of Devon. You are at Stanmer Park, Lord Pelham?'

Amelia called her attention away from searching the crowd but found his scrutiny of her awkward. She looked away again.

'Indeed. You come a long way, Miss Wentworth?'

'Yet we are comfortably placed for a short stay, my Lord.'

Pelham removed his hat, and placed it under his arm. It was hot, but the gesture was a little relaxed. Perhaps this was an occasion when men felt relaxed.

'If you are here to see the Prince, Miss Wentworth, you may be disappointed this year. We are not sure. But there are others with great names and titles. I do not count myself, of course. What grand news it was, do you not think, of the royal child? Charlotte Augusta. Do you follow the court news, Miss Wentworth?'

Amelia thought that she could just see a hat that Thirza might have worn; but the figure proved to be tall and willowy.

'Not especially, Lord Pelham.'

Pelham raised his hand to greet an acquaintance but then made a gesture to indicate that he was occupied here. A woman next to them burst out raucously with, 'Why, he'll pop those buttons, Letty, sure he will!' and then lapsed into quieter conversation again. Pelham began to scan the crowd, but had not exhausted his fund of conversation.

'D'y'hear, Miss North, that Lady Murray has bought Hamilton's house down on the Steyne? Grove House, it is. Now that's where they all wish to be, near the tails of Prinny's coat at the new Pavilion.'

He had become distracted, but had not quite left them. Caroline leaned towards Amelia: 'That reminds me, Melia, that I have given our names to Mr Wade, the Master of Ceremonies, in advance of the race ball.'

'Ladies, with your permission, the riders are up, or so the word is. If you will forgive me... Your servant, Miss Wentworth, Miss North.'

There was a general surge of movement now, the ladies for the most part towards the stand, and a greater number of the men pushing away to the side. Some riders were now visible above the heads, moving slowly through a throng of tall hats, with those joining the crowd trying to ease their way forwards, or peering expectantly over shoulders.

It was then that Caroline saw Tregothen. There was no doubting it, although he had been the last thing on her mind. How her eyes were first drawn to him amongst so many she did not understand, nor could she account for it later. But there was never any uncertainty in her mind. He was un-hatted and the angle of his face at one moment, when he lifted it slightly to look over to the riders, recalled precisely an impression she carried with her from that fateful soirée at Drusilla Marriott's townhouse in Stonehouse, when he had sung so well.

Caroline took Amelia's arm, and began to walk her away to the far side of the stand, slowly concealing them both amongst a mass of gowns, wide hats, and parasols. She placed Amelia's parasol over her own shoulder to shield them from sight with a quick 'May I?' rather to Amelia's surprise.

'Are we leaving?'

Amelia's tone was puzzled, but she had no interest in horses, that was the truth. Her curiosity had been piqued originally by the idea of a race, and up on the Downs too, but it had subsided with her disappointment in not finding Thirza amongst the crowd of unfamiliar faces.

'Well, my dear, if you are growing weary then we might. I think we shall find Benjamin and our chaise. The race will soon be starting, I would imagine, and I hear that many follow it in their carriages. Benjamin will know about this kind of thing. We might choose to change our place before they all do.'

In this she was quite correct. The riders for the race could be seen moving off up the track to a far point along the Downs, some gentlemen following them a little way, but others now turning back. Benjamin was prominently positioned, in plain sight, and only a short step away. He came down off the box, and walked towards them.

'Benjamin, I believe we shall watch the race from a place near to the descent. It has been hot weather, and I would like you to start to take us down when we have seen the horses rush past us. We shall avoid the jam.'

Benjamin's opinion of the lady advanced another notch. He had been here before, and had seen the perils for himself, amongst which were shattered wheels and tumbled, injured men and women. He was quickly back on to his box, tossing a small coin to the boy at the heads, and pulling away as others started to bring their carriages round. It was a case of mind how you go, and not too fast: gentlefolk did not always care to get themselves out of your way. Caroline pulled down the blind on Amelia's side, with a smiled excuse about the sun, and sat back to watch carefully out of her own window. Her heart was beating strongly, but above all she did not want to alarm Amelia. She cast around for a topic for conversation.

'I trust that the letter you received this morning brought you good news, my dear.' There was no sign of Tregothen. He could hardly look inside a carriage, and even if he did, he would surely not remember her of all people.

Amelia broke out of a reverie.

'Oh, not especially.'

'From Chittesleigh, I assume? I hope all goes on well there.'

Amelia looked through Caroline's window at the riders, now distant, apparently lining up their horses. One could make out the course by the carriages and gentlemen on horseback lined up along it, one or two boys running about between them. She could not now see the stand, which lay behind them.

'I think so. No, this was from a publisher.'

'Ah, your writing. The novel. Come, tell me, it is good news, I am sure. Why, you have such a gift…'

Amelia laughed. 'Not according to Mr John Lane, I am afraid. He appears to have a distaste for the French.'

Caroline blessed the distraction. When would the riders put those creatures into a gallop, and be done?

'The French? You lose me? What have they got to do with it?'

That sounded more brusque than was her intention; but Amelia was not troubled by it.

'My novel had French characters, a count and a young heiress, a chateau with secrets. Mr Lane is of the opinion that the reading public at present will only tolerate an Italian setting, and encourages me to recast it accordingly. But I know nothing of Italy.'

'Why, I am sure it is much the same. I know it is all the rage, and there are mountains and grottoes in Italy, and monks and cowls and all that kind of thing. But will you rewrite what you have?'

Amelia folded her hands in her lap.

'I am not sure. He may just not want the book.'

'Look, there they go! Or, rather, here they come! Now I shall say that is a grand sight. Good lord, how some of the carriages are chasing after them, and the riders! Heavens, that is dangerous. My, how they race over the ground! It is most unlike hunting. Do you see, Amelia?'

'I can hear the roar, Caroline.'

'There, they are gone. It is over in a few seconds. We shall not know the winner, but I dare say it will make no difference to us. Men will wager, and women will cry: that was what my father used to say. Still, that will do for us quite nicely, I believe.' She rapped on the roof with the handle of the parasol. 'Forgive me, but it is more dignified than shouting up. And here we go.'

Caroline North looked back through the window nervously, trying to conceal the brief movement from her companion, who had taken her letter from her pocket and was reading it, between the shaking and the swaying and the bumps. Tregothen was not in sight. But he was there, and would be staying either in Brighton itself or perhaps in Lewes, where that young Quaker boy was hoping to see Amelia. She would have to be told, eventually, and above all they would now have to leave, promptly, and away to Devon: there would be no race ball for them this August, and no more sea-bathing.

Amelia had been expecting to see Thirza with her protector at the races, although such a thing had not been mentioned between them. If the new resolution, advanced by Caroline North, was to leave Brighton in advance of what had been anticipated, she could not do so without calling on Thirza and saying farewell, with perhaps a thought as to how they might cultivate their friendship more assiduously than in the past. There was some delicacy in this, although no doubt Miss Farley would not consider that of any great significance, certainly not something to be sentimental about, as she would surely say.

Amelia gained licence from the busy preparations for departure to head into town to see a friend, as she put it to

Caroline, who asked her to take yet another letter to her brother Colonel George North — that was three in as many days — to the post on her way. She noticed that the letter was directed to an inn at Dorking; but not knowing where that was she did not allow herself to be curious about it.

The New Inn was almost as busy as North Street itself, which was like a race-track for coaches, some of which swung into yards with very little consideration for pedestrians. Amelia soon found herself in the lobby, in which gentlemen and ladies and servants of all descriptions came and went or stood, engaged in lively chatter or coarse laughter. She had not prepared herself with a suitable question and wondered if, short of leaving a calling-card for a person, it was possible or polite to ask after a room or a suite of rooms. She hesitated, and as the eyes of one of the graver hotel staff began to settle on her, made up her mind and walked boldly and intently up a staircase.

She recalled that Miss Farley's rooms were on an upper floor, but her memory was frayed beyond that, and her only recourse was to seize upon a corridor and promenade along it, trying to look at her ease. Around a sharp corner she had a conviction that what was in front of her was familiar, so she slowed, and then paused. Would this door be right? She turned around and took several paces. The paintwork was scarred just a little to the left. Did she not remember that, standing and staring at it for a moment while Thirza searched for a key? She insisted on a key, she had said, at that time. Yet the door was open — just a crack, but still open. She pushed at it, and it swung back. The rooms were there, as she remembered them. She edged her way in; they were empty of any personal effects. One might almost suspect they would have an echo. The floor creaked behind her.

'Good afternoon, madam. Have you lost your way? May I be of service?'

The speaker was grey-haired but not old, respectably and soberly dressed, the image of a housekeeper.

'Oh, you must forgive me, I should have sought you out the moment I found them empty.'

'Is your ladyship looking for rooms, then? This is a fine suite, but Mr Dibden at the office would have to confirm that with you. Their availability, I mean to say.'

'Thank you. My name is Miss Wentworth. I... I was expecting to find my friend here, and am a little taken aback to find the rooms empty.'

'Not to worry, madam. I am sorry to hear you are put out. It might be that I can help you with your difficulty.'

There was a brief silence. Amelia began to imagine that she could just catch a hint of the fragrance that Thirza had worn on the day they had met.

'Perhaps I can escort you down to the lobby, Miss Wentworth. It is a veritable warren, and regularly confuses visitors.'

'It was Miss Thirza Farley.'

'It was indeed, Miss. Your friend. They are pleasant rooms for visitors.'

'Miss Farley will be writing to me, but I do wonder if you might recall when it was that she left her lodging here?'

'Why, two days back it was.'

'Well, thank you. We may indeed descend now.'

The woman appeared to hesitate, but then became resolved. 'There was the other matter.'

Amelia became alert to the possibility of an indiscretion; she must not above all fall into the error of encouraging an impertinence. Yet it might be wise to hear what could be said to others. Her voice had a hint of sternness: 'What other matter?'

'There was a report, about Miss Farley's maid — Elisabeth. The poor lass. A local girl, too, from Patcham way. But I expect that you will have heard of this, Miss, and I will not gossip.'

'No, I have not. What about the maid? I did not meet her.'

'Well, madam, it affected her badly, Miss Farley that is. If you did not meet her…'

'No, I wish to hear.'

'They found a body, Miss. I will not say more. It went to a Justice. Why, you look a little pale, Miss Wentworth. I should not have said, but it might explain…'

'No, I am fine, thank you.'

It was another hot day, but Amelia had gone cold. Suddenly, this room was frighteningly like another, and the emptiness in it was completely devoid of scent, devoid of life.

CHAPTER XXI: ASHEY DOWN

Justin had been oblivious to his surroundings as he walked back from the landing in Bembridge and up the slope to the church and the tavern. There was a better room to be had in the farm, the tapster had said considerately, and so he found himself a little later on tucked away comfortably just up the road accepting a plate of food to be brought up to him in the early evening, which would do for dinner. The farm had ale, but he waved it away carelessly, and then called it back, as he realised he had hardly drunk all day. If the farmer's wife was curious, she kept it to herself. The room was plain and homely, with a small window looking out on to the yard.

The child's name was Catherine. That was what Marie-Rose had told him, and he watched to see if she answered to it; but there was no need for them to call her, since she never went far. She had dark hair, and he could see that it was the same tint as his own, more or less: it might change a little with time. From where he sat, to the side of the tiny window, he could not see her eyes, but he heard her cry 'Maman' or something like that when Marie-Rose came out to her. The other woman, her nurse, meant nothing to him.

Marie-Rose had told him that he should go, because the child needed attending to, as children did, and his thoughts went back to his younger brother and to Amelia. He had never considered how they were cared for, not even who precisely looked after them — his mother, who was seen with them in the public rooms, or the nurses they had had, who came and went. He excused himself with the consideration that he had been out of the country for much of the time, but that brought him up against uncomfortable thoughts of a very different kind.

For a man as prey to sharp bites of self-accusation as he was, he ate robustly, and found the ale refreshing, if light and bland. He stared for a while out of the window, which offered him only hens scratching, and then lay on his bed. The sheets were clean, homespun linen, and he wondered if there was a loom in the parlour in place of the embroidering workbox. Perhaps both. He fell asleep early. The following morning when he reached the village, Loic was rolling barrels with a small gang at the far end of Saint Helen's green. The door to the house opened as he approached, and he risked a 'Good morning'. Marie-Rose gave him a quick smile, which surprised him. She led him into the parlour and showed him to a wooden chair, placed to the side of a window. There was a bottle on the table.

'Catherine and Agnès will be back shortly. I shall fetch you a glass. The wine is good.'

The window looked out on the garden, as he called it, although in truth it was merely a patch of grass with woodland to the back of it. She was right, the wine was good. To his surprise, she stayed.

'I saw Loic helping with the barrels.'

'Yes, it is what he chooses to do when he is here. It is only pence at the end of the week, but they have food.'

He could smell the scent of her hair. He cleared his throat, quietly.

'I want to know all about her.'

'You have not earned the right to know all about her. Or about me.'

'But if she is my daughter…'

'If? You say *if*?' Her voice rose, and he could see her ears were red. 'How dare you say that to a woman? To a mother?'

Justin fell silent. He could see the child now at the edge of the garden. She had something in a wooden box, which she was carrying carefully; the young nurse Agnès was with her. Marie-Rose turned away without another word and left him. Moments later he heard the latch, and Catherine cried out and ran up as Marie-Rose came into the garden. They placed the box on the ground, and Marie-Rose reached in and lifted out a small chick, leaving its head poking out from her fingers. Justin could hear it cheeping. Catherine stood up and flapped her arms at her side, jumping up and down. Marie-Rose held out the chick to Catherine, and Justin caught the word '*doucement*' as the child, with help from the nurse, took it into her hands.

Marie-Rose left the garden for the house, and Justin heard her approaching. He was fascinated by the scene outside, so he did not look up. Marie-Rose stood silently in the room, and then spoke softly.

'Tomorrow I want her to see you. Just sitting there, or standing by the window. You should not make any sudden movement, or she will be frightened. I shall be with her, and will show you to her. Briefly, mind. There has been no man in her life.'

At that, he raised his eyes to hers, and nodded.

'And then I shall speak to her?'

She held his gaze. 'If all goes well, you shall speak to her. But you will not tell her who you are — what you are, that is. That is forbidden, for now.'

Justin said nothing and left the house. As he crossed the green, Loic tried to catch his eye, but Justin walked on, head down, eyes on the ground.

The following day, Justin took a walk by the sea, irresolute and deeply troubled. To adopt a child, or otherwise provide for an illegitimate offspring, was always possible, and he had the means to do so; but the mother posed a problem of a different order. While a young wife might just prove over time to be reconciled to the child, it was beyond imagining that there was any place for the woman, outside a vicious betrayal of trust, and clandestine and murky arrangements. Worst of all, he could not fathom what Marie-Rose expected of him, and that caused his head to ache.

He returned to his lodging feeling rather less despondent than when he walked out, although he would have been hard pressed to say why he should feel more sanguine. He found a note from Marie-Rose waiting for him, which carried the information that it was now too late in the day to visit the child, but that she herself wished him to accompany her on horseback on a short journey in order to view something of importance. If he would call at Marshall's farm on Saint Helen's green as soon as he was returned, she would be waiting for him there.

She was as good as her word. The farm was situated at the top of the green, to the far side of the wells, and as he turned into its yard Marie-Rose was inspecting the harness of a large and powerful horse, one that might be grateful for being free from the plough and the market cart. He cast a quick glance around to see if there was another, but she came forward to him with the reins in one hand.

'You will help me up, sir.'

A man stood in the door to the kitchen in a rough, stained jacket and a dark, nondescript neckerchief, and a beaten cap. He gave no greeting, but chewed slowly on a piece of bread he was holding.

Marie-Rose was wearing what he took to be a riding dress, brown, practical, tucked up above a petticoat in front, and short boots of a kind with which he was unfamiliar. There was nothing for it. He clasped his hands together, and she stepped lightly into them, placed one hand on his shoulder as he bent and the other on the saddle. She made no use of the stirrups, and sat back decisively from the saddle, on the end of the cloth on which it was resting. So that was how it would go. Her sleek brown hair was pinned up, with no hat or bonnet, and she had no shawl or scarf for her neck and shoulders, which, like her forearms, showed the influence of the sun.

The man had not moved. For all his impassivity, he might have been thinking that it would be an awkward twist to mount in front of a woman perched like that, which it was. Justin put a foot in the stirrup but then threw himself forward on the beast's neck, holding on to its mane, crooked his right knee and slid the leg down into place on the far side. The farmer, satisfied, disappeared back into the house. The horse was all that it might be in terms of compliance, untroubled by its double burden. There were no other witnesses to their progress.

'We journey away from the sea.' There was hardly a breeze, and she did not need to speak into his ear. The horse rolled easily, flicking its ear from time to time. Justin had a sense that it was familiar with the journey, probably because there were only two roads in and out of the village. The road was in fair condition, although by no means a turnpike, with few potholes. The horse kicked a stone every now and then. The swallows darted.

'Where did you go this morning?' asked Marie-Rose. It was an innocent enough question.

'For a walk by the sea. I meant to go to Ryde to find a bank, as one might.'

'It seems to be that all services of that kind are to be found in Newport, a town in the centre of the island.'

'Yes, they told me that in Bembridge. All roads lead to Rome.'

'Hmm.'

That little acknowledgement was the first relaxed moment they had experienced together. It took him back, with its disturbing sensation of familiarity: he dared not remember intimacy. The horse stumbled, and he felt her hands reach for the back of the saddle.

'How far do we journey?'

'It is of no consequence.'

He turned slightly in his seat. 'Permit me to say that I may be the judge of that. You will find that I should like to be advised of the direction and purpose of our excursion.'

She was unperturbed by his attempted severity and formality. 'That you shall be, in good time. I shall not keep you waiting long.'

There was just the slightest of emphasis on 'you', and so he felt the blow, light as it was. The ground now began to rise gradually to the left, just as it opened up in front of them, and it was clear these would be downs, although he was ignorant of the name they must have. The horse seemed unimpressed by the slope, and kept up its accustomed pace, which was unusually rapid for a beast that measured so many hands.

'We should take the left here.'

It was no more than a track, and the horse slowed as its path wore through to the chalk, the surrounding turf now clear of all other vegetation apart from a single hawthorn, which was stunted, partly from the wind, and partly from the lack of good soil.

'There, that will do. We should proceed on foot for the last, short climb. Here, I shall hold the bridle.' Marie-Rose slipped off the horse's back easily, holding on briefly to the saddle, and stepped round to its head. Justin swung himself down, and she tied the reins to a larger, horizontal branch of the small tree. The horse shook its mane and tried to find something to crop.

The top of the rise was a few steps away. Marie-Rose went on in front, and then turned to face the view, which lay to the north. They were not high, but were raised above what appeared to be a plain, and there was a clear view of water and opposing land in the distance, of ships-of-the-line, quite evidently, and boats of many different sizes. It afforded a grand prospect, and Justin said so. The light breeze blew at his hair, but not hers, which remained resolutely pinned. Without it, the weather would have been judged very warm.

'I believe you English call it a landscape. You try to capture it and fence it in around your homes, I am told. Like a caged bird. Perhaps you have done so too. You never told me much about your home. And we both know I shall never see it. You are now married, are you not?'

'Marie-Rose, what do you want?'

It was a foolish thing to say, and he realised his error almost as soon as the words had been formed. But the reaction was not as he might have expected. She spoke quietly, almost too low to be heard in the breeze, so he had to lean towards her.

'What do I want? What did I ever want? What does your daughter want? She is too young to say. Tomorrow, perhaps, or the day after, or the day after that, she will know she has a father, and then, in time to come, she will know what she wants.'

He clenched his teeth. As he felt now, it was no more than he deserved.

'Yes, but why did you bring me here? Why did we ride out here?'

'To show you that I do not want much. I might have a livelihood, a way of living, close to you. Just off your precious island. On an island off an island. A little England.' She sighed, almost inaudibly, but not totally in regret. 'I am an island girl. A *jersiaise*. My ancestors were islanders. That is strange, is it not?'

Justin tried to be patient. 'You speak of a livelihood…'

'I do.' Her face was now animated. 'I have done my work. This island is an *entrepôt* for your navy. It is not enough to roll barrels of water down the hill. You see, I have spoken to the farmer there, and he is willing. You see, down there — they call it Ashey. And he has said he will speak to others who will bring him cattle.'

'You wish to buy the farm? Is the man not a tenant? Marie-Rose, do you not know about tenancy?'

Animation began to change into agitation.

'What do I care of tenancy? He may sell his beef where he likes. He will sell it to me. And what do I have in turn? You will tell me that. Or what can be supplied to me, do you think, and by whom? You must surely hazard a guess? You know the man I mean, and I know him too. What will be needed for the beef?'

Justin was completely at a loss. He had begun to feel hot, tired and hungry. The last week had taken its toll of his energy and endurance, and he was on the edge of slipping into desperation.

'I do not comprehend your plan. Which man do we both know?'

'Harker. The American. Harker will bring us salt, from Brittany. Some bring contraband, he will bring salt. You see, we could do this together, you and I, for Catherine!' She held both his forearms tightly, which he had raised instinctively when she had swung round to face him suddenly, and in her enthusiasm she fired out the words in her *Québécois* French. He could not think straight.

'I think we should discuss this in the morning, when I have had time to reflect on it. I do not want to say anything now. Will that do?'

He spoke quietly. He had no wish to provoke her. She let his arms drop, and he followed her down the short, steep slope to the hawthorn. In his distracted state of mind, he noticed to no purpose that the horse was a mare, not a gelding as he had assumed. She let him mount first, handed him the reins, and then allowed him to swing her up behind him, leaving the stirrup for her to gain purchase. She was lithe, and her arm was strong.

On the way back down and along to Saint Helen's, she slipped her arms round the lower part of his body, and after a while he could feel the weight of her head and her shoulders resting on his back.

CHAPTER XXII: TRUTH WILL OUT

Eugène braced himself for the crossing from Portsmouth. The sea was unaccountably choppy, since the weather was fine and the breeze light, even on the water. But Eugène had long since accepted that the sea defied any attempt to make sense of its moods and motions, since it was an element on which man did not truly belong. His companion on the crossing was a sailor who helped pull the boat up on to the shore, right by an isolated tower that must have served as a landmark of some kind, and then helped him out of the boat with a generous hand, slapping Eugène on the back and offering to take his bag too. The sailor then pushed the boat off, the boatman showing no sign of appreciation and the sailor quite unconcerned by that.

'Saint Helen's, then, is it?'

'Yes, I thank you.'

"Tis a step, an' no more. Are you to the big house?'

'Well, no, I was thinking of a room. In the village. Simple, plain, bite of dinner…'

'Ah.' They walked on, up an easy road, the sailor scuffling the stones, happy. It was not far. On the edge of the village they stopped.

'Mine's to starboard, sir, yours to port, three door along from me. Lil' Pet we call her, Nat's girl, pretty as a picture, he's to sea, she's rounded, bigger now, near on groanin' time. She will giv'ee room and nammet. G'day to thee.'

'Yes, much obliged to you. Pet?'

'Petronella. Door with horse-shoes on it.'

Petronella was indeed as pretty as a picture, and as rounded as had been predicted, and she was pleased to offer a room, which looked out on the green, and had been her mother's who had passed on, and Eugène would be very pleased for his part to eat with her in the parlour. She blushed at the mention of money, but it changed hands, and that was that. There was soon water in the ewer, and a cloth to dry one's face, and it would all do very well.

With the niceties duly achieved, Eugène pulled the chair over to the small window and settled down to his main task, which was to keep watch on movements. By his calculation, he had three, perhaps four people to look out for, and any one of those would probably be sufficient to lead him where he needed to go. An open green such as that here was an unexpected boon. But he would not rush in: wherever there was mystery, there was also the opportunity for the most devastatingly disastrous mistakes.

Time went on, and the heat grew more intense in the closed room. He yawned and stretched his legs, and then opened the casement. Studying the cottages opposite had revealed little, but he had observed that those people whom he saw mostly came out from behind the cottages, down back lanes. Shambling there was, a little bustling from time to time, the usual greetings and chatter. He thought he could see well-heads on the green. He had an old shirt and a beaten cap, and he changed into them, keeping an eye on the outside. He began to pace up and down, pausing to stare out of the window, and decided he had had enough.

Petronella was taking washing in off the hedge down the side, and he told her he would be back for his dinner. It could be that the village stretched farther than he could see from his vantage point, in which case he might be wasting his time. He pulled the cap down tightly, and walked in a slow, shuffling kind of way along the edge of the green, ignored by a donkey that was grazing, tethered to a spike, and watched by an old woman through narrow eyes who did not respond to his greeting.

There was a farm at the head of the green, and a few cottages beyond that, where the road snaked on down and into the country, blue hills away in the distance. The martins were all over the farmhouse and buildings, in and out. He crossed round behind the farm, to the upper road, with its lanes and alleys leading back from it, and looked in at the farmyard. There was a large and splendid horse standing there, with its head in a bag of hay, and then in a trough. He strolled back towards the far end of the village, casting a sideways glance down the back lanes and alleys as he passed, taking his time.

Justin came briskly out of Marshall's farm and walked down across the green. He was hot, and his head ached, but he was also sour and angry. Every step he took seemed to set him back, pose questions to him that he could not answer. It was not just a matter of money. Marie-Rose's plans made no sense to him, and the child was so young he could not envisage a practicable future for her, let alone for her mother. Whatever he did, or indeed did not do, he would have to inform Arabella, and he could not begin to envisage a discussion of that kind, if indeed it reached the point of being a discussion. Where would one introduce a topic of that kind? In a marital bedroom, or a lying-in room, for god's sake? In a dining-room when breakfasting, in his sober library, full of sound guidance for the mind and morals? Should he tell his mother first, and his sister last?

He turned down the lane leading to the mill, and forced himself onwards, full of fury, and for a moment he thought that he could hear footsteps behind him. He swung round, ready to fight anyone over nothing, fists clenched ridiculously, cursed at himself for being a fool in an empty summer's lane, dodged a dragonfly, and almost stumbled on to the mill and the calm of its tidal ponds. There was no one in sight, and he clambered out along the wall towards the tidal gates, through which the sea was flowing. He sat down, in despondency, and stared out at the harbour.

He heard the sound dimly and distantly behind him, a slow tread ambling and stopping along the wall, but he refused to succumb to his anger and wretched fright. The sea began to rush through the gate, a pleasant, almost soothing sound, as two hands closed over his eyes, and a sly voice whispered in his ear: 'Up to your old tricks again?'

He was up in an instant, his own hands at the throat of his assailant, thinking back to the spies set on him by his father-in-law and god knows who else, to Pitt and his oppression of dissent, and that they should not have him here, not now, of all times.

The man nimbly ducked down, knocking off his own cap into the water, but dislodging the hands that had him by the throat, and then abruptly sat down next to him.

'Well, a very good day to you too.'

Justin remained standing, and his head swam.

'So, they have sent you after me now, have they? Is there no limit?'

Eugène rubbed his neck ruefully. 'Shall I tell you what you are going to do? You will take two long gulps of air, sit down, remove that grotesque expression from your grizzled countenance, and speak to me like a gentleman and a friend, or

I shall with the greatest satisfaction tip you into this seething mass of waters and — I hope — stinking mud beneath. Sit down, you damn fool!'

Justin slowly sank down beside him, and stared out at the small harbour. He was breathing heavily.

'Grizzled? Is it that bad.'

'I should say so. Do they not give out hot water to shave in Saint Helen's?'

Justin scaped his chin with his fingers. Eugène decided to change the subject.

'Now, where are you lodging? That's a simple question.'

Justin waved vaguely across the water, in the direction of Bembridge.

'By yourself?'

Justin nodded.

'Now that is the best thing I have heard for some time. I think you will escort me there, arm in arm like good friends, and we may find that we have some things to talk about. What do you say? On second thoughts, do not say anything, not now. Just do as I suggest.' He patted his friend gently on the shoulder. 'Eugène knows best.'

Catherine chortled as the piglets squealed and ran into the corners of the pen and then on to where their mother was lying on her side, revealing a broad belly which they crowded around. The child laughed and pointed as one scrabbled over another, and then put her finger in her mouth as a squabble broke out, and she could see one of them limping. The piles of dung fascinated her, and she could see milk on the jaws of one or two of the piglets. The sow grunted contentedly, and then, once or twice, quickly reached her head down to knock off one of her progeny who had nipped her sharply.

Agnès looked round as she heard a noise, and then seized the child's hand and began to run towards the door into the farmhouse. But she easily recognised the man who came through it to meet her as the 'guest' who had been visiting the cottage every day for a week. He spoke kindly to her, and knelt to speak to the child in French, who hid behind her skirts.

'Do you want to show me the piglets, Catherine?'

Catherine nodded, and Agnès and the man walked back with her to the pen. The big horse watched over the top of its stable door, and then clumped back into the shade of its stall.

'I can see eight, Catherine.' The man knelt down and glanced at the child. Agnès looked down at her.

Catherine shook her head, and held up three fingers: '*Trois.*'

Justin stood up. 'Shall we go and see the chicks and their mothers now?'

It was earlier than usual, but Loic went with Françoise to answer the knock, the two of them barging each other to reach the door first. It was Françoise who won, and her face went blank as she opened it and stood aside.

'Good morning, I hope I am not too early. I can see you are surprised! How delightful! Why, it is Françoise, I believe, and Loic behind you. Your hand, Loic.'

The French accent was not one either could identify, but the face was familiar, even when surmounted by a fancy hat. Eugène was charm itself, and they were astonished, not least by the elegant waistcoat with its broad lapels and satin-edged pockets into which he had stuck his thumbs cheerfully.

'Well, what luck to find you home, and all of you here! Or do I speak out of turn? Is the lady of the house with you?'

Coline was standing at the end of the short hallway, in the shadow, quite still, her face blank of expression. There was silence for a moment. Then she spoke.

'To what do we owe this pleasure?' It was in English, unwelcoming and unyielding. Eugène responded with his best English politeness.

'May I come in? A little refreshment at this hour would be most welcome, as I am sure you can imagine. Through here? Well, that is most civil of you, most kind.'

He went into what was the parlour, and sat down on one of the two chairs with upholstery. Coline spoke briefly to Françoise, and then followed him in. She wore her hair down, which was not as he remembered, and gone was the faded blue dress with the short sleeves that stuck in his mind from Pontivy, where they had all been together briefly as British agents. In its place was a dark green gown, with its sleeves gathered a little at the elbows. Loic, however, still had that ring on a cord around his neck, but his hair was tied back. Françoise was always in the shadows, busy, but mostly out of sight.

It was Loic, not Françoise, who brought in a small bottle with a glass, and a jug with an old goblet. He put the wooden tray on the table to one side of the small room. Coline poured a glass from the bottle, and handed it to Eugène, and then filled the goblet for herself from the jug.

'You should try the water. The wells here are good. I can see you made the crossing from Brittany successfully.'

'Ah, yes, I am grateful to you. To you all, in fact, for your help. But you would have heard from d'Auvergne in Jersey about my successful escape from Brittany?'

'Yes, d'Auvergne was not much impressed by what you or I had to tell him. But it is clear that something is in preparation.

The suspicion formed from the information he has been piecing together is that there will be an autumn or even a winter invasion of England from France, and he will inform the Admiralty of that; but it will be ill-conceived.'

'When men worry about the colour of the uniform they will use, as we saw them doing in Pontivy, there is not much to hope for from them.'

'So it will be d'Auvergne who told you about my little retreat here?'

Eugène cradled his glass, thanked her inwardly for making that assumption, and lied comfortably: 'Well, he dropped a hint, let us say. Perhaps it was indiscreet. But I thought I would look you up.'

She sipped at her water. 'I do not believe you.'

'Oh, I believe in gratitude, and expressing it.'

She stood up. 'Well, in that case…'

'And I wished to visit a friend too. And, by chance, I heard that he had come down here.'

She was standing still by her chair, and, clever as she was, she contrived to look casually out of the window as she spoke.

'To the Isle of Wight?'

'Yes, that's right. And by a large coincidence, to this north side of the island, facing Spithead and Portsmouth.'

'Do I know of this person?'

'You may; indeed, I rather think that you do. His name is Justin Wentworth, and he is one of us. Has worked as an agent, amongst other things. I should sit down if I were you. The blood drains unpleasantly to one's legs when one is standing for a long time.'

She sat down. Loic lingered in the doorway, and she waved him away. Eugène went on.

'So, you will have to forgive me for becoming curious. As I said to myself, Wentworth is up to his old tricks. And quite possibly up to his old tricks with you, Coline —' here she looked sharply across at him, and was about to give in to rage, but he carried on blithely — 'and your little crew. It began to come together, and make sense to me, as they say. After all, why would d'Auvergne know about this curious little place, and why would the estimable Wentworth with his fund of linguistic abilities be sent down here unless something was afoot, eh?' He was allowing himself to get into his stride, and rather enjoyed it. 'The Isle of Wight has its merits and advantages, and who can deny that boats go from here, clandestinely, to other parts of France: Normandy, for example. Cherbourg or Le Havre. Perhaps even Granville again. Who can guess? All the Admiralty would need for yet another intrigue would be the right people brought together. Now was I on the right track?'

She stood up again; let him think that if he chose. 'Perhaps. Now as I recall, *Monsieur* Picaud, you have a great talent for wasting other people's time…'

Eugène got up and walked over to the table to place his glass on it.

'But then I found out that wasn't it. There was another reason.'

'Is that so? Now, if you will excuse me, I am awaiting someone…'

Eugène poured himself some water, and drank out of his glass.

'Oh, I wouldn't trouble yourself about that. He is counting the chickens with Catherine in the farm across the street, Marie-Rose. It is Marie-Rose, is it not? Not quite as we were first introduced to each other in London, at the Admiralty, when it was Jeanne Heaume, as I recall. But what does a little change in name matter? After all, we have all had so many.'

He heard her feet shuffle behind him, and for just a moment felt like reaching for his weapon. But she put her hand on his shoulder, and spun him round to face her. Her face had blanched, her voice tight.

'You will go now.'

'I am afraid, Marie-Rose, that is the last thing I am going to do. You see, I had occasion to pay a visit to the Abbé Carron, and he told me that you left Jersey before him with a young child called Catherine and an older girl called Agnès. From the orphanage. You had almost adopted the child, he said, but had taught Agnès patiently how to look after her.'

Coline remained motionless, her hands clenched.

'There never was a baby, Marie-Rose. You did not bring a baby with you when you came to Jersey from Quebec. You have been lying to Justin. But it must end.'

She made as if to hit him, but he had been expecting something of that kind, with the emotion that must be seizing her, and he ducked. She spun around, and walked to the door.

'You must go now.'

He looked out of the window, and saw the small child with the young nurse on the patch of grass. The child was carrying a large feather.

'I am afraid there is another matter. I should warn you that your presence may not be well received in Marylebone and its environs at this time. Rumours have spread of a gross attempt at extortion, and of devious arts practised by young Loic out there which might leave him open to the stringent attention of the law. You see, fathers and indeed mothers may be less harsh in their view of their children's morals than you might imagine: those of the *noblesse* most especially. But in either case, you can be quite sure that they do not like those who abuse or exploit them.'

'You have said your piece, now get out.' Her voice was drained of the emotion she had shown earlier. He walked at an even pace, and without profound animosity, across to her, and paused briefly in his stride.

'I hope you will heed my warning. Gratitude has its place. Salt beef may prove to be a better choice for your sense of opportunity: the war is, after all, unending.'

There was no one in the hall. Outside he could dimly hear the little girl laughing.

CHAPTER XXIII: BRANDIVY GORGE

Louis Le Guinec, Laurent Guèvremont's former steward, stretched his legs and looked out of the small, cobwebbed window of the sawmill. The light was fading, and yet it was too early to set his lamps and candles. It was the curse of huddling here in the river valley, overhung as it was almost everywhere by trees. The dyeing works at Pontivy stank, of course, and in that respect the sawmill downriver here was an improvement: but it could be noisy and dreary, with the yards full of woodchips dank from the rain, and the heaped sawdust.

It was undoubtedly a form of banishment for him, although Guèvremont had been at pains to emphasize the degree of responsibility, masking as ever his meanness under a compliment. He was, he had been told, the obvious choice as supervisor for these important factories, and it was fair to say that while the dyeing works had recently been bringing in a burst of solid, unexpected income from the military, the sawmill here on the river would always be well-placed to send timber to Lorient, or to cart it out elsewhere.

Yet the recent letter to him from Guèvremont offered a break from the tedium. It was filled with the usual platitudes thinly concealing commands and expectations on the progress of work. But the ending on this occasion was most satisfactory. He was summoned to appear in Auray and deliver an oral report to Guèvremont himself and to present his accounts to Fourrier, the nose-picking little runt of a clerk who deserved to be fooled if he did not trouble to come and check on the ground what was written in the ledgers. He folded the letter carefully, and called to little Gabrielle to bring him light. He might follow his usual bottle of wine with an Armagnac, because there was something more to savour in this journey than the prospect of a few days in the town. He must have Gabrielle brush off some of his better garb.

In days past, it had been any old excuse. Guèvremont's acquisition of the Kergohan manor and lands had been a blessing. After spending a day in the manor, he would mount his horse and ride over to Brandivy. On one occasion he had loaded the cart from the stables with a crate filled with wine from the cellar, and a small keg of the Breton *eau de vie*, *lambig*, that he had set aside. The following day he had taken Jeanne for a trip around the village in the cart, sat her up in front with him holding the reins, her shawl around her shoulders, just showing whoever might be watching who was in charge here, that she was his and that he would look out for her. She had been widowed from Henri Cariou, but he had paid her husband's debts, given her no choice, and she was his now, to do with as he chose.

The day dawned bright and warm, not yet hot, and there was shade on the road. His saddlebags were full of ledgers and documents awaiting Guèvremont's final attention, an artifice that he had found gave his employer the impression that he was exercising control over everything. He rode on through Baud at an easy pace, and found himself anticipating what he would find at Brandivy. The girl Gabrielle was lively, but she was bony, and her cooking was barely adequate. Still, her washing was diligent, and she remained grateful to him, because the rooms were adequate, far better than what she had been used to. He liked gratitude. When he moved lodgings, from sawmill to dyeing works and back again, she moved with him. It was a convenient but unexciting arrangement; but

Jeanne was quite, quite different.

The cottage caught the early evening light, and he could see some clothing laid out on stones facing the declining sun. He recalled the smell of Jeanne's hair and body, of pulling her close to him. She would be inside the cottage. He tied up the horse, slung his saddlebags over his shoulder, and sauntered in, careless of whether he left the door open or not. Let anyone see or hear if they chose; he was taking what was his.

She was folding clothes, and looked round when she heard him come in.

'*Kenavo*,' she greeted him.

'*Kenavo*, Jeanne. Were you expecting me?'

'I'm not sure. Perhaps I was. Did you send word?'

He came over to her, and stood just behind her.

'The carter, Erwan is his name. He said he would pass, on his way to Kergal.'

'So he did.' But she had the day wrong: how could she remember the days?

'Have you a greeting for me?'

'I have given it.'

He put his hands on her shoulders, and spun her round, took her face in his hands and kissed her fully on the mouth, and then moved down on to her neck. She did not resist, but did not respond either. He released her reluctantly, and she picked up a bag for the clothes.

'Let me finish this, and I'll get you some food. There is water in the pitcher. It has been a long time.'

He pulled the stool across and sat by her, drinking the water from the pitcher itself.

'Yes. Too long in many respects. Too long away from the town as well.'

'You're on your way there, then?' She was not good at concealing things, or at lying, but he failed to observe the hesitant note in her voice.

'I am. For a while at least. I can thank you for that.'

Jeanne finished folding her clothes. 'What do you mean?'

His voice hardened. 'You know very well what I mean. I am where I am now because of you.'

She paused in what she was doing. 'I do not understand.'

'Your refusal to tell Guèvremont that Wentworth was the father of your sister's boy, Gilles. Is that plain enough for you?'

She swept a cloth across the table, and stood back. 'Now for some food for you.'

'I am not hungry. Come over here.'

'I cannot.' She picked up a box with a small metal clasp, placed it on top of the bag of clothes, and then put the bag carefully in the small *armoire*, leaving its door slightly open.

Le Guinec went over and closed the door of the cottage, which left it in partial shadow. He crossed the small room, took her by the wrist, and led her over to the box bed. He sat down on it, but Jeanne remained standing in the half-light.

'I have been waiting for this for a long time.'

He reached for her, but she resisted, pulling her hand away.

'I cannot. It is the wrong time. I am unclean. We should eat.'

Which they did, and as was his custom, he drank some of the good wine he had laid up there. She went outside, and wrapped some cloths around her, to help her fool him. She told him she would sleep on the floor. But he pulled her over to him on the bed, put his leg over one thigh, and tore off the cloths. He was too strong for her, and she turned her face away until he pulled her head round to kiss her violently. Later, he held her wrists above her head and forced her again. She cried out in the night, but there was no one to hear her.

Jeanne had not slept. She had kept still, for fear she would wake him again, and suffer yet more. It was too late now to say she had the day wrong, to accuse herself or Erwan the carter for that, because she knew in misery that she could not leave. Le Guinec had been too powerful for her, as he always was, whether he was with her or was absent, his presence in her life overwhelming. What had she been doing imagining that she could make a life apart from him? The pitiful bag of clothes she had gathered together for her new life, and the few precious things she had in her small box, sat there in the *armoire*, dully and to no purpose, out of reach.

She felt a yearning to pray before Bernard came to the church to collect her, to ask for forgiveness for all her sins and for her weakness. Perhaps God had intended this punishment for her, had sent Le Guinec to her? Her parents had died in pain, her mother screaming about the devil in her belly, her father crushed under a beam. She had thought at the time it was like Christ brought low by the weight of the cross. But it was clear to her now, as clear as spring water, that they were all to suffer for her sister. Her sister's sin had reached out to them all, consuming her first, but bringing harsh judgment to bear on her family for their lack of forgiveness.

He had collapsed face down. She slipped from the bed. She was still wearing her gown from the day before, he had not let her remove it. She stumbled out of the door, and sobbed as she fell on her knees by the bucket at the well, clutching one of the cloths from the floor that had failed to protect her. Water was sent by God, she thought, to wash us all clean. She found some clogs by the side of the cottage, and began to walk and then race down the lane, until she recalled that Bernard might not be there that early: she would have time to pray, and leave before he came.

Le Guinec stirred. His head felt heavy, but his body told him he wanted more of her. He reached out, but the bed was empty. He cursed, and fell asleep again. Outside, after eating the hay that had been spread for it, his horse tried to reach the better grass just beyond its tether, and then gave up, with a shake of its mane.

The small church at Brandivy was bathed in a strange light, its west end looking out over the gorge of the Loc'h, its east end facing the straggling cottages of the village, as if still offering the inhabitants the salvation of which it had been mostly stripped. There was no priest, and nothing was left in the interior, although the door was open for anyone who chose to push it. It was barely dawn.

Jeanne wiped the tears from her face. She would go in because her prayers were private. She had no idea whether they would be received without the intercession of a priest, and was determined to seek out *Père* Guillaume as soon as she could and lose herself in a long confession, if he would permit her to do so. She would have sought solace in the big church at Auray, but that was not now going to happen, and would never happen. Happiness had been a forlorn hope, something that belonged to other lives and not to her own, nor that of her family. Of that, she was now utterly convinced, and she would pray not just for the forgiveness she herself had never extended to her sister, but for the strength to bear what life brought to her, in whatever shape it was presented to her, by God's good will.

As she knelt inside the church, in the absence of any seating, and spoke her prayers under the cooing of a pigeon, Le Guinec guided his horse into the church square, or what passed for one in this humble village. He had seen no one on the road, and it was only an instinct that had led him in the direction of the village, and the church. He was aware of Jeanne's faith, which he regarded as a kind of malady that affected her from time to time, and he was not prepared to leave her just yet after their encounter the night before. He wanted to see her now, and to be able to see her again, whenever he felt the need.

He dismounted, and tied the reins to a small tree that stood on the edge of the gorge. He could hear the breeze rustling leaves down by the river, but the village as a whole was silent. He walked towards the church, which was a mean little building in his view, and round to the door. He peered inside, but she was not there. Perhaps it did not matter. As he turned round, he saw her standing by his horse, stroking its nose. She had always had a sympathy for animals. He came up quietly, treading a line directly behind her back, and when he was a short distance away his horse bucked his head up and down, in a kind of greeting. She stood back, her face pale and drawn. He ran his hand through his hair, and tried a smile.

'Ah, Jeanne. Are you pleased with your prayers this morning? Is it too much to hope that my humble self has an equally humble place in them?'

'I have prayed for both of us.'

'Thank you, Jeanne. I would offer to do the same for you, but I think that after all this time the good Lord might turn a deaf ear to me. I wonder sometimes if he hears the prayers peasants make for their crops, for mending broken arms…'

'Shall we go? I do not wish to hear your blasphemy…'

From his childhood, Le Guinec had detested being called a sinner, having priests or nuns or other lay figures telling him to look into his own heart, to acknowledge the guilt he ought to feel about one small thing or another.

'Ah, I blaspheme, do I? While you have been on your knees praying, still fresh from our embraces? Come, Jeanne, there is time yet before I have to go. Why, let me lift you...'

In a sudden burst of disgust and anger, deep as she was already in raging recriminations against herself, she pushed him away from her with surprising force. To her horror he caught one heel on a large stone behind him, and in an instant his body plunged backwards into the gorge of the Loc'h, rolling over and down at a great speed, crashing over twigs and fallen branches, until he came to rest abruptly with a sharp crack against a boulder just above the stream. He lay completely still, a stillness she had seen at death before. One leg was twisted at an impossible angle under him, and his head hung limply to one side.

Bernard Sarzou walked around the west end of the church. He had brought the cart from his cousin's in quietly, just as he had arranged with Jeanne. The rising sun lit up the east end, but the west was still in a kind of shadow. There was only one figure there, and he could see it was Jeanne: she had collapsed on to the ground just in front of a horse tied to a tree. He ran over, and reached out his hands to her.

'Do not touch me! Do you hear!'

Slowly, and quietly, he knelt down beside her. As far as he could tell, she was unharmed, although what he could see of her face was so anguished it almost pained him to look at her.

'Jeanne. I am here with the cart. It is as we agreed.'

She fell on him, almost grasping at him, her voice rasping amidst the sobs. 'It is not as we agreed! It is over, done, there is nothing left, nothing of us.'

He placed his hand on the back of her head, and stroked her hair. If only she knew how much he loved her; he was overwhelmed and humbled by it. That was all he could murmur to her. She was all he had ever wanted, and the world always contrived to pull her away. It was then that she pointed, feebly. He could not grasp at first what it was that she wanted to show him; but then he stood up, and peered over the edge.

He was never in any doubt, although he was completely astonished: it was Le Guinec. The man always dressed in the same manner. He was dead, stone dead; that much was clear. She must have struck him, somehow, and pushed him over the edge. What came to him immediately was that no one must know. He lifted her up, gently, putting his arm underneath her to support her, and with his other freed the reins of the horse from the tree. Now she was standing, he loosened the saddle girth, pushed the saddle over to one side a little, and slapped the horse smartly, as he had seen others do. Without waiting to see where it went, he put his arm back around Jeanne and walked with her quickly across and behind the church.

She had nothing with her, which puzzled him. So, they would take the cart to her cottage, collect anything she had set aside, and remove anything that belonged to Le Guinec, anything that declared that the man had just been there, which he must have been. Her slack body slumped next to him on the seat of the cart told him a terrible truth about the nature of her anguish. When they reached the cottage, she climbed down and pushed her hair out of her eyes.

'Now you must go.'

He did not know how to reply, so he said nothing.

'Bernard, you must go. I cannot be with you. God has sent this punishment to me…'

'Le Guinec was not from God, Jeanne.'

She put her head in her hands, and sobbed loudly, but said nothing through her tears.

'If there is a God, Jeanne, then he will tell you that I love you with all my heart, and will devote the rest of my life to you, because I can think of none who is more worthy of love, and yet who has had none. That is my God, if you like.'

'Ah, Bernard, where have you been?' She wailed like a child, and Bernard could bear it no longer, but climbed down from the cart and went to her and they clung to each other. Together they went into the cottage, and they came out together with her few belongings. There was nothing of Le Guinec left in there. As the cart drove off, a gust of wind closed the door behind them.

CHAPTER XXIV: PRELUDE TO THE BALL

It was Clémence de Moire who started the ball rolling. One morning in the late summer, on a day when the heat was less oppressive but the weather was bright, she suggested to Joséphine Guèvremont that they should stroll down to *Madame* Hébert, the milliner. She was a little tired by now of the endless *ennui* that affected her friend; outside the house, a different stimulus might shake her out of her endless melancholy. Only that officer Leroux had brought Joséphine to life, although it was hard to see why. He was, admittedly, a handsome man, but aside from a small competence in the matter of the dance he was immune to the benign influence of fashion. Thankfully, he was now a long way off, doing his duty for his country in Germany, across the dreary Rhine; but that did not stop Joséphine pining for him.

Madame Hébert was charm itself, but there was a certain degree of reserve about her manner. She had gloves for the autumn season to display, but her face was drawn and Clémence began to find it distracting. Joséphine became absorbed in the attractions of a blue silk pair, and on the third occasion that she picked them up, *Madame* Hébert spoke.

'*Mademoiselle* Guèvremont, I hope you will forgive me if I raise a slight concern with you over the fate of the masks and carnival costumes which *Monsieur* Hébert procured on loan at your request.'

Joséphine continued in her fascination with the blue silk.

'I believe I do remember.'

'*Monsieur* Hébert was most diligent in his enquiries, although the matter took a number of weeks.'

'I did not know.'

'You had an intention at the time, if I may be so bold, to set in motion arrangements for a ball, and you wished it to be a ball in masquerade, as you explained it to me at the time, *mademoiselle.*'

'I believe I may have done so, if your memory is correct. Tell me, is this the only pair of the blue that you have?'

'*Mademoiselle*, I am most careful never to duplicate my finer goods. That would not do at all.'

'There, you have decided me. Will you send them up to the house for me? I do not wish to carry them now.'

'Assuredly, *mademoiselle*. Katarin will bring them up tomorrow, first thing.'

Joséphine expressed satisfaction curtly, and retrieved her parasol, which lay on the counter. But by now Clémence was by her side, and she placed a restraining hand on her friend's forearm.

'Before we leave, it is evident that we must resolve this matter of the costumes for *Madame* Hébert, who has done us such a good service.'

'Us?' queried Joséphine.

'*Madame* Hébert, we are most grateful to your husband and yourself, be assured of that, for this signal success. It is a request that is quite out of the ordinary, and we are in your debt. Would you say that it is an ample collection?'

Madame Hébert noticeably lifted her shoulders and straightened her back, gratification at the acknowledgement being made after such a long delay mildly qualified by the promptings of pride.

'I do not believe *Monsieur* Hébert would have been satisfied with anything less. They remain unpacked, I am afraid, just as they arrived, although *Monsieur* Hébert and I have confirmed that they are in a proper condition.'

'It is as I would have imagined, *Madame*. Would you be so kind, then, as to have the full collection, masks and costumes, delivered to my father's house at the first opportunity? I shall have his agent speak to *Monsieur* Hébert about matters to do with payment. The agent's name is Jacquot, I believe.'

Joséphine's face was itself a mask. *Madame* Hébert bid them good day, and Clémence took her arm lightly once they were outside in the sunshine.

'Is that not wonderful? Why, it is just what we need! A ball, and in masquerade! Come, you will look wonderful, and you will not have to persuade your father. We shall have the dancing in our grand hall, with the musicians at one end of it. Guests will drive up and alight, there will be torches. Father will arrange a room for cards. It is all so easy. Who would have thought that you had ordered costumes?'

'Do what you wish. I shall not be attending.'

'Oh, Joséphine, Joséphine! We shall write to everybody. My dear, the more who are there, the more your beauty will stand out. You know that is true. Your new blue gloves will look wonderful.'

There was a brief silence while Joséphine considered this. Then, 'I shall not be a shepherdess.'

'No, you shall be Scheherazade. From *The Thousand and One Nights*.'

They walked on, evenly.

The parting from *Madame* Lalande was more emotional than Héloïse had anticipated. As she explained, there was still much to show Héloïse about sewing, notably of linen shirts, but also more on embroidering, and the practical matter of alterations that might need to be made to garments. In addition, there was far more on cooking, on ordering, the payment of minor bills and household wages, and on the magical role of the accounts. Nonetheless, an embrace was called for, which had its tearful moment, and there was bobbing from Nanette and Lise, and a gift from the housekeeper, *Madame* Perrée of a *Far Breton* from the kitchen: nothing much, she insisted, but it would be sustaining on the journey. Katell had certainly been away from home before, but never on her own, even with a maid. She and Héloïse were to stay in Auray as the guests of *Madame* du Plessis, who would also be their *chaperon* at the ball. That was an unexpected kindness, provided by a lady they had never met, and arranged by means of a tactful and courteous correspondence.

Héloïse had been expecting to see Roparzh amongst the well-wishers at their departure, and had indeed been puzzled by the very few sighting of him that she had had after the day of the picnic. Her lively memory kept drawing her back to those intimate moments on that occasion when he had touched her hand, or gently pushed her hair back from her face. Her thoughts drifted from time to time to the promise he had made that he would finish the sketch he had begun in his studio, and then show it to her. She wondered why it might be taking so long, but then admitted to herself that she knew very little about art.

Robert the coachman was cheerful, and the boxes were stowed safely without the need for ballgowns in them, since this was to be a masquerade ball. Suitable costumes were being made available in Auray through the kindness of *Mademoiselle* Guèvremont and her friend, *Mademoiselle* Clémence de Moire. Privately, Héloïse feared that some of the best might have already been selected before she and Katell were able to view them. But since there was nothing to be done about it she sat back in the cushions, and with the increasing heat of the day and the rolling of the coach, she began to doze.

Robert changed his horses at a town called Baud, and reviewed his directions with Héloïse, taking the road towards Grand-Champ at Camors. She did not recognise much of the countryside — just the long, low outline of the forest of the *landes* — until they drew close to the manor. As the carriage swung into the avenue of trees and ground its way up the drive her emotions began to swell. How like and yet unlike that first, gruelling journey from Auray to Plumergat with the carter and that awful boy; how wonderful her first sight of Daniel after so long! Katell perceived the light in her eyes.

'So, is this the manor, Héloïse? What a pretty place it is! Why, I can see the house, up there ahead. Do you know for sure that your uncle will be waiting? I am so looking forward to meeting him, and the lady you mention who is his wife? Oh dear, what is her name again? Quickly, Héloïse, or we shall have arrived and I shall be all tongue-tied.'

'Babette.'

'Ah, yes, I knew I should forget it. It is very charming, but I have not heard it used before. Look we are here, and there is your uncle and Babette, is that not so? Why are there no dogs? I thought there were always dogs at chateaux and manors…'

The wheels came to an abrupt halt, and Robert jumped down and swung the door open with a grin. Héloïse catapulted herself off the step and straight into the arms of Daniel, while Robert helped Katell down more sedately. Daniel whirled around with Héloïse, and then released her to Babette, coming forward with an apology to greet and welcome *Mademoiselle* Floch with some solemnity. Babette curtsied to Katell, who laughed and curtsied back, and they walked hand in hand through the door into the house.

The room was dark and cool. Héloïse knew it as her uncle's office, and it appealed to her because it was redolent of him even if it had little in the way of decoration. He had asked to speak to her alone.

'Hearing about what you have experienced in Pontivy makes me wonder if you have changed.'

'How could I do that? You are all I have.'

'All you have here, that may be so, although you have made friends. *Mademoiselle* Katell Floch is charming.'

'Yes, she is really a young woman by now. It is in her nature to be so light and enthusiastic. I love it.'

'And her brother? I gather you spent time with him.'

For the first time, his niece looked a little guarded. She shifted in her seat, but then looked at him frankly enough.

'He is handsome, if that is what you are hinting at. And he has charm. And sophistication. And he is inspired, in different ways. He is different from the young men I have met here.'

'If you say so. Has he ... shown interest.'

'Would I tell you that?'

'Ah. Perhaps not. Time may tell — which may include telling me.'

At this, they both laughed, and he reached out and held both her hands. She looked again at the fresh scars by his mouth, and above his eye. Now she had his hands, it felt that she might get the truth from him. And she could feel scars on his right hand that she had not noticed.

'So will you tell me?'

'What?'

'You know what. What I am looking at and could not miss. How did that happen?'

'Well, I went to Lorient, as we have said. And the journey went well. Some good people in the port, some not so good.'

'They went for you?'

'Only one or two. Ruffians — thieves, probably. You get them in all ports.'

'But it is only here that they attack you because you are a black man. Did they kick you?'

'No. They were a little drunk. Not so difficult to shake off. There was a man who helped me. A soldier, in fact. He said something about *égalité*, pitched in, and patched me up. We had a drink, and that was that.'

She let his hands go.

'What was it that you wanted to speak to me about? Katell and Babette will be wondering where we are.'

'You remember the documents that you brought with you across the ocean from Saint-Domingue? In the leather pouch?'

'I don't know where I put them after we came here. I'm sorry. Were they important?'

'You should not worry. I kept them in here with other papers. They were the deeds to a number of plantations, of land, in Saint-Domingue. Or copies of them, really. So they were important. Your father signed them over to you, and had me as your guardian should anything happen to him. He was thinking of death, surely, but not as it happened, in violence. It is a simple thing — he wanted to look after you, as he had looked after your half-sister Félice. He had set her up in trade, and with some land too, a few smaller holdings.'

'Is something wrong? Is that why you wanted to talk to me?'

'No, nothing is wrong. But I acted rather impetuously, even if it was on your behalf. I left the original deeds with Félice in Le Cap, and asked her to sell the land when it was possible. Things were so bad, and I could not see us going back there. And there was that man Lafargue too. He wanted everything he could lay his hands on, as we found out. I wanted to apologise to you.'

'For what? Looking after me? But is this why you were away in Lorient? You were with Jacinthe, I suppose. Did she have news for you from my sister?'

'She did. The estates have all sold, apart from one. It was a small coffee plantation, and coffee is what she does. I thought she should have it for all her care for us in treacherous times.'

'I see. So it is all done. It is strange to think of things I did not know, and of my father again: how he looked ahead, but could not see what was coming. And of Lafargue.'

'Lafargue came chasing after you, but did not know enough to find the copies of the deeds we were keeping. We have no need for them now, after the sale.'

Héloïse shuddered at all the memories that came crowding in on her. He understood that. These things were physical. Saint-Domingue was nothing if not physical, brutally so.

'Who bought them?'

'It seems that the rebellion in Saint-Domingue has leaders, and that the leaders and others are now buying up the land. People work for wages now that slavery is over. That is what we are told.'

Héloïse stood up. 'I am glad that they are gone. It is a relief. I think we should burn those copies now, before they do any more harm.'

The coach rolled out of the yard. Robert whistled through his teeth to the horses, and clicked to them. Inside, Héloïse sat back, and stayed silent. Katell could see that she was thinking, and remained silent. But it was not long before Héloïse stirred, crossing her legs because she felt like it. Katell pretended to disapprove of that openly, but secretly she admired it.

'Do you think your brother will take orders?'

Katell was surprised at the question, but pleased to be talking: 'Whose orders?'

'Holy orders. Will he become a priest?'

Katell opened her eyes wide. 'Roparzh? A priest? Whatever makes you think that?'

Héloïse looked at her quizzically: 'Roparzh makes me think that. Quite distinctly. Has he never talked to you about the calling of a priest? He speaks … in an inspired way.'

'Roparzh?'

'Katell, is that all you can say? Yes, I am talking of Roparzh. We do know the same person?'

'Well, yes, of course we do, but I am amazed. I know he likes to think of himself as an artist, a painter, a new Claude Lorrain, but not a priest. Why, I can hardly imagine it.'

'Now you amaze me. What about the praying, in church?'

'Dear Héloïse, I cannot say. Praying? I have seldom known him to visit a church, apart from that time in Pontivy that I told you about. It may be that he did so in Nantes.'

Robert shouted at something in the road, slowed, and then the coach lurched forwards again.

'Tell me about Nantes, then. Do you mind? What was your brother doing there?'

Katell looked out of the window, avoiding Héloïse's gaze.

'It... Well... It did not seem relevant. I thought he might have told you himself... No, that is an untruth, and I am sorry for saying it. I think he may have been giving you a picture...'

'Well, he is a painter after all. And he has promised me a picture!'

Katell laughed nervously but felt encouraged. 'I might have known you would take it in the right spirit. Roparzh was in Nantes working for our father, as a kind of apprentice, I suppose. I do not understand trade and warehouses, so you must forgive me. As a kind of factor, I think they call it.'

'Nantes is a large port. I have heard of it.'

'Yes, he was taking things off the ships, and then arranging for the cargo to be carried elsewhere, up the river, I suppose, or perhaps over land.'

'What kind of things?'

'Sugar, mostly.'

'I see. That would be sugar then from the plantations.'

'Yes, I suppose it would. I did not say so before because I feared it might upset you, Héloïse. You must forgive me! We are not used...'

'No.'

'You see, he came back to Pontivy because the trade collapsed, or so father says. The ... people out there are unhappy, and there is a revolt and... But surely you already know all this, Héloïse. Forgive me again, I...'

'I am not familiar with Auray, but I think we may be approaching it. There are people outside a big church or convent or something of that kind. But we are not stopping. Oh, well. Not Auray.' She leaned back again, and smiled at Katell, uncrossing her legs. 'And — do you mind if I ask? — there is a mystery about this poor young woman who died.'

'Died? I do not know of a young woman who died. Perhaps there was one in Nantes. But he has never spoken of her to me.'

'Katell, Roparzh is mourning a lost love. I do not believe that I can be mistaken in that.'

'Oh, yes, that is true. But Héloïse, I am not sure how much I should tell you if he has not done so himself.'

'You are right. It may be that he will choose to tell me more. That is, when we next meet — if we do.'

'Oh, see there, I think we are coming into the town. How exciting! Yet it is rather like Pontivy, quite small, it seems. No, I think I can confide in you that there was an understanding, but it was with a young lady in Rennes, and it has now concluded. She is perfectly well.'

CHAPTER XXV: THE MASQUERADE

Antoine de Moire was from the cadet branch of an old aristocratic family, which had diluted itself over the centuries to settle finally on a motley array of bourgeois roles in society, with some members active in Rennes, others in Saint-Brieuc, and Antoine himself in Auray. In recent years, he had consolidated the opinions of the wealthier part of the townsfolk of Auray in favour of the Republic, so taking with him those who were less committed but fully pragmatic, such as Laurent Guèvremont. All bettered themselves by acquiring property confiscated under the Republic, and de Moire's own choice was a small and ancient manor without its lands, at a short distance outside the town of Auray.

De Moire was a doting father, and was of the opinion that his wife, Victoire, did not do enough to provide potential suitors for their daughter Clémence. When his darling daughter came to him with the idea of a ball, he was quick to see the merits of it, and keen to patronise the occasion as its host. Clémence was delighted, and entered into the arrangements with a good eye for detail and practicality. The manor had a wonderful space for the dancing in what had been the ancient great hall, which still kept its magnificent roof timbers, and had elaborate and grand candelabra suspended from them. The hall did not have a musicians' gallery, but later ages had added a fireplace at the far end, and the space in front of that would do admirably for them, since the season of the year would not require a fire to be lit.

The costumes for the masquerade were to be laid out on boards and trestles in the great hall itself, and guests invited to come and select what they would. To preserve the spirit of mystery attached to a masquerade, gentlemen were invited on a different day from the ladies, and visitors were formally welcomed on both days by members of the family, but advised in the hall itself by *Monsieur* and *Madame* Hébert. Limited alterations to the costumes were to be permitted, but the costume should be presented to the Héberts in good time so that work might be undertaken or, sadly, advised against.

The array was declared to be *formidable*. There were costumes for devils and jesters, abbesses and monks, and many more, with the characters from *commedia dell'arte* familiar from prints. Some gentlemen who chose to walk through nonchalantly, fingering the occasional item, might then be seen having a quiet word with *Monsieur* Hébert, who would unobtrusively remove a costume and put it behind. Masks were tried on in front of several cheval mirrors, and rather carelessly cast back on the table or even on the floor, and sharp words were exchanged between some of the young ladies, fired by the excitement of impersonation.

The son, Philippe de Moire, had a share in the bank owned by *Madame* du Plessis, whom he welcomed with rather stiff formality in the foyer of the manor on the evening itself, which was warm and dry.

'*Madame* du Plessis, an honour. You are, of course, acquainted with my father, Antoine.'

'Philippe, it is a pleasure to see you both together. *Bonsoir*, Antoine.'

'*Bonsoir*, Louise, you grace us with your presence.'

Victoire de Moire came quickly forward from the hall into the foyer.

'*Mille pardons*, Louise, Clémence had called to me. A very good evening to you. And your charges?'

A neat shepherdess with a small blonde wig and a crook had climbed gingerly down from the carriage, followed by an extraordinary gold mask above a gown of brilliant colours, behind which were attached a pair of tiny gold wings. Both remarkable characters wore long, ball gloves tied above the elbow, in white and blue respectively.

'Well, you men must withdraw. There is nothing to declare to you, and you can make your introductions either at hazard or in the finale.'

Father and son bowed, to du Plessis and to the delightful figures, and walked away some distance, awaiting the next arrivals.

'Victoire, do we wait for Clémence? May I introduce these young people to you without her?'

The shepherdess spoke, between rouged cheeks.

'Permit me, *Madame*, but there will be no harm in a surprise for Clémence later. I am sure that is part of the fun. I know I should like to be surprised!'

'Indeed, there is no harm in it. So, without further delay, I should introduce *Mademoiselle* Floch and *Mademoiselle* Argoubet to you with great pleasure. *Madame* de Moire, our host.'

A deeper voice spoke from the gold mask. It was, momentarily, disconcerting to both du Plessis and de Moire, but the tone was soothingly soft and pleasant.

'We are indebted to you for this invitation, *Madame*, and we shall try to play our part with honour.'

It was an odd sentiment, but an emphasis on honour might always be welcomed by respectable hosts. The small group proceeded into the foyer and stood for a moment at the entrance to the hall. A young harlequin pushed past them, his mask raised on a perspiring forehead, with apologies and the word 'piss' flung at them, and the shepherdess instinctively grasped the other's arm. The noise was extraordinary: it swept out of the hall and engulfed them. Sensing their nervousness, *Madame* du Plessis raised an eyebrow, and smiled.

'Remember what I said to you: the best thing is to "launch" yourselves. Consider that, if you like, you are a small boat on a wide sea and sail from island to island. But make sure you do not venture too closely to land. There are those who will use a crush and a mask to take advantages, I can assure you. I shall remain in sight. The refreshments will give you a respite; but if not, you may find a calmer place right by the musicians, who are idle at present.'

The rouged cheeks and the gold mask nodded at her, for all the world like schoolgirls with their governess, and du Plessis was briefly amused. If she had thought that being a chaperon would be dull, she had been proved wrong. The two 'launched' themselves. What appeared to be a devil came up to them, and made a lewd suggestion to the shepherdess. A Cinderella, with what must be the glass slipper tied by a ribbon around her neck, sidled up with the harlequin at her elbow, and felt the fabric of the coloured costume. The harlequin took the opportunity to speak to the gold mask.

'I trust your wings will not mean you will fly away, *mademoiselle*. We mortals may not follow you then.'

Héloïse turned her back on him, but in doing so lost her shepherdess, who was being invited to take some steps with the devil. Despite the throng, the eyes under the gold mask were drawn over to where Gilles was standing by the musicians. He was unmasked, and talking to a young woman who was simply but attractively dressed, whose face revealed charming dimples. Her own full-face mask felt uncomfortable and hot; irritatingly, it rubbed her cheekbones, and cut into her forehead.

Philippe de Moire appeared; he remained the host, and had not taken a costume, but like his father he was an elegant man.

'I believe we have already met, although curiously we have not been introduced. So the mystery remains intact on my side. Will you take some refreshment? It is quite a throng.'

Héloïse looked about her, and spied Bluebeard with her shepherdess. The devil and Bluebeard in the space of minutes? Was it the attraction of sin to innocence? It was a fine, dark-blue beard with a grimacing mask, but the rest of the costume was nondescript. To her exasperation, she saw Gilles attempting to kiss the hand of the young woman, who withdrew it and spoke in the ear of an older musician.

The refreshments in the room adjoining the hall were hidden behind hot and heaving bodies, with scent and sweat mixed together in the fusty smell of powder from smeared faces, or from hair. Philippe pushed his way through to find her a lemonade, and there just to her left was Joséphine Guèvremont, with jewels in her hair and in a beautiful Turkish costume with a light veil, standing next to a debonair young officer who was protecting them both from the crush with an outstretched arm. Would she be recognised by her? Probably not. Héloïse had seen Joséphine only once in passing through a doorway at the Guèvremont house; but she had already heard disrespectful talk about a penchant for officers.

A Red Riding Hood moving past her stuck out an elbow, which hurt, and Héloïse was sure that she saw the woman's companion slide his hand round her caped waist, and then up above it, while leaning over her. There was a shout for music from the *salle*, taken up by a number of voices, and she recognised the sound of a minuet. Some began to move away from the refreshments to the dancing, but her curiosity stayed with her, and she edged forward. A Pierrot had found his

Columbine, and both were sipping wine decorously: his strange face turned to look at Héloïse as she passed. The officer was standing close to Joséphine, who seemed lost in a reverie. The officer was speaking.

'I wish I could say more. Bring better news to you. But there is no report of him. We should harden ourselves to the fact that he may be lost.'

Joséphine said nothing. There were tears on her face, and lines were forming in her powder under the veil.

'You must allow me to comfort you.'

That was spoken in such a secretive, intimate way that it was barely audible. The officer reached down to take her hand, an invisible gesture in a crowded room. Joséphine withdrew hers from his fingers, and turned away; the officer hesitated, and then made to follow her. Philippe came through the rout, inclined his head to the officer and shouted a greeting, and then presented the lemonade politely.

'We now have the problem, *mademoiselle*, of how you will drink it. And the minuet is in progress. Should we join them?'

'I believe I can tip this mask back a little. There, that will do. Most refreshing, thank you, *monsieur*. You play the part of the host to perfection. But I believe I must now find my companion.'

He had known, of course, had heard of the young woman who had come to Auray in the company of Katell Floch; but the full mask and her shawl had hidden her features, the long gloves her arms and hands. He found the brief glimpse of her dark skin startling. He bowed.

'Yes, let us do that.'

It was even hotter; some of the crowd had pressed to the sides, while others were caught up in the ball. It was exciting. Amongst the dancers were *Madame* du Plessis and Laurent Guèvremont. Héloïse had never imagined him dancing, but the minuet might be his choice. She took a deep breath as she saw Gilles approaching. He shook Philippe by the hand, as one he knew well, and then bowed to her.

'*Mademoiselle*, or if I should call you *madame* I do so willingly, I am enchanted. I find your costume intriguing. Why, there are so many here of great variety, but none, I think, such as yours.'

He has no idea what it is, Héloïse thought. She decided to play the demure *mademoiselle*, and resolved to disguise her voice a little too.

'Why, *monsieur*, you must guess who I am? Let me help you. Were you fortunate, I would bring you a message.'

'How kind. Why would you do that?'

He is making a fool of himself in front of this young *bourgeois*. She was still angry with him: why had he not written to her in Pontivy? But she could not let him humiliate himself.

'I am Iris, *monsieur*.'

'And who, pray, is Iris? I admire these colours greatly. They remind me of a rainbow.'

'Iris is the rainbow, *monsieur*.'

'Ah, that explains it all. Where is Philippe? I did not mean to usurp his place with you. Let me take you to him.'

Now that was a hard blow. Héloïse had hoped to look beautiful, to be enticing, to teach him that he should want her so badly that it hurt, should miss her when she was gone, should see her in the colours of the rainbow: but now she was furious. Messenger of the gods or not, masquerade or not, *grande salle* and ancient timber beams or not, she felt like kicking him.

'So, Iris, the rainbow. Delightful. Ah, I see him there. Let me make a space for you.'

Héloïse stood, rooted to the spot. He would not be taking her anywhere. So he smiled, stupidly, instead. It was not just an impulse: she would kick him, at any moment now.

'Gold mask, and wings. A rainbow. Wonderful mask.' He looked puzzled. 'But why would a rainbow have wings? You have me at a loss there.'

Héloïse sat out the quadrille and the *cotillon*, and was even more infuriated, had that strictly been possible, by seeing Gilles choose to dance in the *cotillon* with the dimpled fairy by the musicians. She was good, mind you, and had a sweet face, but that was not going to win her undying friendship from the messenger of the gods tonight. She saw an Apollo dancing well, his diminutive lyre hanging down from his shoulders on a strap, and wondered if she should join him instead. But she had turned down Philippe and so had no right to do so, which actually suited her increasingly foul mood best. She could also see the officer and Joséphine, not together, but in the same set, at least for a while, and she was pleasantly amused to see her dear shepherdess partnered by Hercules: hot, though, in that lionskin. It was not long before Joséphine sat out; when her father came across quietly to speak to her, she waved him impatiently away.

Then everything began to fall apart. Gilles stopped dancing with the diminutive fairy, bid her a courteous farewell, and grinned vacuously over at Philippe. The room was full to bursting with chatter and laughter, even though the music had stopped, and she saw him look across in her direction. He spoke to Philippe, and stared across at her, quite clearly astonished. She clenched her teeth in anger, and went to look for her shepherdess, who was back with the devil again. The blonde wig was a little askew, but she was still clutching her crook, while the devil had gained a pitchfork from somewhere and they were exchanging implements and laughing. She felt her buttock pinched, swung round to see a friar waddling off with a turbaned dignitary, and then Gilles was right in front of her.

'Well, you had me fooled,' he said.

Héloïse ignored him and kept looking out for the miscreant friar.

'Why didn't you say?'

'It is a masquerade.'

'I know that. There is no reason to be angry with me. How could I know?'

'There is every reason to be angry with you. Now go away.'

'Héloïse, you can't send me away after so long.'

'And why was it so long?'

'I might ask you that.'

'And what do you mean by that? Not one letter, in all that time. Not a word. What were you doing? Cavorting with that prancing imp?'

'That is the dancing-master Duchesne's daughter, Clotilde, and she is a good friend of mine.'

'Well write to her instead.'

The shepherdess was beginning to be concerned, and to lose concentration in her dialogue with the devil. She placed a sympathetic hand on her companion's arm, but Héloïse uncharacteristically shook it off. The remarks about Clotilde made Gilles begin to lose his temper too.

'Well, I doubt that writing could compete with having one's likeness taken by a young hypocrite who takes liberties with your person.'

'How dare you talk about liberties with my person! And what do you know about "likenesses"?'

'Never you mind what I know. Just take it that I do. How is Roparzh Floch, by the way? Has he told you about his fiancée? I am surprised not to see him here, skulking in some corner…'

Héloïse snatched the crook from the hands of the shepherdess and hit Gilles over the head with it. Fortunately for them both it was only made of a light material, so it broke immediately. In the same instant there was a sudden outcry, and a surge of dancers crowded to one side of the hall, where some were supporting what appeared to be a woman who had fainted.

'It is the Scheherazade.'

Some of those around the fainting woman started to point across to the entrance into the hall. The music stopped, and people fell silent. Framed in the doorway stood a man with a bicorne on his head, wearing a domino in black silk, and a black mask. He took one or two steps forward, limping slightly. Gilles stared at him, and then at Lieutenant Vernier across the room, who strode towards the door, only to be imperiously waved aside.

The Scheherazade was helped to her feet. With her veil now removed, Gilles recognised Joséphine in the costume, and knew instinctively who the newcomer must be. Gilles walked quickly back through the crowd and spoke in the ear of *Monsieur* Duchesne. The masquerade held its breath, fascinated, as Joséphine and the domino advanced unsteadily towards each other. At a tap from his violin, Duchesne and the musicians broke into an unfamiliar and beguiling rhythm.

Nicolas Leroux took the mask from his face, dropped it on the floor, and in a sweeping gesture threw his hat aside. As the music from Mozart's *German Dances* filled the hall, Leroux brought Joséphine towards him, gently joined their arms, and began — at first still unsteadily — to dance to the flowing rhythm of the musicians, circling the open space in the middle of the hall. The candelabra glittered, the candles spluttered, and the masqueraders gathered around, captivated, as gradually more and more couples broke ranks to join in the rolling, light-as-air steps of the intoxicating Waltz.

CHAPTER XXVI: CHARLES HOARE SOLVES THE PUZZLE

Colonel North was riding with a young man in uniform whom he hardly knew. They had met for the first time in Dorking, where the Colonel had climbed down from the stagecoach from London, after travelling post-haste from the West Country. With the good understanding born of so many years in each other's company, he and his sister Caroline had been in constant communication since her first, alarming letter directed to him at Stonehouse in Plymouth declaring that Tregothen had been sighted in Brighton.

As he rode on intently, his knees if not his heels conveying to his beast's flanks the urgency with which he rode and the intolerance for any deviation, he could not avoid admitting that he was driven by guilt as much as by intemperate anger. They had sent Tregothen on a commission to the West Indies after his assault on the actress Thirza Farley in the spring, convinced that he would perish there swiftly from the appalling diseases that swept lethally through the British and European troops on the islands. It had seemed a fitting and sound punishment for his gross offences, kept within military hands — and they had been proved wrong. Tregothen had jumped ship, and it was their grave error that had allowed him to be back in England, to attempt the abductions of Mrs Arabella Wentworth and Amelia and even when failing in them to evade capture.

But if they were to find and secure Tregothen now, then above all they would need to have the services of one who could securely recognise him. North's own acquaintance with him was fleeting, and he could not rely upon it. So it was that he was riding as fast as he might from Dorking down to Preston Barracks near Brighton with fresh-faced Charles Hoare. A fledgling when in the South Devon Militia, Hoare had just recently moved with his family to a residence in Surrey, and rejoined the militia there. His great recommendation was that he had seen Tregothen at exercises near Plymouth enough times to recognise him well. But he belonged to a different regiment, and had not been billeted near to him; so the recognition almost certainly ran only one way. Hoare had considered this expedition as something of a lark until his commanding officer took him aside and told him a few things about Tregothen he was not to repeat to anyone, which had made Charles think of his own sister, and how very dear she was to him.

The first day in Brighton was deeply frustrating. Practically speaking, the arrangements were fine, with trained military horses supplied at Preston Barracks for them both, and a short ride down to the Old Ship Inn for rooms. Colonel North could not suppress his impatience, and had sent Charles out almost immediately to use the rest of the daylight walking the main thoroughfares, striding the paths around the open space of the Steyne, casually looking in to the frequented establishments, even visiting the strand itself and staring out at occupants of the odd bathing-machines. But it had all been futile; there had been no sighting of Tregothen, and Charles Hoare returned with an unsettling conviction that the man simply was not there.

He said nothing about that to Colonel North. North was a decent and punctilious companion, even if their relationship was one of superior officer to younger man, which was rigorously understood from the start. He would take his orders from North, and Charles's next duty — which he was anticipating with some pleasure — was to pick up his ticket for the assembly that evening, which Miss North had apparently acquired for him by negotiation from the Master of Ceremonies. Her carefully considered plea to that august figure was that while she and Miss Wentworth would sadly have to be absent, this fine young man Hoare would bring suitable dash to the occasion.

If the MC remembered that promise, he may have found himself disappointed. It was not that Charles was averse to dancing. But he spent all of the evening hanging round the edges of the floor, moving inconspicuously from group to group, and languidly strolling into the card room, even into the corridors, dangling from his fingers a drink in which he rarely indulged. Only occasionally did he allow himself to answer inviting looks from the ladies who would have hoped for a partner, or might just prefer him to the one that they had. He waited for latecomers until well past midnight; there was no sign of Tregothen. By then his ankles were beginning to feel the strain of standing largely idle, and he was worried that he might start to be excessively conspicuous if he stayed longer. He left, frustrated again.

Colonel North slept little, troubled by the feeling that he was looking for a needle in a haystack — or perhaps a snake in the grass — spotted by one person but invisible to any others. Yet his confidence had carried him out of Devon and into Sussex at a pace, and he would not now let it slacken. He rose early, and rode briskly out of Brighton towards the Downs, impervious to the gaiety around him in the town, and to the growing grandeur of the scenery as he left the buildings of the town behind.

Stanmer House was imposing, in every way on a far larger scale than Colonel North's own Polton Court in Cornwall, yet its frontage was to a degree reminiscent of it, simple in design and unadorned. The Colonel did not feel ill at ease, but when dealing with those higher in society than oneself there was always the risk of coming away with nothing. The footman showed him through to the back of the mansion, and he was introduced into a small, private room with little furniture in it, just two comfortable chairs and a side table with a bottle and two full glasses of red wine standing on it. The small window, facing on to a court, gave it a low light. Lord Pelham was standing by it, and turned to face him.

'Ah, North, how d'y'do? Take a seat, will you? Decent journey, I hope? Roads in good order from London, or should be. Turnpiked, of course.'

'Most gracious, m'Lord, obliged to you. A pleasure and a privilege to visit Stanmer.'

'Yes, we are at home here, certainly in this season. Take a sip, North. Don't hang back. I keep a good cellar.'

''Tis very agreeable, m'Lord. Much obliged to you.'

'Now, to keep matters short and to the point — this man you are hunting, Tregorran, bit of a villain, you say?'

'Yes, my Lord. Tregothen.'

'As you say, Tregothen. What do we know of him?'

'A bad lot, my Lord. We can accuse him of assault and … worse. In Plymouth. And repeated those crimes, later. Jumped ship, taking a gullible young fool's fortune with him, and now… There is cause to wonder if he is responsible for another outrage. The young maid…'

'Yes, the Patcham murder.'

'Well, my sister Miss North wrote to me about it, as word of it had gone round the town.'

Here Colonel North sat forward, and placed his hands on his knees, gripping them tightly, his face animated.

'And at the same time, horrifically, she wrote to tell me that she had caught sight of Tregothen, after weeks of going undiscovered, at the Brighton races. This I disclosed to you in my letter, my Lord. I believe I should say…'

'Yes, thank you, North, that will do for the present. I have your letter here, and met your estimable sister at the races myself. Sit back, if you please, and listen to what I have to tell you.'

The Colonel breathed deeply, and determined on silence until bidden to speak.

'It is your belief that this villain may be responsible for the attack on this young woman at Patcham. Now it may surprise you that I have taken an unusual interest in this crime, to the length of speaking with the constable himself. He reports that a man dressed in the clothing of a gentleman, on horseback, was seen that evening by a party of hedge-cutters, one of whom at least was sober, and more especially by an apothecary, riding back from Patcham village. The medical man stated that the rider he saw seemed dishevelled, and appeared to be distracted when hailed in a customary manner.'

Colonel North looked directly at Lord Pelham, but said nothing.

'Let me just say that I have pursued these enquiries on behalf of a person of some standing and influence, recently here in Brighton, and whom I shall not name. It may surprise you to hear that this personage had come to the same conclusion as you: that this act of violation was carried out by none other than this Tregothen. Now what do you say to that?'

'I am dumbfounded, my Lord. We are all in your debt. May I ask why this person was convinced that Tregothen was responsible? Indeed, had heard of the man at all?'

Colonel North was, for the moment, seriously disturbed by the thought that news of the abductions of Amelia Wentworth or of Justin's Arabella had somehow become noised abroad in society. Lord Pelham took a good mouthful of his wine, savoured it, conducted an assessment of North, and came to his conclusion.

'I appreciate your questions. Let us just say that this elevated personage — and I want nothing further said of this — is a friend to a young woman of the theatrical profession, and that the unfortunate victim was her maid. This young woman, or actress as we might call her, will be known to you from Plymouth.'

'Good god! Forgive me, my Lord, I must catch my thoughts... I had not supposed that Miss Farley was in Brighton. I knew she was recovering, but ... the devil! Can it be?'

'Yes, it can very well be, or so my esteemed acquaintance believes. Tregothen had chosen this poor wretched maid to molest for the very reason that she was servant to the actress.'

'The poor soul. Can we be sure?'

'Your letter to me, Colonel North, and your sister's sharp eyes make me think that we can be sure.'

North swallowed the rest of his wine in one gulp, and replaced the glass on the table.

'What is to be done, my Lord?'

Lord Pelham stood up and walked across to the window. After a short silence, he spoke again.

'I believe I may have done all that I can. So, now, apart from the womenfolk, who must not be involved...'

'My sister has left for Cornwall, my Lord.'

'As I say, they must not be involved. I believe that leaves you as the only person we have with us who may be relied upon to recognise him. And so…'

Colonel North turned awkwardly in his seat to address him, and was again animated.

'My own acquaintance with him is slight. But I have another with me, to just that purpose.'

'You surprise me a little, but I am glad of it. You will face great difficulties in finding him, of that there is no doubt. But I have another piece of information, which may be of value to you.'

Lord Pelham came away from the window, and stood at Colonel North's shoulder.

'I take some interest in matters to do with the evasion of revenue. People come to me for authority: I have a role in London, and word gets out.'

Colonel North felt uncomfortable with Lord Pelham standing so close, but he remained silent and still.

'I have spoken to the Riding Officer for customs on this stretch of coastline from time to time, and the officers of the Shoreham Revenue cutter. And to assist them in carrying out their duties, I did place a man of mine in a village called Alfriston.'

Lord Pelham left his position, went to the side-table, and picked up his glass.

'The village of Alfriston is little better than a den of thieves. It is just up the river from the sea. We are speaking of smuggling, North, the rogues who prosecute the trade, making their peace with Frenchmen, landing spirits and whatever they do down there on the coast, notably at Cuckmere Haven. But never mind that. My man tells me that in recent weeks there has been a gentleman appearing regularly at one or another of the inns in Alfriston, the George or Star or somesuch, and that he has been drawing on deep pockets to gamble with leaders of the gangs there. They have taken to him, apparently.'

Here Lord Pelham ceased. There was no indication he would say any more. Colonel North was trying to weigh up all he had been told; he would need a little time to do that. But he was wrong about Lord Pelham's silence.

'Your presence here is fortunate, Colonel North. I shall now be able to inform my noble friend that I am discharging my own involvement into capable hands. I can do no more. You may speak with the Riding Officer, or to others of the Revenue, if that will be of help to you; but on no account may you approach my man in Alfriston. If you will wait in the hall, my steward will attend you, and inform you where you may find the Riding Officer. Good day, Colonel.'

Colonel North stood up smartly, and bowed to Pelham. He strode out towards the hall, his mind whirring, his blood stirred.

Colonel George North and Charles Hoare talked earnestly for an hour or two and were considerate enough not to be excessively impatient with each other. Charles was convinced that the gentleman appearing at the inns in Alfriston scattering coins around must be the man they were seeking. Colonel North proved more cautious. It might well be Tregothen gambling at Alfriston, but the Colonel could not believe that he would be lodging there: he had been seen at Brighton races, on the Downs, and perhaps at Alfriston, but had not been seen in Brighton town itself. North's military mind looked for a central position between the two places, and to his thinking that would be Lewes.

But why on earth was Tregothen wasting time and money in a disreputable hole like Alfriston, and not enjoying himself at the assemblies in Brighton? Charles suggested it might be because he wished to make money out of the smuggling, but the Colonel thought this was madness; Tregothen had money to spare. North's instinctive conviction, which again was military, was that in some way Tregothen was scared. It seemed an odd idea.

'Why would a man like Tregothen be scared, Colonel?'

'All men can be scared, both cool-headed and impulsive, brave man and coward. The totally fearless are merely fools. We should do better to ask what might have scared him?'

Charles scratched his ear. 'Well, Miss North — your sister, that is, Colonel — reported to you that he was at the races, in public, shameless, and apparently fearless. We have that.'

'Ay, we do. He may have seen someone there who knew him, but it is hard to think who that might be. Brighton is well away from the West Country, where he is known.'

'But why Alfriston in any case? We are becoming distracted.'

'Now there's a word,' said the Colonel grimly. 'Think, man, think!' This to himself, in frustration, and in fact the younger man respected him all the more for it: the upper ranks might be human, too. Then the light dawned.

'Why, I am such a fool! It is there in plain sight, sir, and we are going at it the wrong way round. He is not interested in goods being brought in, but in goods that may go out.'

'Say that again, Hoare, or I may not follow you. What goods, going out where?'

'Smuggling, sir, the key is in smuggling. Alfriston and smuggling!'

North was more than mildly irritated, but tried to restrain himself: 'We have been through that, Hoare! What on earth would a man like Tregothen want to smuggle?'

'Himself, sir. He wants to smuggle himself.'

Colonel North looked at this enthusiastic young fellow in puzzlement. Then, gradually, a fixed look came into his eyes.

'You are saying, Hoare, if I am not mistaken, that Tregothen is negotiating a passage, using the land-smugglers to clear a passage for him out on the luggers and schooners. They will be those that land goods at Cuckmere Haven. Why, man, you may be right! That is brilliant, Charles. By God, you may be right!'

North got up from his chair, took two large steps across, and clapped Charles on the shoulder, then returned to sit again on the worn, blue-satin chair. But he was still foxed, and slapped his knee in irritation.

'Yes, yes, but why? What is he scared of?'

'Of himself.'

North stared at him. 'What on earth would make Tregothen scared of himself?'

'It's the Patcham murder, sir. I think he didn't mean to kill the maid, sir. He went too far. He meant to frighten her, to whisper his name in her ear for her to take back to the actress, Miss Farley, sir, as you say, sir, to scare Miss Farley out of her wits. But something went wrong.'

This time Colonel North was muted, as he contemplated the horror of that country lane on a summer evening. Tregothen was out of control. And he was terrified.

CHAPTER XXVII: CUCKMERE HAVEN

If Tregothen was to get away to France, he would need a boat, and if Colonel North and Charles Hoare were right about his plan then it was going to be a boat involved in the smuggling at Cuckmere Haven. What that meant was almost certainly a date for large haul, because these boats surely did not run in to the Haven on their own, or casually. North took himself off to find the Riding Officer, as Lord Pelham had advised, and see what he might have to say about it. The season was surely good for a run, with the evenings shortening but the weather by and large benign. To occupy the time, Hoare rode away to Lewes, but if he had hoped to catch sight of his man, he was again disappointed.

North came back to the hotel primed by the Riding Officer. The Revenue was expecting a cocksure and braggart landing towards the end of the week, perversely when the moon was full. The gangs were apparently already boasting that His Majesty's Navy could come and watch them at it, for all that was to them, and mayhap learn summat an' all. It would be on a spring tide at night-time, which taken with the full moon gave a day that could be more or less certain.

The Colonel took the initiative to approach the commander of the Dragoons at Preston Barracks, who gave it over to a Captain Hardy to get things settled for a little piece of action for his men, who were bored with inactivity. With the Dragoons coming down hard on the land-smugglers, and the Revenue cutter taking on some of the boats, they could set them at sixes and sevens. But Hardy lacked confidence that his men would want to be cutting down Englishmen on the shores of their own country, Revenue or no Revenue. They would be game for giving the rogues a bruise or broken limb, which was no more than they deserved, especially those ruffians they called the batsmen.

Everything now seemed to be in place, as much as it could be. North and Charles Hoare rode out along the coast, and took new lodging in Seaford, to be closer to Cuckmere Haven. They even walked over Seaford Head to look down on the Haven, from a good distance in case they were observed. The only fly in the ointment was their nagging uneasiness about Tregothen: where he was, and what he would do. Whatever they felt, they kept their doubts to themselves. Then the day came, and they were ready.

As the afternoon drew on a light breeze sprang up, rising to stronger on the top of Seaford Head, and by dusk the weather had gone from clear to overcast. Silhouetted against the western sky Colonel North stood with Captain Hardy between their horses, the lines of Dragoons dismounted behind them with not a word being spoken, although grins flashed on some faces in the growing dark. The Riding Officer, sent on ahead, crouched with a Dragoon Corporal, two pairs of eyes being better than one — the Corporal charged with looking up the valley of the Cuckmere River, scanning the marshes with the mist hanging over them, and listening, the Riding Officer peering out to sea, watching for the masts of the Revenue cutter, trusting it did not turn in around the Head too soon. High tide was less than an hour off, but despite being a full sea it was not wild. They could just hope that the conditions were ideal.

Tregothen's head ached. He had never expected this, never known it before, and it was since that chit and what had passed in the lane. He rubbed his eyes, pressed his fingers on the ridge of his nose, ignored the others who stared at him when they thought he was not looking. He drank. The landlord had a brandy that was kept behind, and he had drunk it freely with others. They took his money for riding with them just as far as the shore, and told wily Tam to stand with him on the beach and strike a bargain in the breaking waves with one of the French boats they knew would be there. They would have his horse too once he had secured the passage. His French was no good, next to nothing, and he would not be able to tell one boat from another, as Tam could do. There would be a guinea for Tam, over and above what else he had paid out.

His head ached, and his mind cursed at the memory. The evenings were lighter back then, and she had not taken to him, so he had come on strong with her and the wrestling had him fired. He had meant to scare her, but his blood was up and he could not hold back, not then, not as it was — and then those peasants, most half-gone or more, in the lane. He remembered he had turned his head. She struggled with him, and tore her gown which he had in his hand. He swung round, grabbed at her with both hands, missed his grip; she tripped, he did not push her; she went backwards, fell back, and her head cracked on the gatepost.

He had heard later that she was violated: violated and dead. He had not done that. It was not him. He had wanted to scare her, to get at that Farley woman, he had seen her with the Farley woman, followed her, all that way — why would he do that? — he had not done that. His eyes were like they were made of lead. They must have come upon her body lying there, the peasants. He had heard of that, with dead bodies. Ghouls, foul, detestable ghouls. Or the constable, perhaps, his men, when they laid her out, left her on the slab. Not him. No.

It was time. The landsmen all moved, without a signal, or being told. Picked up their things and slipped out of the inn, and he saw yet another line of ponies coming down towards them. His horse was too large, really, he stood some hands above them, his own head large against the sky, a small pack lashed behind the saddle.

A young man, the whites of his eyes bright in the gloom, looked up from one of the ponies behind him. They had come in from the villages around, drunk ale in the yard. He knew of the gentleman at the inn, had heard, and now he was sure. He would have his man, would find the right time. He had spoken to her about it, quietly, and she knew, she was still there, and a lock of her hair was pressed against his heart.

The landsmen had a lookout at High and Over, as they always did, peering through the gloom, listening for movement up and down the Cuckmere Valley, for trouble ahead or behind, when they were loaded and on their way back, and then on beyond Alfriston and inland. The ponies made their scuffle, which you could pick up a long way off, but military horses had a clatter to them, and they were quicker by half. You had to have an ear to be any good, and a flask against the chill, and it was raised to his lips when a bludgeon hit him on the back of the head and a hand went to his mouth and other arms pinioned him, while yet another tied him up, wrists, hobbled too, a rag in the mouth and a gag tied behind. His eyes had fluttered briefly, but he had gone.

'Be snoring soon,' said one of the Dragoons. 'Peaceful, like.'

The sergeant glared at him: 'Keep it shut.'

The sergeant took his place by Charles Hoare. Hoare was not his officer, but he was an officer of sorts, militia, and that Colonel North with him was a proper man, no doubt about it. He would work contentedly with Hoare, and that would keep Captain Hardy happy. They lay down on the height and stared into the valley, eyes now well-accustomed to the poor light, a full moon filtering through the clouds, but not dark as night.

They both heard it at the same time. The lightest of sounds, and then another, from up the valley, as it should be, towards Alfriston. They held their breath, straining to catch some more. Yes, a harness jingling, and a strange kind of shuffle. No voices. The sergeant looked to Hoare, and put his thumb and his middle finger together in a satisfied gesture. They settled to wait.

The boats came in like ghosts through the mist. It would, in other circumstances, be an almost magical sight, and for a minute or two the Colonel forgot his anxieties and the deep spasms of rage that gripped his chest, and gazed out across the bay. One came in closer than all the others, chose to run along the shore to the east, and then turn back. He did not know the naval term for it, but a flanking manoeuvre came into his head, although he was aware how incongruous it was for a ship. The boat that came closer was one of the smallest, no sail, and it beached. They could just see the oars, and the men who climbed ashore and went to sit on driftwood and larger stones. One of the sailors began to walk towards their slope, and the Riding Officer and the Dragoon Corporal flattened themselves instinctively, the corporal signalling a warning to his captain some distance behind him.

The sailor came to a halt on some higher ground, with a view up the valley of the Cuckmere River, past the marshes. The

Riding Officer knew that the track ran to the western side, almost on the edge of the raised ground: this fellow was watching for the approach of the pony-trains.

A brief gap in the clouds shone light down on the edge of the marshes, and there, quite distinct under the glimmer of the moon, were the first ponies, the men trudging along at their heads and by their sides. Even their faces shone for a moment, and then the breeze took the gap in the clouds inland. The line drew closer; the sailor signalled to the crew on the beach, and walked up to meet the leading pony. The men stopped, talked, and then walked on together. The crew of the beached boat left where they were sitting, and clambered back in, pulling steadily at the oars. Almost at once, other small boats began to come into sight from behind the growing number of ships gathered in the Haven. They were obviously laden; their crews pulled hard.

The Dragoon Corporal and the Riding Officer crept back along the brow. The pony-trains were beginning to accumulate on the beach, men talking at their heads or in groups. The leaders strode along the edge of the waves, and as each boat drove itself ashore, gangs began to go to the cargo, earnest conversation taking place between one or two on the boats and the landsmen on shore.

The Dragoons were filing down the gap, still unmounted, as silently as they were able. The order was to proceed on foot until a cry went up, to leave as much time as possible for the sailors and landsmen to become deeply involved, hands full, minds occupied. Colonel North was at the head of the file, Captain Hardy just behind him. The captain passed word back along the line that they should now go two-by-two. Those to the front, just behind the officers, could see the nearest smugglers, and had their hands ready on bridle and saddle, faces pressed in some cases against their horses' necks. The moon remained buried behind the clouds, darker now than before.

A shout cut through the breeze, across the strand, but the captain held up his hand, sharply. On the other side of the Haven, they saw a scattering of men running down towards the back of the beach, and all eyes turned towards them, with sailors holding ready, and men running away from their ponies holding cudgels, others pointing, and flourishing cutlasses. The Revenue cutter had earlier landed some men to the east at Birling Gap; they had walked along above the Seven Sisters, according to plan, and waited to come down and round from Cliff End on to the beach. They were the diversion; it was a dangerous game, but the Riding Officer had been persuasive.

The Dragoons mounted; Colonel North loosened his sword in its sheath, and repeated to himself that lives were indeed to be spared, men struck with the flat, knocked down, but spared death or maiming where possible. Captain Hardy swung his arm down, and the Dragoons began to ride down hard on the flatter ground below the slope, aware that the shingle beach would be difficult.

The chaos was almost instantaneous. Barrels and tubs were dropped, and rolled madly for a few feet, some tumbling down a short slope into the sea itself. Crates and baskets were discarded, full or empty, and men ran in every direction. Three dull booms were heard out at sea, one after the other, and the Riding Officer recognised the guns of the Revenue cutter, aimed more at causing alarm than at damaging a vessel. Still, there were distant cries as one shot crashed into a larger ship, and the small boats clawed their way off the foreshore and plunged into the waves, the sea now larger than before, the onshore wind stronger. Some rode their ponies hard, heading for the back of the beach where the horses could not go, others trying to cross the river, which was low, to go back up the eastern side, over to Litlington and on. Some men were lying very still on the beach, or collapsed, holding heads or arms, none tending to them; one man was limping, another supporting him, until both of them were knocked down by a horse sweeping back along the strand, trampled on, and left.

Tregothen had his hand on the boat. A boy was holding his horse for him: trust nobody, give nothing away, keep a door open. His bag was in his hand. They were talking in low voices, and he might venture a few words himself on the voyage, but not now. Let the money do the talking. Tam, who looked like a villain of the first order, was not giving the Frenchman an easy time of it. Gestures, dismissive glances over to him, back to arguing. Another sailor chewed morosely, picked at his nose with his thumb, and then suddenly stood bolt upright, shouting and pointing along the shore.

He could hear the shouting, see men running. He spat out his frustration:

'Hurry, man, what is keeping you?'

Without answering, Tam broke off, swung round, and ran up the beach.

He tried to step in over the side of the boat, but the Frenchman stood in his way, pushed him back on the wet stones so that he slipped, and pulled a knife, swearing at him. The noise was bellowing all around him now, but breaking into it was the drumming of hooves, a rolling thud of trembling ground, and there they were, armed, uniformed, and dangerous. He ran for his horse, which the boy had left to pace wildly, grabbed the reins, holding the bag to his chest, swung into the saddle and looked for an opening. The horsemen were all over the smugglers on the beach, riding them down, some striking them on the head with their sabres. But no firing.

A madman came for him. He mounted quickly, and rode right at him, cramping his blow. He had no weapon himself, not even a knife from the kitchen. They collided. The man was covered in braid: a senior officer, who snarled and swore at him, tried to seize his coat, ripping a button. He struck him in the face, and the officer pulled back, the sweeping cut of the military sabre missing his body but slicing down his calf, with sharp and searing pain. He dug his heels into his horse's flanks, laid his head across its neck, and drove a path away from the madman and towards the estuary.

Charles Hoare had seen Tregothen from the back of the beach. He had ridden with his detachment of Dragoons hard along the track used by the smugglers and their ponies, to block their escape: no firearms, just circling back and forth, running men down, turning them back, chasing them into the marshes. He had a sword, and he had drawn it, waiting, standing high in the stirrups, and he had seen the taller rider heading up from the shore, on a high horse, not a pony. He urged his own horse forward, gathering speed, and the other rider pulled up sharply, seeing him, and swung his horse's head away, down towards the river.

It was the marsh which caught him. The horse had an instinct, it tried to turn away, but he kept its head back from that, so it reared and plunged and was mired worse, lashing, kicking, falling back. Tregothen swore at it, saw what he thought was firmer ground, held on to his bag and slid over its rump down on to it, a tuft of greener grass amongst the thin, pointed reeds. His foot slipped down deeply into the mud, and he went over on one knee. There was a voice from somewhere.

'She were our darlin'.'

A figure stood over him, young, probably ignorant, incoherent.

'Give me a hand, you fool! Just pull me out. Leave the horse. Come on, quickly now, what's the matter with you?'

The tumult was less obvious here, probably the rise and fall of the shoreline. There might be time.

'There's a coin in it for you, if you must. Come, take my hand.'

The numbskull had a branch, a cudgel, something like that. That would do, then.

'Here, hold that out. Go on!'

The fool was weeping. What was the matter with him?

'Hold that out to me! Now! That is an order, do you hear?'

The fool cried out, tore the sobs out of his body and offered them to Elisabeth, too late, so, so late, as he lifted her dear, darling limp body and laid it aside and away from him for what he had to do.

'I'm 'ere, sis, I'm here, you'll be right, I'm here now!'

With that, he swung the roughly adzed fencepost back and down on to Tregothen's head and shoulder, cracking it at the collarbone and tearing his ear away, cutting through to the skull. Tregothen gasped, and almost fell, but he seized the young man's leg and pulled him down into the mud, against the side of the desperate horse. There was a knife now, in the young man's hand, and he rammed it deeply into Tregothen's groin, but one bony hand wrenched it from him, and with a monstrous effort thrust it up into the lad's throat, where it lodged. The horse heaved, slipping over on to its side. Tregothen screamed in agony, and levered himself up on to its belly.

Charles Hoare stood silhouetted against a lightening sky. The moon broke though. He spoke very softly, to himself.

'Best to put the beast out of its misery.'

He raised the carbine.

Colonel North heard the shot from the beach, riding wildly as he was, in pain, blood streaming from his nose and cheek, amongst the chaos and the injured. He came to a halt, and the tears ran uncontrollably down his face in the fluttering light, bringing salt into the wound.

CHAPTER XXVIII: BAPTISM AND WEDDING

The baptism of Yaelle's and Grosjean's baby got off to a poor start when old Oanez strayed off the path and got stuck in the marsh. There was a lot of shouting and encouragement to her, each person having a better idea than the previous about the way out to firm ground, before Grosjean inevitably gave the baby back to Yaelle, who told him not to do it, waded out ankle deep, and lifted the old woman out to cries and cheering. They all knew Oanez was half-blind, but in the excitement they had forgotten about her. It was a long enough walk from the village for her to lose her way and blunder, after falling behind, hearing voices farther off around a bend and expecting to follow them straight ahead.

It was Yannic who then found Grosjean's clogs, which had the special leather decoration on them, and put an end to upset about the state Grosjean's feet and ankles were in, which was not pretty. The big man was waving all objection away, and taking swathes of grass to clean them off, much to Yaelle's chagrin. But Yannic had seen him lose his clogs almost as soon as he had waded in, and he managed to find them and retrieve them without getting stuck himself. So there was Oanez and Grosjean and Grosjean's festival clogs all to wash down, with some of the stinking mud on Yannic's arms and legs too, and *Père* Guillaume stood outside the chapel laughing at them, which made Yaelle laugh too, and the baby cry at the noise. Yannic took water from the well there, with the priest's permission, and borrowing Youenn's hat, he dosed them all in turn, although Yaelle made Grosjean hold the baby again while she took care of Oanez, with soothing words and gentle treatment.

Seeing the baby and Grosjean together was a marvel, since if you took away the beard and the bushy eyebrows, they were just the same, or so some of the women insisted: the little fellow certainly wrapped up well against his father's broad chest, encased in his strong arms. As was Grosjean's way, who was light on his feet and stealthy, he was as gentle as a saint with the tender creature, and those who knew always wondered at the ruthlessness he could show to those he considered his enemies. Thankfully, since his wounding, all of that seemed to be over, although some feared that it could come back again, heaven forbid.

As if to remind them, the Chouan captain, Jean Rohu, himself was there on the day, brought in by Erwan, who had more or less carried Grosjean from the fight near Grand-Champ. Not many knew Rohu, but word spread, and he was regarded with awe, his handsome profile backed up by few words. Babette cast a glance at him, wondering if this kind of man ever laid down arms, or could handle a scythe or a pitchfork in peaceful times with satisfaction. For his part, he was interested in her, and since Daniel had remained at the manor to detain any unwanted visitors he began to stand by her. She had little decoration on, but that did not matter to him, because she walked with an ease that for him was like beauty.

Yaelle and Babette were standing outside the chapel, and Babette looked at the baby and at Yaelle's happy face. It was all too easy to be envious.

'How is he?'

'Oh, he's fine, tired already, so he'll cry all-through, that's for sure.'

'Well, he's a dear, and at least he's not asleep for it. But I meant Grosjean. Did he get out in one piece?'

'You mean, does he stink of mud? He's not too bad. Here, hold him for a moment.'

The baby gawped up at Babette momentarily, or seemed to do so, but remained quiet. Babette felt awkward. He was small and warm, and a mixture of smells came from him. She had never suckled or cradled an infant, nor held this one before, merely gazing at him in his cradle before now, or in his mother's or father's arms. He was so tiny, and frail.

'There, best to put your arm like that, and your other one so. *Père* Guillaume wants to speak with us.'

People crowded round, wanting to see the baby, less shy with Babette than they would be with the baby's own mother. There was some pushing and shoving, one or two arms and hands held out to touch him. Suddenly, Babette felt frightened for him. She began to feel hot, and did not know which way to turn. The baby started to cry, and one of the women held out her arms to take him, and others spoke a word or two, and Babette could tell they were thinking that she did not know what to do, was not a mother. She held him tighter, flustered, made the noises she had heard others do, but he cried louder and went red in the face, and then Yaelle was there, smiling, and the women melted away as she took him back.

'There, we are all finished with the priest, aren't we, and you mustn't bawl at your *maeronez*, must you, little one? So, let's hope you don't smell too, or you'll make a right pair with your father, won't you?'

'Not for the last time, I expect.'

The chapel of Saint-Laurent could not hold them all, and they left the doors open for the service. Everything had been brought in for the day, because the chapel had been empty. It was close to Kergohan, although remote in its way, but they still did not dare to leave the forest or the fields to hold Mass in a chapel; the baptism was a shorter service, and that was partly why Rohu was there. He gave them confidence, although Babette had her doubts whether a man such as he warded off danger rather than brought it with him.

The talk subsided. The oil and candle were carried in, and Babette found herself standing next to Youenn, as godmother and godfather to the child. There were tears in her eyes; it was going to be as close as she would get.

When she had left Brandivy with Bernard on that terrible morning of Le Guinec's sudden death, Jeanne Cariou had found lodging again with Bernard's sister Anne Machaud in Auray. Bernard took to calling round there when he was spared from his duties at the Guèvremont house and sat quietly with her, holding the tips of her fingers gently and keeping his own strong feelings for her in check. He had waited half a lifetime for her, without quite realizing that was what he was doing; now that he had found her, patience should not be impossible. What mattered was that she was there; he would not ask for more.

He was dumbfounded when not long afterwards she asked him if they were going to get married. When she repeated the question, he could hardly believe his joy. He took the liberty of kissing her on the cheek to confirm his agreement, but he remained worried about the state of her emotions, and did not want to overwhelm her with his own. On the way back from his sister's house he tripped over a kerbstone, walked into a man around a corner, trod on a dog's paw and finally banged his head on a lintel once he was inside the Guèvremont house. The dog bared its teeth, and snapped at his heels, but he took no notice of it. Had someone poured a pail of water over his head and followed it up with the bucket itself, he would have found it hard not to embrace him.

Little by little, they discussed the wedding together. Bernard agreed to have a religious service despite his own reservations, because he was sure that it would help to lighten Jeanne's heavy sense of guilt. In that respect, it was vital that Gilles would be willing to attend the ceremony, and it was a great relief when he declared that he would be pleased to do so. Bernard's devotion to this anguished woman made Gilles re-examine his own feelings for Héloïse. If those close to him clasped those they loved to themselves without hesitation, why did he himself seem to make a virtue out of equivocation? Was it obstinacy? Or fear? Did he doubt that he was good enough, or that he was loved enough? As usual, and to his endless frustration, he found that he could not make up his mind about it.

Lieutenant Vernier carefully placed his small penknife at an angle against the quill, resting the broken end of the nib firmly on the surface of his worn desktop, and cut just the slightest groove with the blade in the hollow shaft above it. He held the feather tightly between his thumb and his fingers, and began to press down on the blade. There was satisfying feel to this one, after making a mess of two other quills which lay at his feet.

There was a sudden knock at the door, which was banged back against the wall heavily by a careless hand. The knife slipped, and the end of the quill split against the surface of the table. Vernier looked up angrily at the burly Sergeant of Gendarmes standing in the doorway, his bristling moustache drooping down on either side of his mouth like the tail of a stoat, bicorne hat under his arm, and a pristine red and blue uniform. An idiot, Vernier concluded. He swept the useless quill on to the floor alongside the others, took up his knife and snapped it shut.

'Sergeant. What can I do for you?'

'Thank you, sir. Obliged to you, sir.' The gendarme had not moved.

'Well, man, out with it, I haven't got all day.' Which was hardly true, if one excepted a date with a glass of wine and an excellent lentil soup at the Lion d'Or in about an hour's time; but a note of impatience would help to hurry things along. 'Do come away from the door, and while you are there, close it, if it is still on its hinges.'

'Yes, sir, excuse me, sir.' The sergeant gingerly pulled the door back and shut it quietly, and then came forward to stand just as stiffly in front of Vernier's desk. Vernier leaned back, yawned deeply, and placed his hands flat on the table.

'Lieutenant Noyet has sent you, no doubt. A message, information. Out with it.'

'Indeed, a bit of both, sir. Message and information. You asked after the priest, *Père* Guillaume, the one from the Landes.'

'Ah, yes, Guillaume, the renegade. What have you to tell me?'

'There has come to us word of a wedding. We heard of a baptism, but too late. As for the Masses that they hold, they move around…'

'And it is all too difficult. Oh, I am quite sure it is. Your men, being local, would never know in advance of something like that, would they?'

The sergeant shifted uncomfortably. Lieutenant Vernier ignored him, and carried on.

'So, there is to be a wedding. Well, we shall offer them a reception. Tell Lieutenant Noyet that I shall accompany you. I want some men on foot. The wedding will be held in the forest, I have no doubt, just like all these gatherings we somehow fail to find. Never mind the peasants — it is Guillaume I want. The couple, whoever they may be, can be left to come creeping back to the civil clerk, if they can wait that long. Is that clear?'

'Certainly, sir.'

'The day?'

'It is *quartidi*, sir. That coincides with one of their old Sundays. That is, in three days' time.'

'They still keep to their old religious calendar, do they? Why should we be surprised? That will be in the morning, I presume?'

'Yes, sir, about the eleventh hour. In the Landes — the forest that is, sir — above Brandivy.'

'Good. That will do, Sergeant. I shall discuss our deployment with Lieutenant Noyet, in a day or two. We do not want a little bird singing to the enemy about what we intend, do we?'

'No, sir. Lieutenant Noyet has been very strict, sir...'

'I am sure he has. Good day to you, Sergeant.'

Vernier looked down at the butchered quills by his feet. There was a lad in confinement who could sharpen pens, and his mother had been very obliging. One more little job for him, and perhaps one a little more intimate for his mother too, and then the boy could be released. Vernier liked to be known for keeping his word. He leant down, and swept up the feathers with his fingers.

Two days before the wedding, Gilles drove to Kergohan from Auray with Jeanne and Bernard's sister Anne in the carriage from the Guèvremont house. Jeanne had no maid, but did not need one, since Anne and Babette were determined to attend to her. Anne had insisted that Jeanne should have a Sarzou family wedding-gown, which had been handed down from her grandmother, and which she had worn herself. As a gesture of goodwill, Laurent Guèvremont provided money for a pair of shoes for the bride, aware as he was that she had no father or brother living, and Babette promised a shawl, should the weather begin to turn.

Bernard had no hesitation in taking Breton dress for himself, and on the morning of the wedding he was laughing with his brother Mael as they strode through the woods to reach the glade where *Père* Guillaume would be waiting for them. Babette was to bring Jeanne up from the manor where they had dressed her separately, along with Anne. Just to complicate matters, Gilles and Héloïse were nowhere to be seen, and Daniel had gone looking for them, with some urgency. They hoped that Gilles would step forward with the bride, releasing her from the past into a new life; but he had just said he would think about it, and no one had risked asking him again.

The rain came lightly, just as suddenly lifting away, leaving a bright but gentle sunshine. Gilles saw the women leaving the manor for the woods, but he was aware that Héloïse was not with them. After wandering around rather aimlessly, he came across her up by the cider press, through the orchard. She had picked an apple and was holding it in an absent-minded way. He called to her, and she lifted her head and bit into it, chewing as she stared at him. She did not move.

'What do you want?'

'I've come to fetch you. Babette and the others are leaving. We don't want to be late.'

'We, is it?'

'Well, we could walk up together. Like old times. It would be pleasant.'

'Do you want to hold my hand, then? Or is that too bold for you?'

Gilles stood still, staring at her, unsure what to expect, and scratched his head.

'Well, I can see you find it difficult to make up your mind. Just let your mouth hang open, and that will complete the picture.'

Héloïse laughed, tossed the apple to him, and began to walk past him. He caught it well, and bit into it himself.

'Be careful,' she said, 'there's a worm in it.' He took her by the arm as she passed, and she raised her head to his and kissed him fiercely on the mouth, then as quickly detached herself.

'It tastes sweet, though.' She tossed the words over her shoulder as she walked away down the path.

The gathering in the woods for the marriage ceremony between Jeanne and Bernard was small, since the women had decided it was better that way. As much as the villagers loved Babette, they remained cool about Jeanne, who had deserted her nephew Gilles for so long. On the bridegroom's side, the Sarzou family all attended: Anne was chatting to Babette and Jeanne, while Mael Sarzou stood to one side of the clearing, talking to their brother Bernard and laughing with him. They all looked up as Héloïse walked out of the woods, dressed in bright green and white; Babette ran over and kissed her on the cheek. Gilles strolled in arm in arm with Daniel, and they all gathered together.

Mael had been told that they would hear just one owl call, and that it would be soft. He had been listening out for it, and had heard the barking of a deer, way off behind the distant rocks, and the harsh call of a jay more than once, but nothing else. Yet there was the owl, faint but unmistakeable. Mael tapped Bernard on the arm and waved his hand to their sister Anne. Babette paid some final attention to the bride's hair, which was tied up 'like a silly young thing' as Jeanne had said, but beautifully, with a few ribbons and a little cap perched on top. Héloïse had picked a small posy for Jeanne of corn marigold and poppy, still surviving in the fields, which she had wrapped in a neat little handkerchief that she had found in a box in the manor.

They all knew instinctively that they were now being watched by *Père* Guillaume's lookouts, but there were no more owl calls. A man stepped out on the far side of the clearing and stood with his arms crossed, just as *Père* Guillaume could be seen coming slowly along the narrow path in front of them, with apparently none in attendance on him, but already robed. In fact, there was a lad just behind him, who was carrying the battered old bag used for the vestments and for the small cross. *Père* Guillaume came over to Bernard and put a hand on his arm considerately; he then went to greet the bride, who immediately sought a favour from him. The priest agreed. The boy brought up holy water in a small flask from the well at the chapel of Saint Lawrence, and poured it into a bowl, and Jeanne was blessed.

They made the decision to divide, with Babette, Daniel, Héloïse and Gilles on the bride's side, and the Sarzou family standing with Bernard. They shuffled a little, and fell silent, looking to the front towards *Père* Guillaume, who was facing the small cross now pinned to the trunk of the large beech tree, with his back to them. The air was warm, and the sounds of the forest mute, the sun warming their necks. *Père* Guillaume turned benignly towards his congregation, and Gilles offered his arm to Jeanne as the priest stood waiting for them, Bernard just to one side.

A sharp cry came from down the track to the manor. Owl calls came in from left, right and all around, and they heard what had to be horses crashing through the undergrowth, with shouts and curses intermixed. A lookout raced across the clearing, swept off *Père* Guillaume's chasuble unceremoniously and hustled him a short way into the woods, while the boy snatched down the cross and crammed the chasuble into the bag. He then took to his heels, leaping over fallen branches, his bag slung over a shoulder, while the lookout pulled a smock down over the priest's head and almost threw him into the hands of another man, who began to run with him along the path.

The horses could be heard loudly now, but from the sound there would only be two of them, three at most. Babette quickly fastened Daniel's belt around Jeanne's gown, tucking it up and in, and Bernard pulled her swiftly away, while Mael took Anne by the arm and quickly disappeared into the woods. Babette and Daniel followed them; by now, Gilles and Héloïse were nowhere to be seen. The first of the uniformed gendarmes broke into the clearing on foot, and stood there indecisively, as others slowly joined him. They had come through the gorse and the brambles, and slipped on mossy stones, and had tears in their uniforms and mud on their breeches, their hats awry or off. More came in on the opposing side of the glade, and stood there awkwardly, unsure of what to do.

The horsemen finally broke through and burst into the clearing. One was evidently a gendarme officer, dressed in a similar unform to the men on foot, and he reined in by them, mostly concerned with checking their number, as it seemed, which was not large. The other man rode his horse roughly and urgently around the clearing, pulling up and peering into the woods, and then driving hard into the undergrowth, cursing when the horse bucked and refused to go further. He swung round in the saddle and shouted furiously across to the two groups of gendarmes, and then rode up to the officer and swore blindly at him, pointing off into the woods. The gendarmes began to jog reluctantly down one or two of the easier paths; their officer pointedly ignored the other rider, and trotted his horse unhurriedly down a wide and empty path, until he too decided to come to a halt.

Lieutenant Vernier rode wildly around the clearing once again, looking through the trees hopelessly for signs of a straggler. He then muttered something to himself, and leapt from his saddle, holding the reins in one hand while he bent down to pick up a small object. It was the flask with the holy water. He opened it and sniffed, and then poured a little out into his hand. He tasted it with his tongue. He was hot. He poured it out over his head.

CHAPTER XXIX: THE WAITING IS OVER

Gilles and Héloïse had escaped from the raid on the clearing together; Héloïse had quickly tucked her skirt up and run like a hind. Gilles was no slower and no less agile, and they found it exciting to stay close together at a pace through the almost imperceptible gaps in the undergrowth. They began to head down and around towards the woods that stood some way above the manor, and they came out near one of the outcrops of rocks which they knew was called the Devil's Crag. Here they paused for the first time, a little out of breath, gasping, but exhilarated: Gilles stood still, listening. Héloïse came to stand by him. Then in the distance, and unmistakeably, there was the sound of hooves.

'Coming or going?' she whispered.

'Hard to tell.'

'Run or hide?'

He looked around. 'Hiding would be better. Whoever it is would not know we are here, unless we give ourselves away.'

Héloïse began to make her way around the rocks, and he followed her. There was a gap at one point, where the rocks were highest, and although narrow it led through to a kind of chamber. She led, squeezing through the crevice, and Gilles remained outside for a moment longer, listening. Then he put a palm on the rock and eased himself in. There was light from above, and no animals had sheltered in there. Héloïse shook her dress free, and spoke without looking at him.

'What was that about?'

He sat on his haunches, grateful for the rest.

'Hard to say. Maybe they were after the priest. They hate them most of all.'

'Who were they?'

'Mostly gendarmes, but I think I saw Vernier. The army lieutenant from Auray.'

Héloïse sat down too, but on a small, rounded outcrop.

'What will they do now?'

'Who? Oh, you mean Bernard. I cannot imagine.' He picked up a small stone, and bounced it in his palm.

'Frustrating.'

'Yes, I should think so. But he's waited a long time.' He began to scratch a mark on the rock to his side.

She got up, angered, and stared directly at him for the first time. 'How can you say that? How do you think they feel? How would you feel?' Then she made up her mind, irritated by his aimlessness. 'I'm going. Let me pass.'

He was upset by this outburst because he did understand: Bernard was his friend, and he himself also knew about waiting. She never allowed him any feelings; he was just a dolt, of course. He dropped the stone abruptly, stood and put his hand up, as if to stop her passing him, his face flushed.

'You do me an injustice.' She tried to push past, and he held her back briefly, which was exciting: her eyes were wide with anger, her breasts rising and falling. He could smell her warmth. She was increasingly irresistible once again, but he had to respect her, not give in to impulse. He clamped his teeth, released her in excruciating self-denial, and spoke instead: 'Look, I came to see you in Pontivy.'

If anything, her eyes were even wider; he had not noticed that she had not sought to free herself from him. 'What? You came to see me? Where were you, then?'

'It was by the chateau, on a day when you were there with Katell Floch and … her brother. I…'

She did not move away from him. 'And?'

'Well, I turned around and went away. He was sketching you, and … I was jealous. Like a fool. It does not matter. But I wanted you to know that I did come to see you.'

She considered this for a moment, her eyes not leaving his face.

'You know, I had wondered about that. You said "likeness" at the ball.'

'Yes, and that was another disaster, the ball. But I have nothing more to say. I do not want to get in your way. Anyway, it's probably safe now to…'

She seemed to edge closer to him. 'You have nothing more to say?'

He could smell her perfume against the dull but satisfying odour of the earth. He knew it would be on her neck, and he knew he could not even think about that, or he was lost.

'No, I…'

'Nothing?'

She was so close now. There was no doubt: it was the same perfume.

'Still nothing?' she breathed at him.

He put his hands flat against her shoulders, feebly, as if to keep her away from him. 'Oh, God, I want you, Héloïse. I can't help myself. Please don't torture me. You must have Roparzh if he is the man you desire, I know that. I keep telling myself, but it is very hard…'

Her mouth was close to his, her voice low. 'Roparzh Floch traded in sugar at Nantes. Sugar from the plantations at Saint-Domingue. His sister told me. He deceived me, totally.' Her lips were almost touching his, and she spoke softly, feather-light, fading away almost to a whisper, still gazing into his eyes, her own still very wide: 'Besides, I want to live at Kergohan, and you come with that property — or that's what I've been told.'

'So…'

She was a moment away from him, an intake of breath, and she kissed him with warm, sweet lips, and his head swam. She pulled back, but only for an instant, because he would not let her leave him, not now, putting his arms around her waist and letting her words drift voluptuously into his ear: 'Oh, for heaven's sake, what does a woman have to do?'

Outside, just as they lost all sense of time in a rush of blood, they could hear Daniel's voice calling to them, as if from another, distant world. By then they were locked together, and neither of them wanted to hear him, but Daniel was now only a few steps away, as if he knew instinctively where they were. Before they shouted to him through the gap, and squeezed out through it, they rested cheek to cheek, breathless, their hands entwined, and Héloïse agreed that she would be with him, that they would live at Kergohan, and Gilles swore to her in a surge of passion that he was devoted to her, and that the fragrance of her sweet body was in his heart and soul.

Laurent Guèvremont stretched out his legs underneath his desk, took out his pocket watch and looked idly at it, yawned, and listened for sounds of movement in the house. The young people were gone, as he had always expected. There had been an inevitability about his daughter's choice of Leroux, one that perhaps was part of the spirit of the changing times. It was at least a relief that the man had distinguished himself in battle, a rearguard action of some significance it was said, and had subsequently been promoted and appointed as an advisor to none other than Lazare Carnot, an *éminence* of the Republic charged with military affairs in the new, ruling Directory.

It was a significant advancement, for the time being, at least. Although later he might have to travel, Leroux was temporarily settled in Paris, and Laurent had allowed Joséphine to stay in the city with a Guèvremont relative of unimpeachable reputation, who had contrived to do enviably well in that dangerous environment. But he was absolutely determined that the couple should be married in Auray, where he could organize matters to his satisfaction.

The news of Bernard's disrupted wedding came as a surprise; but he had made a point of never asking too much about anything of that kind, since the military had been involved, futilely, it seemed, which was probably for the best. In any case, Bernard was now installed as a vintner down towards the harbour with that woman Jeanne, after a far more sensible civil ceremony. He would no doubt benefit from the assurance of his former master's patronage, and his influence amongst the better class of citizens in the town.

But the fate of his ward Gilles proved to be the most satisfactory. For him to choose, freely, to unite with young Héloïse Argoubet was, as the proverb had it, killing two birds with one stone. Laurent could now see why that sly rogue

Lafargue had pursued her with such enthusiasm. She was an heiress of no mean proportions, and had wisely now sold her properties in Saint-Domingue — or, rather, Daniel Galouane as her uncle had done it for her. The mortgages which Laurent himself had settled on the larger plantation meant that she would not inherit that; but the lands passed over to her by her father before his death had not been similarly entailed. He could wish that he had known of their existence before; but in truth it was well enough as it was. Kergohan could belong to Gilles and *Mademoiselle* Argoubet, and it would cost him nothing more: her money would sustain them both.

Laurent sat up more imposingly behind his desk at a knock at the door, and called out his permission to enter. The young maid Gaëlle trod in carefully, dressed in a neat petticoat, apron and cap, holding the tray on which were his habitual morning coffee and its sugar. She looked up at him nervously.

'Excuse me, *monsieur*, but where should I place this tray?'

Her voice was pleasant. He had come to appreciate that local accent, so long as it was not too marked.

'You might place it on my desk here, Gaëlle, for I shall be continuing with my papers. Bring the tray round, next to me. There, that will do very well. You need not pour; I have everything I require.'

She curtsied to him quickly, and just as quickly tripped back across the polished floor towards the door.

'Ah, Gaëlle, I recall there was something else.'

Gaëlle turned, and replaced a lock of hair under her bonnet.

'Yes, *monsieur*.'

'Come a little closer, I do not wish to shout.'

The maid stepped cautiously forwards, to stand just across the desk from Guèvremont. He steepled his hands, and looked at her severely over the top of them.

'It has come to my notice that there is a young man who is seen here rather frequently. Is this the case, or would you deny it?'

Gaëlle started to tremble. She did not know what to say, and in her terror could not have formed the words.

'I see. This is no relative. A young man who makes a nuisance of himself around the kitchen, and has adopted — what should we call it? — a familiar air.' Guèvremont scratched his nose briefly between finger and thumb, and then placed both hands flat on the desk, and leaned forwards slightly.

'Let me be quite clear: there must no improper behaviour in my employ. Nor, indeed, any suggestion of it. There are others, many of them I am assured, who would be flattered to have a position in this household. Do you understand me, Gaëlle?'

Her 'Yes' was only a squeak, but they both heard it.

'Good. This young man must not be seen here again, and I shall have you attend more closely to me now that your mistress is away in Paris, to make quite sure of your conduct. We must make something of you. Do you understand?'

She nodded, bent her head, and curtsied.

'Do not disappoint me, young woman. That would have most unfortunate consequences. Now, you may go.'

The door closed behind her. He found that he felt a little warm. He removed his coat, sat down again and poured himself some coffee, dropping the sugar in piece by piece.

Babette crept off during Bernard and Jeanne's cheerful wedding feast, which they held at Kergohan, after a civil ceremony in Auray. Even though it was nothing, as the tears came into her eyes she found herself being sick. When she went back inside Old Gwen stared at her and cackled, slicing the pat of fresh butter with a broad knife, and muttering to herself. Babette silently wished her at the devil, but caught Daniel looking over at her, and smiled at him shyly as she wiped her eyes. Yaelle wisely said nothing, but put her arm round Babette's shoulders, and squeezed hard. Héloïse pulled the rolls and the tarts out of the oven in the kitchen, and tossed one to Gilles, who grinned back at her. Babette did not wait, but bit into a roll greedily, never mind the butter, and for some odd reason she found herself laughing and crying at the same time.

CHAPTER XXX: HMS *AMPHION*

The press of people on board was remarkable, and Amelia wondered if naval life was all like this, wives and sweethearts and children welcomed and feted in laughter and tears, and then sent away for heaven knew how long to fend for themselves. It was, for the time being, very much like a party, with gay dresses and ribbons abounding, children running up and down the decks and stairways, babies held in arms and kissed by doting fathers along with their mothers, who might make a show of protesting mildly, or simply ignore any looks they were given. Indeed, who in a gathering of this sort would bother to give the time away to staring at others when a dear one was close at hand? Short of impassioned caresses there was much warm intimacy, not least on the public decks, helped in many cases by the contents of flasks and bottles, thrown gaily overboard when empty to find their way down to the glutinous harbour mud.

Justin had come with her, and she was glad of it. They had found Eugène, under guidance, in the gunroom of the frigate, which was packed with junior officers and loud and warm, and although he had laughed and clasped Justin joyfully by the hand, he had given a small bow to Amelia, and addressed her in a sober way as Miss Wentworth. His face looked sombre, and their conversation had been of formalities. But he had relaxed briefly when he had introduced one or two of the naval officers with cabins next to his, if you could rightly call a small, boxed tent a cabin with any confidence. Privately, Amelia was appalled by the cramped and airless conditions of their mess, the tight corners and low ceilings of the ship in general, and what was undeniably the strong odour of too many men gathered together in too little room.

Eugène must have felt her discomfort, because he suggested a turn on deck, heading for the steps, which were steep but which appealed to Amelia's childhood memories of climbing. Justin waved the two of them away, since he was engaged in some kind of discussion with one of the naval lieutenants. It was refreshing to be out in the air again, and Amelia grasped at her bonnet as the breeze caught at it, with Eugène quickly holding her steady. The ship was lying alongside another one that was mast-less and quite close to what they called the jetty, so it was hardly rolling, but occasionally it heaved and groaned a little.

'Come with me,' he said.

They climbed up at the rear of the ship, on to what Eugène called the quarterdeck, and as they did so Eugène whispered in Amelia's ear 'Captain Pellew'. The captain was standing with another officer at the front of the quarterdeck, and both men bowed to her while not much interrupting their own earnest debate. Eugène helped Amelia up on to the small deck behind, right at the back of the ship, on which there was a slanting flagpole. She stood with her hand on the rail, looking out over the bright extent of the harbour at Plymouth, up the Tamar river and then across to the land opposite, with its glimpses of a large house at the top of the slope. She thought she might have crossed from there by ferry when she had first come to Plymouth. The sun was bright, the sky clouded in part, the air warm in the light breeze. The curls in her hair danced around her cheeks; Eugène stood beside her, and she spoke to him in as light a tone as she could devise.

'My brother tells me that you are to serve as a marine. I am not sure that I know what that is, except that I can see you have a different uniform. Justin said something about a marine being a soldier at sea.'

Eugène smiled at that. 'In my case, I should think that is an apt description. All at sea, I should not wonder. Yes, your brother helped me secure the commission.'

'And there was a friend, he said. At Chatham. A Major Houghton?'

'Francis. Francis Houghton, Major of Marines, the Chatham Division. He found an opening for me here, in the Plymouth Division.'

Amelia nodded, but her thoughts were elsewhere. She gazed across at the inert bulk of the ship next to them and spoke with a tremor in her voice.

'I did not know, Eugène, until Justin informed me. Of your plans, that is. It was remiss of me. My memory does not always serve me well, but I believe I may have… There may have been something wanting in the manner in which I addressed you when we last met. If so, I owe you an apology.'

Eugène's face was like a mask. Behind them, Captain Pellew and his companion left the quarterdeck, to be replaced by a younger naval officer with a young woman and a child of seven or eight years, the officer pointing out the sights. Amelia tightened her hand on the rail, but her eyes remained on the horizon.

'Why are you doing this, Eugène? Am I to blame? It will be dangerous…'

Eugène plucked up the courage to face her.

'It will be exciting. The Americas are unknown to me, I am young, I may discover something there that will further my ambition, lift my spirits. But that is enough of me, Miss Wentworth. How did you in Brighton? I have heard it is lively and fashionable. All the world goes there now.'

'So they do.'

So much remained unspoken and unresolved that there was a silence. Eugène cleared his throat.

'We must soon go down again. Let me take your arm. But I am forgetting myself. How goes your writing? Justin mentioned a disappointment a little while ago with a publisher, for which I am most sorry. All that effort … but I expect you have an answer to that.'

'It is kind of you to ask. But I have just recently received a letter from the publishers of *The Lady's Magazine*, in acceptance of the story I submitted to their judgement.'

'Why, that is wonderful! May I congratulate you, and heartily? You deserve no less.'

He had taken her hand in his enthusiasm for her triumph and held it between both of his. She looked down at their clasp, and he slowly lifted her hand to his lips.

'You are a marvel.'

'If it is marvellous to change the setting of a story from France to Italy, since Italy is in fashion and France is not, then I shall accept your compliment, sir. Yet the truth is that I know nothing of Italy apart from what I have read. That will have to do.'

'You may say that, but will France be anything more than a memory soon for either of us, or for many more?'

'That is all too true. You will write to me, Eugène, if talking will no longer be possible. I shall be waiting for you… For your letters to arrive, that is.'

'I hope they will entertain you, Miss Amelia. I have but a rough style. We should go down, and Justin will be wanting to leave.'

He took her hand in his, but with a quick glance behind him Amelia used his grasp to pull him towards herself. They stood inches apart. She brushed his hair from his face, placed her hands on his shoulders, and kissed him passionately and breathlessly on the mouth. He gasped, but before he could respond she released him, and walked tearfully past to the head of the steps.

Justin had met Colonel North in London, and heard from him of the ghastly end met by Jowan Tregothen. They had identified the lad who had followed and fought with him at Cuckmere Haven as the brother of the maidservant whom Tregothen had assaulted and killed; but no one could be sure how young Ned had first found him. Lord Pelham had spoken with Colonel North again after the events at the Haven, and they had agreed to provide means for the burial of the brother and sister. North had stood by the graveside to pay his respects. Charles Hoare wished ardently to be there, but he had been summoned back to his duties now that his presence was no longer required by the authorities; it was a harsh and unfeeling decision, but predictable.

Subsequently Pelham made inquiries, and it seemed most likely that Ned had heard talk of an unfamiliar gentleman on horseback seen on the fateful evening of his sister Elisabeth's death, and from there had worked things through from Lewes — where he was a stable lad — to the inn at Alfriston. It was indeed possible that Tregothen had been identified by his horse. The poor creature did have some distinctive markings, which could well be remembered; but all remained quite uncertain. The matter of the shot that must surely have brought Tregothen's life to an end despite his other grave injuries was also left unexplained. Pelham undertook to write to Tregothen's father and his brothers with an account that made brief reference to the action of the Revenue men. He received a reply which insisted on further provision being made to the family of the brother and sister, and Pelham undertook to see it done.

Colonel North knew from Pelham that the young woman Elisabeth had been serving as maid to an actress staying at the New Inn in Brighton, under the shadowy patronage of a person of some standing. Whatever the identity of that individual, North made it clear to Justin that the actress was no other than Thirza Farley, whom Tregothen had assaulted so abominably in Plymouth. George and Caroline North conferred on this topic, and their terrible conclusion was that Tregothen had seen Elisabeth in the company of Miss Farley, on whom he must have been spying as he had been on the Wentworths before the abductions. Quite what he had intended by pursuing the maid down a lane near Patcham heaven alone could tell; but his actions might possibly be connected with frustration in finding Miss Farley in the care of a powerful protector.

They eventually decided that Caroline would inform Amelia of the death of Tregothen, and give her some account of the circumstances leading to his end. That it had been sudden, none could realistically conceal. With some luck, word might spread that associated Tregothen with the trade in contraband on the south coast, and specifically at Cuckmere Haven. Such a story would be near enough to the truth to remove any occasion for further curiosity, and might well develop over time into something of a local legend.

Justin had found that carrying the news of Tregothen's demise back to Arabella in Devon had conveniently obscured the need to account for his own extended absence on the Isle of Wight. Arabella listened to what was a fuller account than that given by Caroline North to Amelia, with a face that betrayed no emotion. When Justin had concluded, and tentatively held out his hand to hers, she had folded hers on her lap.

'The poor child,' she said. 'And that poor boy, too, her brother. I would that I might meet their mother, albeit consolation is not possible.'

'There is no mother. Nor father either. Only the grandmother. George North has been to see her. He stood with her at the lad's grave. He and Pelham will do something for her. Tregothen's father, too.'

'What can they do? The memory stays with you, and will not fade. She has lost her life, in truth, and no doubt feels she has betrayed her daughter's trust completely. When it comes to the point, there is so much you discover that you could not prevent.'

Justin rose from the end of the chaise where he had been sitting.

'I must see my mother. There are certain things that it is better that my sister does not know, and my mother may be in touch with Amelia herself.'

'Yes,' Arabella replied absent-mindedly. Then, 'Why? What should she not know?'

'That Tregothen died in the way that I have described to you, leaving little out. That the young woman he assaulted fatally was Thirza Farley's maid. That kind of thing.'

Arabella sounded harsh: 'Why should your sister not know what I can know? Do I not have her sensibilities?'

Justin perched once more, this time on the side of the chaise, and nearer his wife. 'You may well have an equal sensibility, but Amelia has no companion.'

'Twaddle, sir! So I shall not have my nerves trying me because you sit with me at breakfast and lay your head on my pillow at night, and that only when I choose to permit such a thing in the lamentable condition in which I find myself! Off you go, off to your mother, and see if she will indulge your fancies better. Leave me to my dullness of spirits. No more, go!'

Justin and Amelia stepped into the carriage that was waiting for them at the Dock. He found himself unaccountably dwelling on that conversation with his wife, wondering how it was possible to get so much wrong when one said so little. Arabella had been contrite when she spoke to him later that day, and he had held her hand, but she was flushed and abstracted after dinner, and would not join them at cards. That was, no doubt, to avoid further attention from the vicar, Cradock Glassnott, who had dined with them that evening — as Arabella chose to believe — in gleeful anticipation of more cannon-fodder to come for his baptismal font.

While the carriage rocked them easily along the streets near the harbour, and away toward Plymouth itself, Justin mused inwardly on a growing conviction that both Arabella and Amelia had been harmed by their violent experiences at the hands of Tregothen and his followers. They might well be damaged beyond appearance in ways that he had seen with some men who had been involved in the horrors of warfare. Why should that not be the case? He risked a glance at his sister sitting across from him, and recognised that he did not know what she was feeling, as thoughts and emotions flickered over her expressive face. How could people be so dear to you, and yet remain so enigmatic?

The carriage lurched round a corner, and the driver shouted at an offending pedestrian, who raised his stick and made an attempt to strike at the side of the vehicle. They were nearing their destination in the townhouse of the Norths, and Justin broke out of his brown study, leaned forward and spoke to his sister.

'How long shall we be staying with George and Caroline, do you think?'

Amelia started slightly, and then smiled at him.

'Why I had not thought about it, to be honest. But you must be wanting —'

She broke off and instinctively reached out a hand to a side-strap, because the whole carriage was astonishingly shaken on its wheels as if by a monstrous earthquake, which was accompanied by a deep, growling boom of a kind she had never heard before. The carriage pulled to one side abruptly, and in that moment they stared at each other in astonishment, surrounded by shouts and running feet. Amelia felt her heart pounding, and her eyes searched those of her brother for understanding. He took her hand and kissed her on the cheek.

'You must go on to the Norths, and stay inside the house until I come back to you. Will you do that for me?'

Amelia nodded, not knowing what else she might do.

Justin sprang out of the carriage, gave instructions to the driver, and then spoke to his sister again as he threw his coat through the open door.

'Stay inside the house. I shall be with you shortly.'

The driver clicked his tongue urgently, the carriage pulled sharply away, and Justin started to run back towards the Dock. There was then a second explosion, and the red glow of flames lit up the sky in that direction, with black, oily smoke snaking up amongst the obscured white clouds behind. More were now running with him, men, women and children too, although some mothers held back their excited young sons while others stood at their doors with fear in their eyes. The nearer he came, the greater the terror and the throng, and the roar of the flames mixed foully with the screams of the wounded and dying, and the shouts of those who were desperately tending to them.

What lay in front of him was, incredibly, the remains of the *Amphion* — on which he and Amelia had just now been standing — blown all to pieces, a charred, reeking and flaming wreck, as was the hulk moored next to it. The deck of that ship was a charnel house, and he recalled that no skirmish or even a battle was as appalling as the effect of an explosion, which tore limb from limb and bathed the remains of bodies in blood and entrails. At a glance he could see that there were some who were whole but already quite dead, while others were horrifically maimed but still clinging miserably to life, as hope inexorably ebbed away. The noise was hideous, of screams and begging and cries of agony, while the men and women who had found their way on to the hulk were frantically searching for their loved ones, or could be seen clasping a child to their breast, and wailing piteously.

An experienced eye gradually told Justin that there was little that could be done. Most were dead, in so far as there were even partly intact bodies to be seen, and there were, ominously, no cries for help issuing from the water. Carts were taking away the dead, and even the crowded deck of the hulk could not conceal that many must have been consumed by fire in the cramped confines of the frigate, already crushed or torn apart by the force of the explosions. But if he could not save many, he might look for one, and he tried to avoid slipping as he moved forward, looking urgently for a red uniform. But how to search for red when so much was red, stained from a different source? Here there was a uniform, blackened on a savagely torn torso, a marine, it could be no other — but there was nothing on it to signify an officer.

Something made him turn, to look away from the fierce heat of the *Amphion* under his scorched feet and out beyond the end of the jetty. There were too many floating bodies there for any comfort. Suddenly a voice at his shoulder said: 'Do you see him?' He became aware that there were now uniforms on the hulk's deck, and the speaker was a young marine corporal, whose face was white and drawn.

'Is that thing alive?'

It seemed like the bloodied mimicry of a human face, blackened too, but surely showing expression. A mouth that moved. Justin ran forward, threw off his burnt shoes, and dived off the deck away from the jetty, surfaced, and swam toward where the corporal was pointing. He went under in order to come up from below on whatever was left of a human being, but to his relief his hands felt legs, knees, an arm in a red sleeve flailing at him, and above it a head that floundered in and out of the wreckage gathering by the jetty, badly cut, and with hair burnt away on one side. The face spluttered and sobbed, and then that arm came round his shoulders, and the head rested against his, the voice gasping but unmistakeable.

'Better … late … than never, *Monseigneur* Franglais.'

A small group of marines now gathered around the corporal on the hulk in their red coats raised their arms in a cheer. Justin eased his way from the timbers of the jetty and swam slowly on to the waiting shore, his arm wrapped tightly around his friend.

CHAPTER XXXI: THE LIMITS OF DECORUM

The ceiling, if that is what it was, was misty, and moved up and down, and at times around, so he closed his eyes again. It would help if he could be sure where he was. At times it looked like the ceiling in his old room in the house in Tours, at times like Dick's room in London, and at other times like the captain's cabin on the ship, low and menacing. His head, too, seemed to swell with throbbing, and then to shrink back in as the pulses ebbed, and his eyes were adrift somewhere in that sea. But that was nothing to the excruciating pain in his leg and his shoulder, which at times blinded him in its searing fury, and then seemed mysteriously to vanish, and leave him in peace. The noise in the room was odd too: hissing at times in his ears, but then complete silence. Should it be that silent? If he could be certain where he was that would help. London it might be, not France — that was surely mad, merely a memory — but why did he not know where he was when he could remember the fire, the acrid stink that came with it, the bodies…?

Eugène could hardly turn on this bed, but he heard the footsteps, then some soft talk outside, the door creaking and more footsteps. But why on the wrong side? He could not turn his head to look. A cough, certainly, but why on that side? The pain twisted his mind into a blank paroxysm, and then…

'This is a rum go, old man.'

The voice he knew, quite certainly, but it was not his father, it was…

'Hair will grow back, mind you. Right as rain. No complaints there. No bones…'

'The other side. The wrong side.' His own voice was a croak, pitiful, pathetic.

'What sort of side? No, no, I am on your side. One of yours, you know.'

Francis, it was Francis. It had to be Francis, no mistaking… What was he doing here, in Tours, of all places? No matter, but…

'I know who you are. Come here, Francis, dammit man, on this side, here.'

Houghton levered his long frame up, lifted the small wooden chair on which he had been perched up above his head and walked round to the other side of the bed. He could now see Eugène's face, and most of it seemed to be in place, which was not always the way it was in these cases, and was a relief to him to see it, the soft-hearted, square-jawed, lanky gentleman's son of middle-years that he was. He pushed his fingers through his thinning hair, put one bony hand on the bed, and pulled the chair under him up to be more or less level with that blistered, mottled mask inside which his friend still breathed and spoke, and was amazed.

'Well, I'll be damned, the creature has a voice. I won't be listening to you singing a ballad, my dear fellow, if you'll forgive me that. But from the sound of it you're on your way back to barking an order, I'll be bound.'

Eugène felt the sting of tears in his eyes. His head ached as if it would burst, and stabbed at him as he turned slightly, a change from the seething torments of his leg, whatever might be left of it.

'All in one piece, then. Bloody miracle. "Somone looking down on him". That's what I said when they told me about it. Bit of a dent in the skull, but might shake some sense into you, you never know. Told your father I'd write to let him know how you are getting on. Thought I should stop in on the way here. Odd cove, your father, if you'll forgive me. He seemed worried you might take against him, blame him for everything — wanted to know how things stood between you before he ventured down here, believe it or not. You'll best know about that. He'll be here in a jiffy if I slip him the word. Still, manners of a gentleman, I'll give him that. But I'm tiring you, mustn't go on like a parade sergeant.' Houghton stood up again, one hand on the back of the chair, lifting it slightly. 'Damn glad to see you living and breathing, old man. Now don't you trouble about anything. I've had permission from your commanding, and I'll be watching over you. Guardian angel, and all that.'

'Thank you, Francis.'

'Think nothing of it. On second thoughts, I'll leave this here.' Houghton placed the chair in what he thought was a sensible position, not too near and not too far from the bed. 'There's a lady waiting outside to see you. Send her in, shall I?' He turned away, and then half back again. 'God bless, old boy.'

What lady? It couldn't be his mother, she was dead. He knew that. Yet there was a memory ... he was lifting someone young out of the water, clasping her, dripping, but she felt ... as if she was part of him.

He had closed his eyes in the strain of remembering, and the fire was scorching at his shoulder again, but he heard the rustling of skirts, the quiet: was there breathing? And a scent, a scent of flowers, not the stench of burnt flesh and tar seared for ever into the scorched cavities of his nose...

He forced himself to open his eyes.

He knew who it was suddenly. But he could not see her, because she had walked past him, on the wrong side, to the window. He could hear her breathing, as if she was standing by him. That was strange. But he dared not speak. The sun broke through, and the room shone with light, so he winced and half-closed his eyes, and strained to hear any sound. She gasped, he was sure of that, but then the footsteps came back towards him. Like Francis, she stood on the wrong side. Her voice was like balm to him.

'Eugène, they have let me see you. I pleaded with them, with Justin too.'

He did not know how to reply. How could he say that she was all that mattered, now he was alive again? How not to offend her, as he had done before? He had no need to answer because she continued.

'I … heard. Oh my God, I thought you were dead, with those poor…'

'Amelia, I cannot turn over. As yet, it is too painful. Come to my other side, I beg you, then I may look upon your face.'

He heard her movement, and there she was in a russet gown and no bonnet, her eyes wide, her cheeks flushed, it seemed to him. She leaned forward to kiss him, on the side of his head where he still had some hair, and few burns. Her scent was an elixir that he drank in, and as she lifted her head, he felt her tears on his face.

'How many lived, Amelia? No one has told me. And where am I? For the love of God, I have to know. You were there, you saw…'

'Captain Pellew … and a few more, I have been told. No more than that. It is ghastly. I am so sorry, Eugène. This is all my fault…'

His voice was still a croak. 'Where am I?'

Amelia sat down, and placed her nervous hands on her lap.

'The hospital, Eugène. They have put you in the Royal Marine Barracks. We are in Plymouth, where you were.'

'Ah.' Some relief flowed into him. Despite it all, he had not lost track of things.

'How long, Amelia? How long have I been here?'

'Some days, Eugène, perhaps nearly a week. Justin and then Francis were by your side. I like Francis greatly; he is a good man. You have good friends, Eugène.'

She stood up, and walked past the head of the bed once more to the window.

'Do you know, Eugène, I was here in Plymouth, not so many months ago — just over there, I think, in the assembly rooms. They call it the Long Room, I believe.'

She caught her breath again, in that strange way.

'He is dead, Eugène. Tregothen. They found him and … he is dead. So it is over.'

She came back to sit by him.

'I cannot leave you, Eugène. I will not.' She reached for his hand, which was less scarred than much of his body, and placed her other hand over it. 'You are far too dear to me. I should have known. I should never have sent you away. You said you would protect me, do you remember? Well, my love, I should have protected *you* from all this, to my shame, and now… We shall heal. We shall heal together.'

He squeezed her hand.

'Amélie?' He spoke faintly, so she bent over. 'But your suitor? Mr Richard Bevington, I believe? Forgive me, I must not…'

She looked at him closely, and for the first time, she smiled. 'My suitor, is it? Oh, Eugène. Mr Richard Bevington has sailed for America, to save more souls. And as I recall, I did not kiss him goodbye. Passionately, on the mouth. A liberty which I ventured to take with a handsome young marine officer of my acquaintance, not far from this very spot. Quite beyond the limits of decorum, as I recall.'

'Yes, quite beyond the limits,' said Eugène. 'But —' and his words were barely perceptible, he was now so utterly exhausted — 'the two of us have never been very strong on decorum, have we, Amélie?'

'I sincerely hope not,' she said.

Amelia and Eugène were married in the church in Marylebone. Francis was Eugène's best man, while Justin gave his sister away, and laughed with her at the silliness of the phrase. The Comte had provided a place for Eugène in his various enterprises, mostly to do with import and export; they might live comfortably in Bristol, or if they were lucky, in London. The Comte had fortunately not been listening when Eugène described himself sardonically to Justin as now being a *bourgeois* in the making. Dick Courtenay sent his love to the couple, and at the reception Alphonse was talking gaily to a lively Thirza Farley, sporting a flamboyantly ribboned hat.

It was a matter of only a week or more later and the Wentworth family was gathered together again at Chittesleigh, not just for the beginning of Christmas on Saint Nicholas Day, but also in attendance for the birth of the child. There had been no other way, because Sempronie and Amelia had insisted on being on hand in the house, and Arabella had to stifle her objections to 'dropping her calf in the middle of the herd', as she had so tartly and improperly put it to her husband.

Justin himself was pleased to have Eugène under his eye, as well as his sister, and he began to set his friend to fencing for the exercise. There was a short gallery at the back of the house that was ideal for that exertion, with some of the older paintings hanging in it. Justin had discreetly asked for the mirror to be removed from its place on a wall nearby, although the terrible burns were healing remarkably well.

So it was when the cry of the child was at last heard, and those in the house could finally relax on reassurances from the doctor and raise a glass to the baby, that Justin climbed the stairs to the gallery with a letter to his father-in-law in his hand, signed by both him and Arabella, with the name they had chosen for their daughter: Hortense. It would be sent in the morning, and Arabella's groom Andrew would carry it in person on Black Diamond along the edge of the moor to Alverscombe Hall.

Justin stood for a moment quietly in front of the portrait of his maternal grandmother, her bountiful fair hair gathered up high in the style of the time, an open volume of the letters of *Madame* de Sévigné in her lap. It was supremely comforting to have the family around him. He breathed in deeply, and wondered lazily what his daughter Hortense would come to look like in time. Then he turned, and walked back down the gallery, tapping the letter thoughtfully on the back of his hand.

HISTORICAL NOTE

There is so much of historical interest in the 1790s that it is hard to know where to begin. There are always facts, of course, but I am myself struck by the web of unfinished business, such as the new egalitarian French government's wavering attitude to the liberation of slaves in its colonies, and the grindingly slow campaign for the abolition of slavery in Britain. What matters is the struggle that is required, and those who become involved in it, which lights a way through the dark tunnel. These four books hardly scratch the surface of what happened in Saint-Domingue or in the British abolitionist campaign; but they acknowledge characters who are caught up in events or play their small part. Similarly, the internal politics of England are bound up with the revolution in France from the beginning, and repression and suspicion and surveillance can enter lives unexpectedly. The 1790s are by any standards a turbulent period, and issues of loyalty, duty, allegiance and morality under pressure will become prominent in individual histories, which is, incidentally, how I see this saga, as a set of individual and interlinked histories forming part of the substance of that larger and better known 'history' that you find in books.

How people live is the stuff of fiction in many ways, if we also add how people feel, and that will depend weightily on status. In Saint-Domingue, as in other colonies, a large class was known as the *gens de couleur libres*, which might translate into the modern phrase 'people of colour'. This was a social category in a colonial code, so it should not be separated from a grim and oppressive context; but its primary purpose in the laws of that regime was to indicate those who were free, not enslaved, and who might own property and be involved in transactions and trade. In the novels, Héloïse and her sister Félice are both freed *gens de couleur*, children of a white planter and a black woman who was formerly a slave; but Daniel might be considered one too, since he has been freed. It is a status that the plantation overseer, Lafargue, chooses to ignore and attempts to override, but his time of power has gone.

The military campaigns of the Chouans, and their resistance to conscription and the Republican appointment of priests, come to a climax in the first novel, at the battle of Quiberon, and in many ways are in decline after that. The great names of the resistance, Georges Cadoudal and Jean Rohu, carried on the struggle for many years; and the bad feeling between Bretons and the French army is reflected throughout the saga, and at times revived sharply by Captain Leroux and Lieutenant Vernier. Even more influential in the novels is the matter of confiscation, not particularly here that of church property, but far more notably that of the estates of the former nobles. The manor of Kergohan, in the possession of the de Guèrinec family, of which Sempronie is a direct descendant, lies at the heart of the issues of dispossession, ownership, and inheritance. Without exaggeration, it is fair to say that the foundation of the wealth of much of the nineteenth-century bourgeoisie in France was derived from shrewd purchases of property at that time, and the use or disposal of it — much as those who were later classed as gentry in England had benefited from the purchases their predecessors made of lands and property sold off under the dissolution of the monasteries and church lands in Tudor times.

Behind both sets of disturbance and turmoil on either side of the Atlantic lies a struggle for property and the wealth that comes from it, and for those who might not have owned property providing finance was a path to laying hands on some of the profits that came from the exploitation of those who worked on it. In the novels, Laurent Guèvremont emerges as the spirit of a new age of entrepreneurship, related to the de Guèrinec family but not in the direct line of inheritance, who proves to have interests in Saint-Domingue through finance provided to Octave Argoubet, owner of the Galouane and other plantations and the father of Héloïse. It is Laurent who purchases Kergohan through dealings with agents of the Republic, and he sees Kergohan as an opportunity to supply the Republican army profitably, if it is ably managed — as he hopes — by Daniel Galouane, who takes his surname from the plantation to which he was formerly attached. Laurent also manages to acquire other kinds of enterprise, a tannery and a saw-mill, as part of a pledge to support the orphan Gilles. Guèvremont is some part of the spirit of the age, as indeed and more surprisingly is the vicomte de Biel-Santonge, Eugène's father, who has anticipated events and developments by disposing of most of his inherited lands and investing in trade in wine and various other enterprises, one of which is the new printing works in Tours.

Turnpikes, toll-houses, mail coaches and good roads; a relatively reliable postal system; the watering and victualling of the Royal Navy, in the Dock at Plymouth, or at anchor in the Solent opposite Portsmouth; the seemingly endless provision, or recycling, of military uniforms, and their dyeing; summer training camps for the militias, so often up on the Downs above the south coast; the flight of French monarchist refugees through the Channel Islands to America; the plight of the émigrés in London, and the charity of such as the Abbé Carron, an historical figure; the lighting on Westminster

Bridge, clearly seen in the ink-drawing by Thomas Malton from 1792, held by the London Museum; the watermen, ferries, and hackney carriages of London; the assemblies in the Long Room at Plymouth, a building still to be seen in Millbay; and indeed horse racing, catching on fast at about this time, up on the Downs above Lewes, or at Whitehawk on the Downs above Brighton.

And above Brighton at Falmer is Stanmer House, one of the residences of the Pelham family. I have given Lord Thomas Pelham a role in the concluding novel here, based on his office of Surveyor-General of Customs of London, a role which I hope is consistent with compassion and the exercise of responsibility. He also makes a brief appearance at the races on the Downs, from which he could look down on the extraordinary development of the fishing village of Brighthelmstone, to the point where it would soon overtake the ancient town of Lewes in scale. It is a reminder that so much is in flux in this period, that the constructions of the subsequent Regency that we see in the imposing exteriors of both Brighton and Bath are like the dust and uncertainties of Sanditon in Jane Austen's unfinished novel about speculation. It is a theme to which I hope to be able to return in a subsequent book.

A NOTE TO THE READER

Dear Reader,

Moonlight at Cuckmere Haven is the concluding novel of four in the Wentworth family saga and I am confident that the stories have worked through to a point where they draw to a close satisfactorily. As readers, we are all aware that a single, stand-alone book tends to round things off in a rather abrupt fashion, and even when the author is none other than Jane Austen there is a strong demand for more of the characters in her novels, either in continuations, humorous parodies, or additions, such as the novels that cast Jane herself as a sleuth. Either the story or the characters of a stand-alone can burst out at the seams in our imaginations, which may be why a series is now so popular with readers, in which established and familiar characters recur in different scenarios. Some authors will allow a relationship to run through the series as a thread, or as a mystery, but one that will tick along without too much emotion invested in it. A saga is bound to be very different.

This set of four books has been called by the name of the most prominent family, which embraces Justin, Amelia, their mother Sempronie, Amelia's friend Arabella who marries Justin, and Justin's friend Eugène, who marries Amelia. But it quickly became apparent as the story developed that the involvement of this family with Brittany, which came with Sempronie's birth and inheritance in that region, brought with it many other characters. So there is Sempronie's cousin, the investor Laurent Guèvremont who becomes involved in the family manor of Kergohan, and his daughter Joséphine, who becomes entangled with the French army captain Nicolas

Leroux, and does finally marry him. But perhaps the most appealing of the Breton or French characters for many are the feckless orphan boy Gilles, the woman who has given over her life to being a mother to him, Babette, and the two characters from Saint-Domingue in the Caribbean, Héloïse and her uncle Daniel, who falls in love with Babette at a point when both of their charges are growing up and becoming independent.

There is a lot to weave in. Readers who have started with the first novel have had to wait patiently for the second and the third, and I offer my apologies to them for the delays (which should be laid at my door and not the publisher's) and my thanks for that patience. A saga is bound to carry a large number of characters with it, and will trace out a set of stories, not all of which will be resolved at once. That is all fine, but can be frustrating if you have to wait, and risk forgetting storylines and the interlinking of characters. In fact, it seems to me that a saga has now become something of a rarity, perhaps for those reasons. My impression is that people read very quickly, and burn on to the next title, which accounts for the popularity of series, for which there may already be a backlist with the next one ready to pop up soon.

In contrast, a saga that appears gradually will eventually have a moment at which it can be grasped, and if so this would be it: all four novels can now be read in succession, with no gaps or delays, and the pace of the writing may settle in comfortably, as tends to happen in longer works, or so I have found myself as a reader. As an author, I do know that I have a tendency in all of the novels in the saga to start off the story relatively quietly, as if life is normal and there is nothing particularly fraught going on, and then to let the pace pick up and the action gather speed and trauma, emotional or physical. I suppose it is partly a trick, to lull the reader; but it is also my sense of how things are, that life goes on in an ordinary way, and then suddenly things start to fire off. That rhythm of each novel should now be part of the saga as a whole, and how it comes across over the two years in the 1790s in the lives of the characters.

I would also hope that the whole saga will reveal a continuing and changing sense of place. The story is written across two regions in particular, which I know very well and love, Devon and Brittany, and in many ways it is embedded into them — the countryside, the moor, the woodlands, and the small towns, with at times a strong feel for the sea. It would be possible, if you are so inclined, to follow much of the action on the ground, and certainly a holiday in either region might add some of that sleuthing to the enjoyment that is bound to come with being in such beautiful places. In the countryside, close to identifiable places but belonging solely to the story itself and its characters, are the two manors: Chittesleigh in Devon, close to Hatherleigh, and Kergohan, in the countryside to the north of Auray, and not far from the villages of Plumergat and Brandivy.

But the saga is not exclusively confined to the countryside. Much of the second novel, *Heir to the Manor*, is set in the city of Plymouth, with its busy naval port of the Dock, and reflects the society of the time in the 1790s, with a theatre, fashionable shops, circulating libraries, and the Long Room for bright, candle-lit assemblies. Much of the third novel, *Lady at the Lodge*, is set in London, in the suburban village of Hampstead and then down by the Thames, along the shore of what was known then as the Port of London, with its 'stairs' leading down to the waterside. This, the fourth and final novel, finds itself with Amelia in Brighton, on the Steyne, in the hotels, at the racecourse on the Downs, and finally on the beach at Cuckmere Haven, where there is horror in the moonlight.

I hope you enjoy all four books together: there is much to reward a reader who follows the journeys of the characters to the end.

Do take a look at my website and blog, if you have a moment: **grahamley.com**. I hope to meet you again there.

If you enjoyed the novel I would be grateful if you could spare a few minutes to post a review on **Amazon** and **Goodreads.**

My mother was the romantic novelist Alice Chetwynd Ley, and her Regency novels may be found at:

saperebooks.com/authors/alice-chetwynd-ley.

Graham Ley

Sapere Books is an exciting new publisher of brilliant fiction and popular history.

To find out more about our latest releases and our monthly bargain books visit our website:
saperebooks.com

Printed in Great Britain
by Amazon

57153864R10175